THE LAWMAN
AND
THE LADY

THE LAWMAN
AND
THE LADY

By Tera Lee Mattera

CODY BEN TAYLOR PUBLISHING
Fresno, California

Published by

CODY BEN TAYLOR PUBLISHING

3841 North Orchard Avenue
Fresno, California 93726-4210

Printed in the Unites States of America

Photo Credits
Photo of Evelyn Nesbitt by Gertrude Kasebier, Courtesy George Eastman House
Photo of train courtesy Central Pacific Railroad Photographic History Museum,
© 2002, CPRR org

To my husband, Ralph, who kept me writing and made me believe I was a good writer even though I wanted to quit.

For my late mother, Sue, who, on her deathbed, made me promise I would publish my novel and told me how proud she was to have a daughter who was a writer.

My beautiful granddaughter, Alexandra, who told me my novel was good even though she could not yet read.

Acknowledgments

This author has sincere appreciation to the following for their assistance:

David Marion—friend and mentor for his invaluable talent, extensive knowledge of the English language, and his many words of encouragement.

C.L. Cake, author, friend who kept me on track all the way to the completion of my novel.

Richard Camerena, museum supervisor of Tuolumne County Museum for reading my manuscript and checking for historical accuracy. His help, one chapter at a time, made him "worth his weight in gold."

Audie Buckler, historical researcher of Columbia's history. Without Audie's wealth of knowledge of Columbia's former times, I would not have felt my novel was ready for publishing.

Frank Palma, for his extensive knowledge of computers and his patience whenever I asked for help.

*T*he mob roiled, shuffling between moonlight and shadow. The air reeked with fear, excitement, and alcohol. Words, uncertain in origin, rang out, high-pitched and stammering, hesitant, then booming with strained confidence. Dynamite is unpredictable.

"Harris is gonna swing! Don't you get in our way Deputy!"

"You ain't gonna stop us, Taylor. Harris is gonna dangle from the end of this here rope. He's good as dead."

"Yeah, he's gonna be the guest of honor at our string tie party."

Winchester rifle clutched in his left hand, a loaded Walker Colt .44 riding free and easy on his hip, Cody Taylor, the Deputy of Sonora stood motionless on the front steps of the jailhouse. Sweat soaked the band of his Stetson and streamed down his face. The mischievous grin that had become Cody's trademark was ominously absent. His piercing blue eyes scrutinized the taunting mob. But Cody did not see killers. He saw farmers, shopkeepers, and ranchers, respectful folk, men who earned their living in the town of Sonora.

These men of Sonora had reached their own verdict. Having spent the evening fortifying their courage at the saloon, they had talked each other into a fever pitch. Stuart Harris, shackled in the Sonora jail, had brutally murdered a young miner. Now, on the basis of the apparent evidence, the men had become self-proclaimed executioners and, come the witching hour, they had vowed to hang Harris from the nearest tree, with or without the deputy's approval.

In 1848, the discovery of gold in California, from Coloma in the north to Oakhurst in the south, had brought many innocent men not into the vast riches they had anticipated, but into their graves. Greedy men, too lazy or impatient to work the sluices or to pan for gold, ambushed and killed them, often for the pittance in their pockets. But by 1875, law and order had finally seemed to take root in Sonora, and Deputy Taylor represented that law and order. And, he demanded fairness and the full administration of the law, even for a man like Stuart Harris.

"You gonna stop us, Deputy? You and who else? Sheriff Sanders ain't here and we don't see no one else on your side. Come on, men. Let's lynch him!"

The badge on Cody's vest reflected the glint of the torches. He directed the barrel end of his Winchester toward the crowd and took one step forward. As he spoke, softly and clearly, the deadly control of his voice stopped the angry men in their tracks.

"Harris won't hang tonight or any other night, not by you. That's for damn sure. He'll get a fair trial. If you try to hang Harris, you'll be worst than him. You're good men, not killers. I'm sworn to protect my prisoner. The first man that tries to take him from me, I'll stop that man."

The sudden flash and roar from Cody's Winchester stopped the lumbering forward movement of the mob like a wall. The moonlight cast Cody's six-foot body into a sixty-foot shadow that loomed over the mob like an omen of disaster.

In the last four years since the tragic gunfight at Crow Canyon, when the deputy badge had been pinned to his blood-soaked vest, Cody had defended law and order to the letter, just like his late father, Sheriff Andrew Taylor. The Taylor family history was littered with lawmen, and the family traits of inherent strength and instinctive cunning had seeped into Cody's blood and prospered there.

With deadly casualness, Deputy Taylor recocked his Winchester and every ear recorded the click of the shell into the chamber. Cody's voice resounded deeply now, as if it had emerged from the cold, dark barrel of a field cannon.

"If you think I'm going to turn my prisoner over to you, Paul, or to you, Joe, your dead wrong. Go ahead, try to take him if you've truly sold your souls, but you'll have to step over my body to get him."

. . . .

On the previous Sunday afternoon, a young miner rode his packhorse into Sonora and tethered it in front of the saloon. He had spent weeks in the hills panning gold out of the streams. He needed supplies and wanted to mingle with other miners in town. Now, with his pockets full of gold dust, spruced up in his blue shirt and new brown pants, he hankered for a few beers and maybe a poker game.

In the saloon, the miner noticed a tall; hardy looking fellow, dressed in black pants held up with a wide leather belt, dirty worn boots, and his shirt was drenched with sweat. He was leaning against the bar, drinking from a beer mug. The man was speaking quietly, his voice redolent with a Swedish accent, to an older man in city clothes, black trousers, a vest, and real shoes, his white shirtsleeves held up by red garters.

At a corner table in the back of the saloon, a languid buxom lady of the night sat across from a burly mountain of a man who darted suspicious glances at various patrons of the saloon.

The young miner ambled up to the bar, "Name's Jake," he said, removing his dusty hat and flashing a friendly smile at the bartender, "I sure could stand a beer."

Jake took the proffered foamy glass and drank deeply; then turned and directed himself generally to the patrons in the room, "Anyone here like to play a little poker?"

"Yeah, me," the huge man at the corner table snarled. "Been sittin' here for a damn hour waitin'. Who else is gonna be sittin' in? We ain't got all night."

Jake sauntered to the corner table, a whisky bottle cuddled under his arm, and reached out his hand.

"Name's Jake."

"Name's Harris, Stuart Harris," growled the giant at the table. He ignored Jake's outstretched hand.

As Harris shuffled a deck of frayed cards, the two men who had been talking at the bar, joined Stuart and Jake, and introduced themselves as "Per Johannsen, blacksmith" and simply "Gus, the saloon piano player."

Some people call it "beginner's luck"; Jake raked in money one winning hand after the other. The tension at the table mounted with each hand, and Harris' hands began to clench and unclench, his red eyes surveying Jake's growing pile of loot. Finally, when one the saloon girls praised the miner's skill at poker, Harris exploded in fury.

"You gotta be dealin' off the bottom of that there deck," he roared. The veins in his temples beat with every word, "Nobody wins every hand. You got cards up them sleeves? I say you're cheatin', stranger, and there's only one way to prove you're not. Draw that pistol, you yellow belly! Draw coward! After the smoke clears, the man standin' gets the money."

The venom and contempt in Stuart Harris' words would provoke even the most patient person and send him over the edge. When Jake's chair went flying, the Swede and piano player dove for cover. Hell bent for trouble, the simple miner played right into the titan's hand. Harris was the fastest draw in town, even with his Dragoon Colt, and deadly accurate. Jake had no way of knowing; he only wanted to prove he wasn't cheating.

"I ain't cheatin'," Jake stammered, as he backed up, his right hand poised over his revolver, "but I guess there's only one way to prove it to the likes of you. Stand up. Let's get this over with."

A slow grin spread across Stuart's face and his eyes burned into the young miner. His six-foot four bulk loomed over the miner as he moved his chair out of the way and took several steps back, eager and willing to answer Jake's challenge and to spill Jake's blood.

Just as the two Colts were about to clear their holsters, the swinging doors to the saloon burst open and revealed Deputy Taylor, leveling a shotgun in the general direction of the only two people in the saloon who were not cowered behind protection.

"The first man who draws eats buckshot," Cody said calmly.

Well into the hush of night, as the bartender and piano player were stacking chairs, Jake finally staggered out of the saloon in the direction of the Sonora Hotel. For this one night, the first night in many months, he will sleep in a bed with sheets and pillows.

Feeling richer than a Midas and on top of the world, Jake reeled passed an obscure form leaning against a side wall in the shadows of the alley next to the saloon. Moments later, the bartender and piano player also passed the hulking form, and they nodded to one another. In the distance, they glimpsed Jake stroll unsteadily into the thick gloom.

As he rounded the corner just yards for the sanctuary of the Sonora Hotel, Jake found his way blocked by a Goliath. Harris' mighty forearm encircled the miner's neck and held it like a steel band.

"Tried cheatin' me once," hissed Harris, "but ya ain't never gonna win at cards again."

Cold, hard steel sank into the miner's ribs again and again. Then the razor-sharp Bowie knife was raised, and the miner's throat was slashed open with a flick of Stuart's wrist. Jake dropped face down in the dirt while the lifeblood oozed from his neck and back. A sardonic smile twisted Harris' lips as he sheathed his bloody knife and stalked from the scene.

Tormented by their consciences and terrified by the thought that Harris might know what they had seen, the bartender and piano player spoke to Deputy Taylor three days after the killing. Cody promised them around the clock protection, but he required two contingents from the informers. They must help to snare him into admitting to his fiendish crime, and they must testify against Harris in a court of law.

Near closing time at a secluded table in the Sonora saloon, the bartender's hands shook as he set a bottle of whiskey and a shot glass onto the green felt surface. Harris scowled as he poured the amber liquid and quickly bolted several shots of the best whiskey in Sonora. The bartender held his towel in a death grip as he watched Harris drink. Silently, cautiously, he noticed the piano player edging his way toward the table.

When the whiskey had mellowed somewhat the potent fury that seldom left Harris' face, the bartender broke the silence, "Harris, me and Gus here seen you watching that young miner when he left the saloon the night he won so big playin' poker. He was dead the next day and he didn't have no money on his body. We think you killed him and took his loot."

"I weren't following him," said Harris. "You tryin' to get me hung? Cause if you are start prayin'."

Strong meaty fingers shot out and locked onto the throats of the bartender and piano player. Harris pinched off their breath of life while he described a long, painful death each man would suffer if they talked. When he had intimidated them sufficiently, Harris loosened his grip and smirked as he recounted every gross detail of the young miner's horrible death.

Cramped in a closet behind the three men, Deputy Taylor listened. It was moments later that Harris was charged with Jake's murder, hand-cuffed, and escorted to the Sonora jail with the deputy's Walker Colt aimed directly in the middle of his back. After hearing the testimony of the witnesses and other evidence brought forward, a jury will pass their decision to the judge who will give Stuart Harris the ultimate verdict: Death by hanging.

· · · · · · · · ·

"Think again before you point that peacemaker at the deputy, Buck," the bartender roared from behind the mob, "my scatter gun will take both you and Joe. I'm sidin' with Cody. I want Harris hung for this killing as much as anyone. But he's gotta get a fair trial. Like the deputy says. We ain't murderers. You men know we ain't."

"Before the deputy goes down," shouted Gus as he stepped out from the shadows on the side of the jail toting his Winchester and revolver, "three men standin' here will die. You can start shootin' anytime, Pete. Your jaw's been flappin' all night wantin' to hang 'em. Listen, if we hung Harris we'd be the ones to suffer, not Harris."

Murmurs rumbled throughout the crowd, Deputy Taylor and the men that courageously stood with him made good sense. Cody held his Winchester ready as each man slowly lowered his rifle or revolver, nodded to the deputy, and silently walked away.

But even as the mob dispersed, there will be no rest for this lawman. Cody will guard the prisoner night and day until Sheriff Robert Sanders rode back into town. And Cody swore an oath to himself that Harris would still be alive and in his custody to face justice for his heartless crime.

$\mathcal{2}$

$\mathcal{R}$elishing in the comfort of the plush velvet cushioned seat; Gina Tufano luxuriated in the Wagner Palace Car and admired the elaborate ambience it extended to the traveler. After months of heart-wrenching sadness and weeks of backbreaking work, she was favorably anticipating her long train ride on the New York Central. She will journey from New York to Chicago, detrain from the elegant Wagner Palace Car in Chicago, and board the Union Pacific to Ogden, Utah. For the remainder of her trek to California, Gina is pampered in the exquisite Pullman Car.

After a locomotive change at Ogden, Utah, the Central Pacific carries her non-stop to Sacramento. One final train takes Gina from Sacramento to the Milton-Sonora Road station, south of Stockton. After an overnight stay, a stagecoach ride will convey her to Sonora.

A "First Class Through" ticket from New York City to Sacramento, California lay on her lap. With a final destination at Sonora, California, the fare of $136.00 included a drawing room for the entire journey. For two dollars extra per night, she had secured a bed and the exclusive use to a bath closet. In the late afternoon, the chamberman would convert one of the chairs in the Palace Car into a bed while Gina strolled to the dinning car for supper.

The best comforts of home adorned the Wagner Palace Car. Exquisite paneling, beautiful marquetry, and inlaid tables complemented by overstuffed chairs made the living space elegant. Ornate gold mirrors graced every wall, bordered by large curtained windows complete with silver-plated rods.

Breakfast, lunch, and dinner were prepared in a special coach adjoining the dining car. Of the ample choices offered on the menu, Gina selected breaded veal cutlets for her first meal. Total cost was sixty-five cents, including French coffee.

The dining table, adorned in fine bone china, snow-white linen, and fresh flowers, matched the luxury and exquisiteness of any first-class restaurant in New York City. Three other passengers shared her table and partook of the wine and conversation as the train sped along at thirty-five to forty miles per hour.

In 1865, when Vincente and Mary Sciaroni, Gina's uncle and aunt, left New York for California, trains did not travel across the country. When Vincente and Mary left New York harbor, crossing the Panama isthmus was the fastest way to the West coast, and the sea voyage still took over one month before the ship docked in San Francisco Bay.

However, railroad tracks were finally completed in 1869, and the journey from New York to California would take Gina a mere seven to eight days.

In the last four weeks, Gina had sorted, crated, and packed a museum's worth of household furniture, clothing, and miscellaneous articles from her parents' home. She had hired a house agent to sell the three-story house and everything else that would not be going to California. In less than one-year, Gina's father and mother had both died and only a small group of close friends and colleagues remained in New York.

Anthony E. Tufano, M.D., had been a brilliant doctor, far ahead of his time. Tony met a beautiful young woman, Constantina Rotunda, who was tending to patients when he visited a hospital in London. Dr. Tufano's attraction to Tina pressed him to asked her to be his assistant when he set up private practice in New York, and Tina agreed. Most doctors frowned upon women in the medical field, but Dr. Tufano knew how much help, support, and comfort a nurse gave to a patient.

Tony and Tina fell in love and were married after a brief courtship, and they became Gina's parents. From an early age, Gina was instilled with an innate love for the medical profession. At age nineteen, after one year of intense nurse's training, Gina had left Bellevue Hospital in New York City with her certificate, one month after her father's death.

Tina had nursed Tony before his death and during the six months prior to Tina's death, Gina had nursed her mother. One month after Tina's funeral, Aunt Mary suggested that Gina move to California.

The thought of moving across the country staggered Gina and she dismissed the idea straightaway. But as her tears persisted and her aching heart continued to grieve, Aunt Mary's suggestion echoed and re-echoed in her brain. The move to California gradually became a dire necessity.

Miss Tufano put pen to paper. "It will take me a few weeks to sell most of the furniture," Gina wrote to Aunt Mary, "and hire a house agent to sell our house, but I have decided to move to California.

"I miss you," Gina continued, "and I am so terribly lonely here without Mama and Papa. Too many memories surround me here; I have to get away. I think that California might be the change that I need, for awhile anyway, although I do love living in New York City. I'll wire you the approximate day of my arrival. I look forward to being with my family again."

Although friends were highly critical of her decision, Miss Tufano was adamant.

Sally, a school chum, alerted Gina of expected trials and tribulations with disparaging remarks, "California is no place for someone like you, Gina; it's so primitive, it's dirty and it's ungodly. California is the worst place you could move. And the men that live there, well, I've heard tell the men in California are wild and soulless beasts, rough and rude miners. They'll ravage you. They surely will!"

"Everybody is telling me the same thing, Sally," Gina replied, "I know Sonora is full of vulgar coarse miners. And, I also know it's a different world than New York City."

"They wear pistols and carry large knives," Sally retorted, her big blue eyes solemn, "and there are no conveniences, no theaters, no restaurants. California is savage, a horrible place for anyone to live, especially you. Why, you'll go positively mad in just a few days. There is nothing to do there, Gina."

"Sally, listen to me, when Papa, Mama, and I visited Uncle Vincente and Aunt Mary in Sonora five years ago, there were grocery stores, banks, restaurants, and theaters all along the main street. Sonora was civilized then; it will be better now, and there will be more to see, more to do. And, you are also forgetting I will be taking over Aunt Mary's duties at the doctor's office. I will be busy."

Sally dropped heavily into a slipper chair next to Gina's bed. "I will miss you so, Gina. Please don't leave. You're my closest friend."

Gina walked to the opposite side of the bed, and slipped her arms into the sleeves of a soft blue wool sweater that her mother had knitted shortly before her death. She took a deep breath and brushed thick, dark curly hair out of her face as warm tears filled large almond-shaped eyes and slipped down her cheeks.

"It breaks my heart to leave New York. I hate to leave my home, my friends, Sally," she murmured. "But I have to leave. Everywhere I go in this house, everything I see reminds me of Mama and Papa. I break down and sob when I see Papa's favorite chair or the pan in which Mama used to make Italian sauce. Every time I pick up a cup or a dish, there is a memory and it makes me cry. I am too sad living here; I cry most of the day and night. No, I need to go away; I will not stay in New York, Sally, not this year."

"I know it's not easy with both your parents gone," Sally said, wrapping her finger around a long yellow curl lying on her shoulder, "but I must remind you, the men in California are desperate and I'm afraid for you. There can't be that many women living in Sonora. Who'd want to? Maybe you conveniently forgot, but I do remember what you told me about that Cody Taylor person when you were in Sonora. Surely, you cannot dismiss how he treated you five years ago. Tell me he wasn't a barbaric rogue."

"He was; Cody Taylor was a crude and obnoxious young man. But not every man will be like him. Why did you bring him up anyway? He can't possibly live in Sonora. It has been five years. I am leaving New York, Sally. *Hai capito*? Nothing you can say will change my mind."

While waiting for the other passengers to board the New York Central, Gina gazed out the window with tears in her eyes. Men and women hugged loved ones tightly before they waved good-bye and disappeared inside the train. Corded crates going as freight were loaded into a special car for transport.

In a few of these crates, held Dr. Tufano's medical books, credentials, and important documents, as well as possessions that had belonged to her grandparents when they left Florence, Italy in 1820. Some people might call this freight, but to Gina it was cherished memories, keepsakes, and mementos.

Disquieting questions continually broke into her thoughts. Had she made the right decision to leave the city of her birth? Would it be possible to find happiness in a place like Sonora? A young woman is born to parents who loved the medical profession. How could this person brought up in the City of New York to nurse and care for the sick and dying, adjust to the living conditions in California? But her reaction to these questions was always the same; Gina had to leave New York.

Holding Aunt Mary's last letter in her hand, Gina was comforted by the words, "…you will be happy in Sonora, Gina dear, I know it. Your uncle and I fell in love with California, and you will too. I will be looking forward to your arrival and I do need your help."

The Conductor shouted "All Aboard", two short whistles sounded, the train jerked forward, sending out billows of white smoke. Soon, the New York Central train station was a memory, as rolling hills and meadowland took the place of familiar buildings and streets.

The tears flowed down Gina's cheeks as she choked down the lump in her throat. A new chapter in her life had begun; she must confront whatever awaited her. Mama and Papa had taught her never to look back, and even though her heart groaned and burned deep within her, Miss Tufano whispered good-bye to New York City.

3

A single passenger stepped off the stagecoach into the heat of Sonora, California-Miss Gina Tufano.

She looked for Aunt Mary up and down the main street, listened for her voice, but in vain. Gina removed her dust-covered traveling coat and hat, loosened the top three buttons of her black dress, and stood fanning herself in front of the Sonora Hotel alongside her baggage.

It was Sunday; the town swarmed with visitors. Gina watched as miners fastened supplies onto their pack horses or frequented the saloons. Children played games on the board walk in front of supply stores, waiting for their mothers to emerge. Elegantly dressed ladies, arm in arm with men in black suits and hats, smiled as they stopped to speak with acquaintances.

A door, painted in white letters "Mayor's Office," opened across the street from where Gina was standing. Two men came out, walked toward the Sonora Hotel, but stopped directly in front of Gina. The younger of the two wore a sheriff's badge pinned on his vest. Gina guessed him to be thirty to thirty-five years old. Dressed in brown pants, blue shirt, and brown boots, he was one of the few men in town that wore a holster and revolver strapped to his hip.

The other man was dressed in black, and nodded a friendly welcome to Gina. As he lifted his hat, a mop of white wavy hair appeared.

The man wearing the gold star introduced himself; "My name is Robert Sanders. I'm the Sheriff of Sonora."

He had kind, liquid blue-green eyes. He removed his hat revealing diminishing brown hair, and flashed a sincere smile.

"And this man is William Thorton; he's the Mayor here in Sonora," Sanders said.

"I am please to meet you. My name is Gina Tufano. I just stepped off the stagecoach, and I am waiting for my aunt."

"Are you expecting Mary Sciaroni?" Mayor Thorton asked pointedly.

Gina was taken aback by his question. She knew Aunt Mary had failing health and she now feared Mary might be seriously ill. "Yes." She replied, "Is there anything wrong?"

"Miss Tufano, do you have papers with you to prove you are related to Mary Sciaroni?" Robert asked.

"I have a letter in my purse with her signature. I received it a few days before I left New York. Will that do? I have papers in my trunk to prove my relation to her, but it will not arrive for about a week."

Mayor Thorton glanced over the letter and handed it to the sheriff.

Sheriff Sanders quietly perused the letter and then in a hushed voice said, "We're sorry to have to tell you, Miss Tufano, but Mary Sciaroni died five days ago. Since we didn't know when you were to arrive, we buried her. She's in the cemetery on the edge of town.

Gina was stunned. She turned her face away and wept bitterly, muttering softly between sobs, "I only wish I had arrived sooner."

William and Robert carried Gina's baggage to the Mayor's office and waited patiently until she regained her composure. The Mayor read Mary Sciaroni's Last Will and Testament, which Mary had entrusted to him one month previously.

As the only living heir, Gina inherited Mary's home and property, including a small amount of money. The majority of Vincente and Mary Sciaroni's savings had been designated for the construction of an adequate, up-to-date hospital, which was desperately needed in Sonora.

Kindly, compassionately, Sheriff Sanders and Mayor Thorton allowed Gina time to grieve, and then escorted her to Mary's home.

When they arrived at the Sciaroni residence, Robert opened the front door and handed Gina the key, while the Mayor carried in her baggage. Gina walked into the silent entry hall, void of any family, to the center staircase, sat on the bottom step and wept.

Robert waited in the open front door, "Is there anything we can do, Miss Tufano," he asked, "I can bring you some food. Are you hungry?"

"No," Gina answered, "I am not hungry. Thank you for your kindness Sheriff Sanders and Mayor Thorton. I will manage."

Now utterly alone and feeling totally lost, Gina watched them walk down the front steps to their waiting buggy.

4

Cody dismounted in front of the jail and tethered his horse. The townspeople smiled at him as they walked by, pleased to see the deputy back on duty.

There were times when Deputy Taylor felt restless living in Sonora. Recently, when he was in Sacramento for Harris' trial, Cody had received a tempting offer to work for the government. He had declined the offer, but not without some regret.

He walked into the jail. A large window in front of his desk afforded a clear view of the main street and a building that had been vacant for several months, but was now teeming with activity. Doctor Matthew Gibbs, elderly, with tons of gray hair and compassionate hazel eyes, the most popular and trusted doctor in Sonora, and people impressed into the doctor's service, carried heavy boxes, books, and furniture through the front door.

Dr. Sciaroni had drawn up plans for a new medical facility two years before his death. But for now Doctor Gibbs needed larger accommodations until the new hospital was constructed. This temporary site was located across from the jail on Washington Street, the main street of Sonora.

When a patient detained Matthew from the work at hand, Billy, an orphan and willing helper, saw Cody standing outside the sheriff's office. He took the opportunity to step across the street and visit with Cody. Billy was not yet fifteen years old, but a lad with strength, bulk, and height for his age. His mate, Cody's brother Andrew, was smaller in size than Billy and three years younger.

Ted and Sue Martin, Billy's guardians, encouraged him to help the older residents in Sonora with chores that they could no longer accomplish alone. Today he was helping Doctor Gibbs carry heavy boxes and furniture into the temporary hospital.

"Hi, Cody." Billy said, smiling broadly, his brown eyes fixed on the deputy's face, "When did you get back from Sacramento?"

Cody leaned against a post and returned Billy's smile. "Last night, late," he said.

Eager to impress Cody, Billy took a step forward and said, "Did you hear that Nurse Mary had died while you were in Sacramento?"

"Yeah, the sheriff told me about it. Too bad. I sure
liked her and ol' Doctor Sciaroni. The town'll miss her."

"How did the trial turn out, Cody? Was he hung?"

While Cody was a lawman and sworn to protect the people of Sonora, he did not enjoy seeing any man hang.

He replied quietly, "Yeah, four days ago."

"I wanna help you capture a prisoner or a killer someday, Cody," said Billy, "I'd like to be a lawman like you. You think I'd make a good deputy? Maybe I could even save somebody's life?"

"Yeah, you'll make a good deputy someday, Billy."

"Thanks, Cody. Well, I gotta go. I'm helping the Doc move boxes and furniture into that empty building. See ya."

Cody called over his shoulder to the sheriff inside the jail. "Doc Gibbs sure has people carrying a lot of boxes into that empty building. He moving in?"

Robert came outside and leaned on the opposite side of the post. They watched as the doctor picked up a box containing small bottles and carry it back inside.

"The town is finally behind Matthew and pushing for the new hospital," Robert said. "The Doc and William been working day and night on the plans Dr. Sciaroni left."

As Robert and Cody chatted, a striking young woman with dark hair piled high on her head opened the front door and emerged. She wore a blue-striped uniform under a long white apron. Her well endowed, hourglass figure, even in the unflattering nurse's attire, was unmistakable.

"Micah," she said, holding the door open, "please can you come inside and help Luis place my desk in front of the window. It's too heavy for Doctor Gibbs and Billy."

The deputy straightened up, riveting his blue eyes on this exotic creature. She had not been in Sonora three weeks ago when he had left for Sacramento, this he knew.

"Well I'll be damned. Who is that?" Cody asked.

"Matthew's new assistant, Gina Tufano," Robert replied. "Mary Sciaroni's niece. She's been helping the Doc, like what Mary use to do. Helped him deliver the Humphrey baby last week.

"She come all the way from New York City and got in town the day after you went to Sacramento."

Cody stretched his neck to get a better look. He was about to stride across the street when Robert held him back with his hand and a warning, "Hold on, deputy. Not so fast. Don't you go heading in her direction. Matthew's pretty protective when it comes to that nurse. She's causing a stir in this town, and the Doc doesn't like it when the young bucks come by and stand around watching her."

"Doc doesn't like what? What the hell are you talking about, Sheriff?" Cody asked, staring blankly at Robert.

Sheriff Sanders continued, "Matthew told me Gina was raised by Italian parents. She wasn't allowed to be alone with young men, you know what I mean. Her father and Mary Sciaroni were brother and sister. Before Nurse Mary died, she asked Matthew and your mom to watch over Gina, if anything ever happened to her."

Deputy Taylor listened patiently as Robert explained. "So don't think of sweeping this girl off her feet. You can't come on strong with Gina."

Noting Cody's raised eyebrows, Robert made him hear the entire story. "It's like this deputy, first her father dies and then her mother dies. When she's on her way to Sonora expecting to live with her last relative, Mary up and dies."

The sheriff and deputy watched as Luis and Micah positioned a large desk in front of the window. Whoever sat at that desk would see all the activity on Washington Street and be seen by anyone passing by.

Robert read Cody's expression and felt obliged to repeat himself. "You tread careful, hear me? This girl's got a temper. I've seen it. You can damn near have any woman in this town, but that doesn't mean the nurse is going to fall head over heels for you. She's different, she's the type of girl you should think about when you finally get ready to settle down."

As Sheriff Sanders was finished speaking, the Mayor crossed the street toward the jail. He was anxious to document and chronicle the trial of Stuart Harris for the town's permanent records. Cody's curiosity and eagerness to see the new nurse would have to wait.

Mayor Thorton approached Cody with a firm request as the sheriff walked inside the jail, "Deputy, I need you to come to my office. You have to read over the documents concerning Harris' trial and verify them since you witnessed the hanging."

"I should have been to your office first thing, William. I knew I had to sign those papers," said Cody.

"Take your time Cody," the sheriff said, grinning. "Your work'll still be here waiting for you when you come back."

"Any problems getting the prisoner to Sacramento, Deputy?" asked Mayor Thorton,

"He went quiet enough, Mayor," Cody replied, "but I had shackles on him. Harris knew I'd shoot him if he tried anything."

"We watched Harris when he was led to the gallows. Before the black hood was put on his head, they asked if he had any final words. You know what he told them?'

The Mayor stopped walking to focus on the prisoner's final words. Cody shook his head and said, "He said, 'You want me to give you a damn speech? I ain't gonna do it. I come here to get hung.'"

"I knew Harris was a killing fool, Deputy. It sounds like nobody's death fazed him, not even his own. But if it's any consolation to you, people of Sonora have told me they feel safer now that Harris is gone."

"Thanks, Mayor. I sure hope folks appreciate how hard the sheriff and I work to protect this town."

$\mathcal{5}$

$\mathcal{C}$ody left the Mayor's office and headed toward the temporary hospital. He wanted to ask Matthew to lunch and meet the new nurse.

Billy, true to his habits, flew out the front door of the hospital in a hurry to meet up with Andrew, and left it wide open. He swung up on his pony and rode away.

Cody stepped into the disorganized waiting room without disturbing the bell recently nailed to the front door and stared at a puddle of ink dripping down the side of an empty desk and spotting the floor. He saw a movement through a partially open door and, thinking it was Matthew, he headed toward a back room. But, it was not the doctor; it was his new assistant.

Bent forward from the waist, head near the floor, feet apart, the new nurse murmured as she twisted her curly thick, long hair into a coil to pile on her head, her back to Cody.

While engrossed in writing down a patient's complaint to present to Matthew, Gina's long heavy hair had slipped from her hairpins, and when she raised her arms to pull it away from her shoulders, she knocked over the inkwell. However, before she cleaned the desk and floor, her hair had to be secured. Priorities are priorities.

Cody extended his arm and pushed the door open silently to get a better view. In Cody's estimation, not many women had a perfect figure, but this young woman came pretty close.Suspended from a hook and chain, a large mirror was positioned over a small table and reflected the front and side of Gina's body. From his vantage point, Cody could take in every detail of her lovely figure, the amply endowed breasts, a tiny waist, and her perfectly formed, round hips.

Gina straightened up, but kept her eyes fixed on the tabletop where a quantity of hairpins waited to be used, mumbling words the deputy did not understand. When the last hairpin was put into place, and her gaze focused on her reflection in the mirror, she saw a man leaning on the doorframe grinning from ear to ear. His lively interest took in the full panorama, from her bosom to her face, the full lips, large, dark-brown, almond-shaped eyes, and long dark eyelashes.

"Who are you?" Gina screamed in alarm as she turned to face the visitor. "Get out of this room!"

As she flailed her hand directing him out, Gina bumped the table and sent it crashing to the floor along with everything on it.

One dominant characteristic of Gina's personality, not that she was proud of this feature, was an Italian temper that erupted at the slightest provocation. The words she wanted to vocalize to this impertinent intruder bubbled in her throat and almost made her choke. When Gina's lips parted to tell the stranger what she thought of him, the back door suddenly flew open and Matthew rushed into the room.

She waited for the doctor to reprove the stranger, but instead he extended his arm, "Cody Taylor," he said, "you're back. But why aren't you wearing your deputy badge? You scared my assistant. When did you get back?"

The deputy shook Matthew's hand while he grinned and gazed, unashamed, at Gina's every curve. "I'm wearing my badge," he replied, lifting his vest to show the deputy badge on his blue shirt. "I got in last night, late."

While the doctor questioned Cody about Harris' trial, Gina picked up the table and retrieved the hairpins from the floor. It was hard for her to believe, but the young man who had vexed her five years ago was now the deputy Sheriff of Sonora.

Matthew interrupted her diversion with two questions, "Gina, do you remember Cody Taylor? Sheriff and Millie Taylor's oldest son?"

Gina remembered him, although she tried her best to forget their last meeting. Both times she met this man, his boldness had irritated her.

"Cody, this is Gina Tufano," Matthew said, "Mary Sciaroni's niece and my new assistant."

Something stirred in Cody's memory. He had met this young woman before.

"How do you do, Gina?" Cody said, flashing his mischievous grin.

"Cody is the deputy of Sonora, Gina." Doctor Gibbs announced proudly.

Miss Tufano restrained the anger she wanted to vent and extended her hand to the deputy, "I am fine, thank you," she replied, tersely. "Next time you walk into a doctor's office unannounced, pin your badge to your vest so someone can see it."

Kind words to indicate that she was pleased to see him again would never issue from her lips. That was entirely out of the question.

Cody took her hand and held it tightly, in no hurry to turn it loose. Gina tugged, gently at first, and then she yanked her hand from his grip the instant Cody loosened it. When she fell back, the table crashed against the wardrobe and again the hairpins were scattered all over the floor.

Without moving a muscle, the nurse sat on the floor in a most unladylike position, peered at the men through long ringlets as she seethed. Matthew and Cody were ready to bust out laughing at Gina's ungraceful landing.

Doctor Gibbs helped her into a standing position. A torrent of words that would express her opinion of the deputy rushed into her mind as she turned away to straighten her uniform, but she bit her quivering lip.

"Are you hurt, Gina?"

"No, Matthew, I am not hurt. But I hope you both will soon be leaving this office."

The corners of Matthew's mouth twisted upward although he tried not to smile. To hide his amusement, he lifted the table and repositioned it against the wall.

Eager to bait her, the deputy picked up a single hairpin and handing it to her, he said with a twinkle, "Gina, I would like you to bend over again in front of the mirror and fix your hair. If you wouldn't mind."

"*Abba'stanza*! Enough!" She shouted, and threw her arms into the air, hissing Italian words at Matthew and Cody. She flung open the back door with such intensity that it slammed into the wall, and after Gina had stalked through the doorway, mumbling in Italian, the door slammed shut with equal intensity.

Stepping over boxes, hammers, and tools scattered on the floor, the two men left through the front door.

Cody snickered as he expressed his opinion of the new nurse, "Robert told me she had a bad temper. He was right. She's something. I didn't think anybody could slam a door so hard."

"She has a temper, Deputy, this is true, but you sure didn't help her control it."

When Gina's temper cooled, after her hair was tucked into a coil once again, and she removed the ink stains from the desk and floor, she sat in a chair and stared out the window toward the jail.

"Cody Taylor is the Deputy of Sonora," she grumbled, "I never would have dreamed it. He would be the last person I would chose to be the deputy, and the last person I expected to see in this town. Maybe I can have Matthew reposition my desk. I cannot stand the thought of seeing him going into and out of that jail every single day."

$\mathcal{M}$ounted on his Appaloosa pony, Sammy, the deputy headed south. A risky predicament had developed on Ted Martin's spread. One of Ted's ranch hands, Owen Clark, caused animosity among Ted's workers from morning to night. It was only a question of time before someone was killed in a heated argument. Deputy Taylor had spoken to Clark earlier about his malevolent behavior, and he decided he'd warm him again, but for the last time.

Stuart Harris and Owen Clark assured Ted the day they were hired on at the Martin ranch, they would work hard for him. Cody questioned Ted's promptness in hiring these two strangers, the deputy wanted to know more about them before they were residents of Sonora. Harris and Clark liked to work, it was their only good quality, and they were big, brawny men, they could do a fair amount of work in a day. But from the moment Harris and Clark rode into town, their goal was to incite trouble.

Harris was now out of the picture, but his cousin Owen Clark still wreaked havoc in Sonora. Clark's antagonistic attitude needed to change quickly, but if it did not, Deputy Taylor planned to escort him off of Ted's ranch and out of Sonora.

Cody slowed Sammy to a walk; the new nurse filled his thoughts. Why was the urge to tease her so overwhelming?

He remembered someone else that kindled his mischievousness and the light flashed, "Gia, that's who she is," Cody said to himself. "That Italian girl who visited here a few years ago from New York."

. . . .

Five years ago, Sheriff and Millie Taylor invited Dr. and Mrs.

Sciaroni, along with Dr. and Mrs. Tufano, and their daughter, who were relatives of the Sciaroni's and, visiting from New York City, to Sunday dinner. At that time, Cody was a rash, impulsive eighteen-year-old, and Andrew, his only brother, was seven.

When Cody walked out of the stable and into the confines of the back yard, after he had given Sammy a rubdown and his portion of oats, Cody saw Andrew, and a young girl with long dark hair. The girl was sitting on the Taylor's swing holding Andrew's hands, while Andrew stood with his right knee raised, pleading for approval to nestle on her lap.

The girl protested, "No, *bambino*. I will not be able to move my legs back and forward and swing you if you are sitting on my lap. I'll get off the swing and push you."

"No, Gia. Please let me sit on your lap. We can swing together."

"We will try, *bambino*, but you hold on tightly to the ropes. *Hai Ca'pito, Capisci?*"

Even with a small boy sitting on her lap, this spunky girl got the swing to mount. However, as it slowed, Andrew and Gina toppled over. She landed on her back and Andrew ended up sitting on top of her.

Cody's hat was tipped back, revealing his sandy-colored hair. He approached the jovial pair and stared at the young lady. His blue eyes scanned every detail of her behavior and figure. Gina's long, ebony hair had collected dirt and leaves from the grass, and one foot was caught in the rope, exposing her young, but shapely leg.

Andrew spotted his brother, jumped up off of Gina and exploded into Cody's arms. "Cody," he shouted, "you're home."

Gina's modesty prevented her from lying flat on her back in front of any young man. She scrambled to her feet, straightened her dress, and attempted to remove the leaves and grass from her hair.

Andrew pointed a finger to Gina. "This is my new friend, Gia, Cody," he said proudly.

"Gina," she said, "Andrew does not pronounce the 'n' in my name."

Cody gently set Andrew onto the ground. "You go inside and clean up, Andrew," he said, "before Mom sees you. You're a mess."

Gina started to follow Andrew, but Cody had different ideas. He grabbed her left arm with his right hand and held it firmly.

"Come on, Gia," Andrew called.

Cody reprimanded his brother, "Go in the house and clean up by yourself pronto, or I'll clean you myself!"

Cody was fascinated by this girl and compared her in his mind to other young women in Sonora. He was enchanted by her half-closed almond-shaped eyes, which at that moment seemed to flash warnings to the audacious young man who held her arm.

Gina wrenched free from Cody's clutch and announced, "I am going into the kitchen, now, to help with supper."

She turned to leave, but he blocked her way, stretched his arms out to the side to prevent her from leaving and grinned playfully. Gina glared at him and swore beneath her breath in Italian.

On an impulse, his hands went around her waist and lifted her off the ground. He sat her on the swing and covered her hands with his, holding them tightly around the ropes. Then, Cody took several steps back and let the swing fly.

"This swing is going too fast and too high. Stop it now!" Gina shouted as Cody pushed the swing higher into motion.

Since her English commands were ignored, she spoke in Italian, "So'stare. Fi'nire."

He pushed again with all his strength and folded his arms across his chest. As she struggled to control the erratic movements of the swing as it slowed, he did nothing to help her.

During Sunday dinner, Cody regretted his impetuous behavior. He sat across from Gina, smiled, and tried to speak to her from time to time, but she was aloof and ignored him.

When farewells began, Cody watched Andrew climb on Gina's lap, seize her neck and bellow, "No Gia, don't go. Don't leave me. Not ever."

Sheriff Taylor was a patient and kind man, but he was not a father to let his son display a fit of temper. He pulled Andrew away from Gina, and carried him off kicking and screaming. Gina collected her wrap and purse.

It was now or never. Cody felt that he had to apologize for his actions to this young beauty before she left Sonora. After all, no gentlemen would put a lady on a swing against her wishes and ignored her pleas for help or stared at her face and maturing young body from the moment he set eyes on her.

But when he opened his mouth to speak, Gina could take no more of this cheeky young man's impertinence. The words exploded from her lips. "I am not interested in anything you have to say to me now or if we ever meet again, Cody Taylor. I think you are a crude and obnoxious person and I hope I never see you again as long as I live."

She pushed by him, calling over her shoulder, "Good-bye!"

. . . .

Now, pleasant memories surfaced as Cody recalled his difficult meetings with Gina both five years earlier and just recently at the doctor's office. "When I get back to town," Cody said to himself, "I'll make it a point to see the Nurse Gina every day."

Then, Deputy Taylor nudged Sammy into a gallop.

Gina debated Millie's invitation; her encounter with Cody before lunch had been bad enough. She was certainly not in the mood to see him at suppertime the same evening.

Millie insisted that she come, "You do not eat enough child. Living in that big house all alone is not good for you. Matthew will drive you home after supper. You will drive her home, won't you, Matthew?"

"I'll drive you home, Gina," Matthew promised, "but remember, Millie, Cody rode out to Ted's ranch today. He probably won't be home for supper."

"You're right Matthew. Well, Gina, even if Cody won't be there, do come. Andrew so much wants to see you this evening."

The doctor added, "We can leave from the hospital, Gina. I'll bring you to Millie's house. After supper I'll take you home."

When Matthew stopped his buggy in front of the whitewashed picket fence surrounding the Taylor's house, the aroma that drifted into Gina's nostrils made her realize she had not eaten all day. The beef stew and cornbread Millie heaped on her plate was consumed in record time and a second helping requested.

After supper, Gina cleared and washed dishes; Millie put away leftover food. When the deputy walked through the back door, Andrew and Matthew were eating custard pie.

"Son, you're home. We didn't expect you for supper. I'll get your stew, dear, but you need to wash your hands."

While drying his hands, Cody looked at Gina, but said nothing. He sat down at the table.

Matthew took the dish with his custard pie and moved next to Cody.

"How was the confrontation with Owen?" he asked.

Millie, Gina, and Andrew left the kitchen, preferring the comfortable chairs in the living room. Andrew collapsed on the floor and in two minutes was fast asleep. After Gina's hectic day and eating an enormous supper, it was time to go home.

The men were talking head to head in the kitchen. Obviously Matthew forgot about his promise.

"I do not want to disturb Matthew," Gina said to Millie, "I can walk home tonight. Thank you for supper; it was delicious as usual."

She kissed Millie on the cheek, collected her purse, and left quickly.

Although Millie had cooked her son's favorite food, Cody's mind was not on his supper. It was on the conversation with Owen.

"Were you able to speak to Clark?" Matthew asked.

"Yeah, finally. He wasn't around when I got to the ranch," Cody answered, "he was with Jed digging postholes. We talked when he got back.

"Ted told me Clark's always throwing that Arkansas toothpick at opossums and squirrels. He's quick, has a pretty good aim. He makes the kill, pulls the Bowie out and starts hacking away. Then, he leaves the pieces to rot in the sun. He sharpens the knife, puts it back in his boot and starts laughing. I can't figure Clark. Why does he have to kill small animals? They don't hurt him. Why does he do it, Doc?"

"Who knows, Cody. Maybe he just enjoys killing. Why? I can't tell you. I do know Dr. Sciaroni observed people like Owen Clark in New York and San Francisco. I have his notes; I'll read them over. Clark does need treatment, but I don't know any medicine that'll calm him down. Did you tell him this was his last warning?"

"Yeah, I told him. He said he'd put his knife away, and wouldn't wear his six-shooter around the ranch. Told me he only wanted to tease the men, he didn't want to hurt or kill no man, and he sure didn't want to give me any trouble. But he was smiling the whole time, and wouldn't look at me when I was talking to him. I knew he was lying."

"Now, he may be afraid of you, Cody. He knows you're the one that took Harris to the gallows."

Cody pushed his supper away. "I don't know what's wrong with him, Doc," he said, "but he's got something working. Until I figure out what he's up to, I know I've got to watch him close."

"If I can help, I'll do whatever I can. Tomorrow I'll start reading Dr. Sciaroni's observations."

The gabled, white two-story house and wraparound porch built by Vincente Sciaroni shortly after he arrived in Sonora, rested on a small hillock. A black wrought-iron fence circled the house. Huge rocks, some jutting out from the ground at an angle, dotted the property. A grove of tall oak trees, fragrant honeysuckle vines, and wild roses woven through the fence made the picture complete.

Gina stopped at her gate. She decided to let John and Myrtle know she was safely home. Doctor Sciaroni had hired John and Myrtle Alexander two years before his death to be caretakers for his acreage. Vincente built a small cottage on Sciaroni property. John and Myrtle lived close, but still had privacy.

After Mary's death, the caretakers approached Gina and asked to stay and keep up the property for the new owner. She agreed and appreciated their diligence in taking good care of the land and in watching over her.

If Gina rattled the gate to alert the dogs that she was home, Rex and Butler would come running. They were diligent protectors of property and possessions. But as she touched the gate, a shuffling sound in the oak trees across the footpath caught her attention. She peered into the grove, but saw no movement.

"Hello," she called, removing her hand from the gate, "is anyone out there?"

There was movement and a shape formed; somebody stood behind a tree.

She called out again, "Hello! Who is there? Is someone there?"

A large man emerged into the clearing leading a horse, advancing toward her with a slow, deliberate walk. Born cautious, alert to peril, she sensed that this man was evil. Gina's heart thumped in her chest. Every instinct in her body screamed danger as he walked closer. A barrier was needed between him and her, but she stood frozen with fear unable to move.

Long muscular arms and a big barrel chest were obvious, but his hat was worn low on his brow, and his face partially hidden. The brawny man walked steadily closer. Something about him was familiar. Gina had seen this man before.

"Can I help you? Are you looking for someone?" Gina asked.

A diabolical grin slowly spread across his face, but he did not answer her questions. Gina felt vulnerable outside the gate. Forcing her body to move, she opened the latch with as much noise as possible, slammed the gate shut, and stepped backward. Involuntarily, a shudder went up her spine and stirred the hair on the back of her neck.

Reaching the fence, the man stared at Gina, sweeping every inch of her body from top to toe, his massive fingers curled around the wrought iron gate. She tried in vain to scream for help, but no sound would come.

Rex came running from the back of the house, barking furiously until he was by her side, protecting Gina with his intimidating stance. Butler followed and stood with his head lowered, snarling at the intruder. John trailed, closely behind Butler, holding his rifle.

The stranger looked at the dogs and John, walked to the left side of his horse and mounted. "Won't be tonight," he said, shoving the toe of his boot into the stirrup, "but I won't forget. I'll be back. You'll see me again when you least expect it." He nudged his pony with his spurs and rode off.

"Who was that man, John?"

"Owen Clark."

"I have seen him in town. What was he doing here?"

John looked at her, concern marking his kind face, "Go inside the house, Gina," he said, "and lock your doors. I'll keep the dogs in your yard tonight. They won't let anyone close to the house without barking first. You'll be safe, I promise. Go inside now. Get some rest."

She went into the house, locked the front door and peered out the window. John was at the gate, rifle held steady and his eyes focused on the path that led to Gina's door.

Gina wrapped her lunch in a clean towel and stuffed it in her tote. A knock at the back door made her heart jump in her throat. She turned and saw John on the back porch.

"I'll take you to work, Gina," he said. "You ready? I'll bring the wagon around."

"Yes, John. I'm ready."

"Meet you in front of your house. The dogs will stay in your yard today."

When Gina had seen Owen Clark emerge from the trees, her immediate response had been, "How do I defend myself from this giant of a man?" She felt helpless in the presence of this monster. Obviously, John realized she felt that way.

· · · · · · · · ·

The treatment of the mentally unstable was dishearteningly primitive in 1875. Doctor Tufano objected to inmates who were committed to an institution being shackled to a bed or a chair while the public was allowed to visit and laugh and jeer at them.

Dr. Tufano spearheaded a new treatment: Observe the criminally insane people, probe into their minds through questioning, and learn why they had violent tendencies. His ultimate goal, along with that of Dr. Sciaroni and a few other enlightened doctors in New York City, was to find the reason why men like Stuart Harris and Owen Clark had some kind of a desire to harm or kill another human for no apparent reason.

· · · · · · · · ·

Leaving Gina at the doctor's office, John walked to the jail hoping to see the deputy. To his surprise, both the sheriff and Cody were sitting in the front office.

"John," Robert beckoned him forward, "come in and have a seat. Is there a problem?"

Sheriff Sanders and Cody listened as John told of Owen's visit to Gina's house. "I wanted you both to know so you can watch him," John said. "He's up to something. The way he looked at Gina disgusted me. I don't trust him and I'm worried about her. If I'm not around and he gets into her house, well, I'm afraid of what could happen."

Cody stood up and walked to the window. While Robert continued to question John about Clark's erratic behavior, the deputy reached for his hat and headed toward the door, "I'm going to talk to the nurse. I'll let you know what I find out, sheriff," he said.

Gina stood at the examination room door talking to Matthew when the bell sounded. She turned and saw the deputy standing by her desk.

"Got a minute?" he said, boldly pulling around her desk chair and taking a seat.

She closed the door, moved one of the waiting room chairs close, and answered, "Sure."

Cody pushed his hat back, "I hear you had a visitor last night after you left our house," he said. "Tell me what happened."

"Nothing really happened. As I approached the front gate, a noise, then a movement in the trees across the path, caught my attention. A large man stepped out from behind a tree and walked toward me, leading his horse.

"I was terrified. He reached my gate and just stood and stared at me. I tried to call the dogs, but the words stuck in my throat. Finally, Rex ran from the back barking, then Butler followed growling. John was just behind Butler and stood by me with his rifle. The man mumbled something, then mounted and rode away."

Cody sat with hands together, elbows on his knees, and his upper body tilted forward. His head inclined in her direction, Cody listened intently and observed closely Gina as she spoke.

When Gina had finished relating the incident, he stood up to leave. However, he paused as she related another encounter she had with Owen. "A few days after I started working for Doctor Gibbs, a man came in to be treated for a cut to his left arm. I think the man I saw last night in front of my house and the one I treated with the cut was the same man."

Doctor Gibbs walked in from the examination room, saw Cody standing by Gina, and took a seat near Gina.

"Tell me again," Cody said to Gina, "about the man that came into the doctor's office, the man you patched up."

"I think it was the same man I saw last night standing in front of my house."

Matthew was not getting the whole picture. "Gina," he asked, annoyed, "what is going on? Who was standing in front of your house last night?"

"A man named Owen Clark, Matthew, an evil man, a very frightening man. One afternoon, not long after I started as your assistant, you left the office and a few minutes later a big man came in to be treated." Gina's arms opened out to show the enormity of the man. "He had a fresh cut on his left arm. The wound was bleeding, so I washed it carefully, applied antiseptic, wrapped it to keep it clean, then bandaged it securely."

"Why do you think it was Owen Clark? Did you get a good look at him?" Cody asked brusquely.

"I checked the register this morning. His name was listed as a patient examined soon after I arrived. The man I treated when I first arrived stared at me while I washed and cleaned his arm, the same way Owen Clark stared at me last night. Something has always bothered me about that patient. I remember he had a wicked smile, evil, and the cut on his arm had pieces of what looked like old flesh and filth in it. I had to wash the opening several times, because although it was a fresh cut, there were signs that infection was starting. I think the knife or whatever cut him had to be filthy."

Cody was aware that when Harris and Clark sheathed their knives, they never cleaned them.

In her first two meetings with Cody, Gina had not picked out the qualities in the deputy she sensed today. He was playful and mischievous, yes, but now she saw that he could also be thoughtful, stalwart, and daring.

Dr. Tufano and Dr. Sciaroni had possessed those qualities, along with what she remembered of Sheriff Taylor. Cody had aggravated her enormously the first two times she met him, but today she saw a different side to Deputy Cody Taylor.

In spite of Miss Tufano's bad temper and aloofness, Cody also noticed qualities in Gina that he admired in women, goodness, guts, and compassion. As he watched her speak, he noted her quiet beauty and, above all, her innocence. And, he realized that something evil had formulated in Owen Clark's mind. Whatever it was, it included this nurse.

9

"This coming Sunday? Yes, I can assist you, Matthew," Gina said as she locked the dispensary door, "I would be happy to help."

"Thanks, Gina. You need your time away from the doctor's office, but Mayor Thorton said this Sunday with the promise of free food and the need of supplies, the town will be chock-full of miners. If they gamble and drink like they usually do, and stay for the parade, it's likely they'll get into some kind of trouble and need doctoring."

Although Sonora acquired new residents daily, the town council had four vacant positions, treasurer, city attorney, recorder, and clerk. *The Sonora Herald* had printed an invitation to all the residents in and around Sonora: "Everyone is invited to a parade and picnic on Sunday, June 2, 1875. Come one! Come all! Hear! Learn! Listen! And, get to know your favorite candidate! After the parade, food will be served."

Gina checked the house for unlocked doors and windows while waiting for John and Myrtle. She heard Rex growl and saw him run toward the cottage. Butler followed.

What did they see? If Owen Clark was close to the house, Gina was safer outside with the dogs than in the house alone. She stepped out the back door and a strange feeling swept over her. Someone was watching and it made her feel both frightened and cautious.

She turned her head from side to side as she slowly walked forward, scanning the yard, until she saw branches move on a large oleander shrub by the side of a shed. It was a calm day; wind surely did not move those branches. She ignored her internal warnings and started walking quickly toward the bush to investigate.

However, she heard John calling from the front of the house where he and Myrtle were waiting to take her to town. It was time to collect her purse and tote. Gina made a mental note to speak to the deputy about the movement of the branches in the oleander bush.

Washington Street was crowded with people, horses, and wagons, so John parked the wagon on Stockton Street. Gina walked the two blocks to the doctor's office. As she entered, Matthew was moving antiseptic, bandages, and dressings from the dispensary onto a tray. The nurse put away her purse and tote and went to assist the doctor.

The bell pealed as the front door of the doctor's office burst open. Deputy Taylor stood in the doorway just behind two men, who had their hands lifted high and Cody's Colt was pointed directly at their backs. Gina could see that Cody toted two extra pistols in his belt. All three dripped blood from their faces, hands, and knuckles.

Doctor Gibbs stood by the door to the examination room and beckoned Gina. Deputy Taylor wiped the dripping blood from his chin with the back of his hand and prodded the men forward with his Colt. He stepped inside the room, closed the door, and leaned against it.

On this Sunday morning, hundreds of young men, lean, hard, and tough, and most in the prime of their life had ridden into Sonora. The consumption of whiskey and the plethora of pretty young maidens filled them with false courage and an excess of bravado.

The bell sounded again. Gina excused herself, left the examination room, and found Robert in an agitated state.

He asked Gina, "Have you seen my deputy?"

"He's in the examination room with Matthew and two miners. All three of them have obviously been in a fight. One miner has an deep gash over his left eye, and I believe Doctor Gibbs has just finished stitching that wound closed. He should be sewing a tear on the cheek of the other miner now. Come in, sheriff, we won't be long."

"I'll wait outside," Robert said, looking a bit queasy, "I'll watch the people. Make sure there's no trouble. Tell Deputy Taylor I'm out here if he needs me."

Nothing sombers a man faster than seeing a needle and feeling pain. When the examination door finally opened, the two bloody, bruised miners were eager to leave the doctor's office and follow the law to the dirty cots in the jail. Sleep would put them right by morning.

Robert escorted the prisoners across the street. Doctor Gibbs made Cody stay to be treated for his injuries. He wondered what had caused the cool-headed deputy to lose his temper.

While Cody gave a brief account of the fight, Matthew dabbed antiseptic on a deep cut across the deputy's chin. "I saw two drunk miners dragging off a young girl, who obviously didn't want to accompany them. I pulled her away and they started fighting with me. I had to take them down. They were bleeding, and I didn't want the jail dirtier than it is already, so I brought them here to be patched up."

"Good for you, Deputy," Matthew said. "Imagine someone dragging off a young girl against her wishes. It's good you were close when it happened. Do you know who she is?"

"Never saw her before. She sure didn't want to go with them. When I pulled her away, she started running and screaming for her mama. Then the men jumped me."

Matthew smoothed ointment onto the deputy's chin. "I bet their stitches will teach them to fight with you, Deputy," he said with a snicker. "You'll be fine in a day or two. There's no permanent damage."

"Thanks for the patch-up, Doc. I'm gonna lock up their pistols. See ya, Gina."

Cody left the prisoners groaning on their cots. He stood on the front steps of the jail, overlooking the crowd of people waiting for the parade. Robert mounted his pony to get a better view of the townspeople and visitors.

Gina hurried across the street to tell Cody about the mystery of the oleander bush. She waited at his side until he acknowledged her presence. "Cody," she said, "I need to speak with you, please."

He nodded, but did not take his eyes off of the cheering and, at times, jeering crowd. Unsure if Cody was listening, Gina started her tale. "This morning, before I left the house, the dogs were restless and started barking. I walked outside, and when I got near that big bush close to John and Myrtle's cottage, I saw the branches moving. It was calm this morning; there was no wind. Someone was inside that bush pushing the branches apart to watch me. I think it was Owen Clark. Who else, I ask you, would want to watch me?"

"Gina, there are dozens of bushes in your yard and by John's house. Which bush had its branches moving?"

As she spoke her arms made a large circle overhead with her fingertips touching describing the enormous size of the bush; "It is that big bush with the red flowers. The one behind the back fence, and just in front of John and Myrtle's cottage."

Gina's frequent descriptive gestures always made Cody smile. He glanced away, but questioned her further. "What do you think was causing the branches to move?"

"What I just told you," she said, her left hand on her hip, the right hand shaking a finger at Cody. "I think there was someone inside the bush watching the house and me. I think it was Owen Clark. There is no one else. Something was moving the branches and it sure wasn't the wind." She looked at Cody, silently demanding an answer from him.

Cody did not answer, but he turned his head and said to her, "I'll check out the bush with John."

Fainting at the first sign of trouble or crying for sympathy was not Gina's way of getting attention. Her anxiety was real. It was obvious that Clark had a passionate desire for Gina and trouble was imminent.

"Thank you. I feel better now," said Gina.

Deputy Taylor watched her float down the steps, dodging carriages and horses as she headed toward the doctor's office. As she passed by four young men, her long dark curly hair bounced on her shoulders and down her back. They all smiled and gazed in admiration at the natural way her hips swayed from side to side.

When Robert had said this exotic maiden was causing a stir in the town, he was right on the money. Gina stirred Cody's insides, too.

From the first day Cody had met Gina, she demonstrated a spirit that challenged him. For some reason, he liked that feature of her personality. Since his return from Sacramento after Harris' trial and hanging, and seeing Gina again after five years of separation, Cody realized he was content living in Sonora.

From his window in the jail, to the window in the doctor's office, he could see Gina work at her desk. This young woman was a quandary to him. She was certainly out of the ordinary and one in a million, like a precious jewel with many brilliant facets, colorful, intense, and alive.

Cody turned his attention from the nurse and tried to concentrate on the crowd, the parade was in progress.

*C*ody's efforts to stay one step ahead of Clark dominated his conscious thoughts. He had to know what Clark planned.

Owen Clark had been prone to violent fits of temper to the point of doing harm to others from a child to adolescence, but a depraved outlook toward women had surfaced when he turned twenty-one years old. He met and fell in love with Ruth, a woman thirty-years old and intensely desirous.

Ruth had married at the tender age of seventeen. Bored to death with her first husband and annoyed that his earning did not keep her in the luxuries she thought a necessity, she left him.

Clark filled Ruth's lap with tawdry jewels and clothes. In return, she promised love and marriage to Clark. But when he learned she had many pursuers that she encouraged, he confronted her. Ruth made a mockery of him.

The final blow came when she divulged, "You are a nobody, Owen, a bloated giant, insignificant, and poor. Why would I want you when I could have any rich, good-looking man I want?"

Clark was unstable before his affair with Ruth; now he was treacherous and unpredictable, dangerous and violent. A maiden like Gina had no chance of escape from Clark, not if he caught her alone. And, who was able to predict the actions of Owen Clark? No one. Not Matthew, Cody, Sheriff Sanders nor John; they must wait for Clark to initiate his plan of action and pray that their help would not come too late.

It was well past the lunch hour. Cody reached for his hat and headed to the doctor's office across the street. He held the door open for Mrs. Humphrey and her new baby as they were leaving.

Mrs. Humphrey was known as the town's busybody, and since Cody was not getting any younger, she ventured her opinion, "Gina is such a dear, Cody. We all loved Mary, but Gina does have a way about her. Don't you think? She's caring and an excellent nurse; she might just make some man a good wife." She winked and walked away smiling.

Cody touched his hat at Mrs. Humphrey's departure. The married ladies in town all wanted to make plans for him. He appreciated the interest, but he was not ready to marry.

Matthew was in his office, Gina at the dispensary, when the bell pealed. The deputy got right to the point. "Can you have lunch with me, Doc?"

Gina heard Cody's request as she walked into the front office. "Bye," she said, turning around, "have a nice lunch."

Unaware that she was also included in the invitation, she heard the deputy call out, "Gina, I want you to come with us."

Eat? With the doctor and the deputy? Alone? With the two of them? This sort of thing was just not done in New York City.

"No, thank you, Cody," she said, "I brought my lunch. I will stay here. You both go; enjoy yourselves."

Reaching to grab her hand, he pulled her to face him. "You're coming with us," he said. "Lock up, Doc."

"No, really, Cody, I cannot go," she protested.

"You need to eat," he said, thus, ending the discussion.

Cody confessed his reason for the impromptu lunch after they had ordered. "I want you to find a medicine for Clark, Matthew. Is there anything that'll calm him down?" Cody's appeal bordered on desperate. "I know Clark is up to something. I have a gut feeling what it is, but nothing I can pin on him."

While Matthew reviewed different treatments in his mind, Gina threw caution to the wind and spoke out, "Cody, Owen needs to be in an institution; there is no medicine that will help him. To understand what causes a person to act like him, doctors have to observe his actions constantly for many months or years in a special hospital for the insane."

Gina continued explaining the problem that confronted doctors. "Six months before my father died, he protested the release of a man brought to the sanitarium for threatening young women with death when they passed him on the street.

"My father initiated a new treatment and used it on this patient for almost one year. He observed him, questioned him, got him to talk about his life, and tried to learn from the patient why he wanted to kill people, especially women. But even after eleven months of these intense measures, this man was still too dangerous to release into society.

"The other doctors disagreed. They thought the inmate had adjusted, had made progress. My father was overruled.

"Two weeks after his release, the man killed a woman and her child as they walked along Madison Avenue in New York City. He had fooled the other doctors completely. The deaths of the woman and her child grieved my father until the day he died."

Matthew added his conclusions. "It's true what Gina says, Cody, Clark should be in an asylum, permanently, where he does not have the liberty to harm anyone. The truth is, we as doctors don't have answers for people like Clark. Sadly, however, when confined to an asylum, sometimes the treatment the inmates get makes them worst than they were before.

"I have learned, however, that recently in sanitariums in New York and San Francisco, doctors have been observing the mentally ill, using Doctor Tufano's methods. Hopefully, in the near future, we will have an answer. I'm still reading Dr. Sciaroni's observations, and I hope to have some recommendations very soon."

The waiter placed lunch on the table. Cody and Matthew had ordered steak, and Gina had decided on the restaurant's famous fried chicken. She picked up her knife and fork and ravenously devoured her lunch.

Cody watched her scraping the dish with the bottom of her fork to get the last of the crumbs. "Are you still hungry, Gina?" he asked.

"Oh, no," she said, a bit embarrassed, "the food was delicious. Thank you for lunch, Cody. I must have been hungry."

Since the nurse had arrived in Sonora, Owen Clark had not been the only person on Cody's mind. He recalled the first time he met Gina and the event on the swing.

"I like when you smile and laugh, Gina," he said, leaning back on his chair. "Remember five years ago on the swing with Andrew? When you came to our house for supper?"

Gina blushed when she recalled her haughty attitude toward Cody. "I did enjoy sitting on the swing with Andrew that day. He was so upset when I had to leave and return to New York. I was also very rude when you tried to speak to me. I am sorry, Cody."

Mesmerized at Gina's sincerity and charm, Cody collected his thoughts and responded, "I remember that day and I know I wasn't polite to you, either."

Matthew and Gina thanked Cody and walked toward the exit. But with a sudden fancy, Gina turned and went back to face the deputy. Standing up on her toes, she placed her hands on the top of his shoulders, raised her head, and kissed him on the left cheek.

Robert opened the front door to the restaurant just as the doctor and nurse were leaving. He nodded to them, and then went directly to Cody. He handed the deputy a telegram and said, "I just came from the telegraph office. We received this from Mariposa a few minutes ago."

"I remember this guy," Cody said as he read the telegram. "He was always taking his six-shooter out of the holster and pointing it at people. He even aimed at the Doc once."

"I'll go through some of the wanted posters," Robert said. "Do you remember if he stole anything?"

"I don't know. The sheriff of Mariposa wants to talk to one of us. I'll ride over tomorrow, but I'll be gone two, maybe, three days."

Robert plunged his hands deep into his pockets and fidgeted. "It has to be done, Deputy," he said, reluctantly. "I sure don't want you to leave Sonora. I need you here. I'll watch Clark. Come back as soon as you can."

Sheriff Sanders turned to head back to the jail, just as Nancy Johnson was about to enter the restaurant. He opened the door wide, always a man with a polite gesture and a friendly smile for a pretty lady.

"Thank you kindly, Sheriff," Nancy said, flashing her beautiful smile. She wore her usual low-cut dress, and a trail of perfume followed her as she drifted around the tables toward Cody. He stood by the proprietor of the hotel, waiting to pay for the meals.

Widow Nancy is what everyone in Sonora called her. Pretty, young, not thirty-years old, she was soft and round in all the right places. She had been married to a man twenty-five years her senior, but for the last six months she had been a widow.

At his death, Nancy's husband left his pretty young wife with a beautiful home, some money, and a healthy appetite for young men. One in particular caught her fancy-the deputy. She had invited him over many times in the last five months, and many times Cody had accepted.

Eager to satisfy the needs of men, especially the deputy of Sonora, she now nestled close to Cody and requested his company for the evening. "Come by for supper tonight. I'm making your favorite, beef stew, cornbread, and custard pie. What do you think, Deputy? Can you come tonight?"

Seldom was Nancy's offer refused. "About six o'clock. I'll see you then," she insisted.

Nancy turned from the deputy and glided toward the door.

"Can't make it tonight, Nancy," Cody said. "I have to check out a bush."

Rejected because of a bush? Perplexed, crestfallen, she pivoted to face him with an alternative proposal. "Can you come over tomorrow, then?"

Cody countered, "I'll be in Mariposa tomorrow. Be gone two, maybe three days."

Nancy was a beguiling lady, with grace and beauty, and she had the ability to enrapture virtually any man with little or no effort. She floated back to Cody's side, linked her arm through his, and gazed deep into his azure eyes. "Well," she said, "I guess I will have to wait two, maybe, three days."

As he watched Nancy's young, shapely body glide around the tables and out the front door, Cody touched his cheek and recalled Gina's kiss. That kiss burned his cheek the rest of the afternoon.

When he found himself standing in front of the hospital as the doctor locked the office door for the night, Cody was not surprised.

11

Since her encounter with Owen Clark, Matthew, Millie, and John agreed that Gina should not walk anywhere alone.

"This arrangement is unnecessary," Gina said. "After my parents died, there was no one to walk me to the hospital, emporiums, or market. Surely I can walk to or from the doctor's office by myself in Sonora."

Her pleadings were ignored. She waited in the buggy for Matthew to lock up the doctor's office, and then watched Cody's horse, Sammy, strut across the street following his master's lead. He was the perfect specimen of an Appaloosa. Long, muscular legs and a powerful body, a well-shaped head, beautiful spotted rump, and a long shaggy mane and tail.

For over two months, that Miss Tufano had lived in Sonora, she had yet to sit on a saddle on a horse. But if she ever got the chance to ride, her preference would be Sammy.

The deputy reined up and rode along the side of the buggy, asking Doctor Gibbs questions regarding Owen's unstable behavior.

Matthew was still limited in his search for information, but he gave Cody hope. "I had a discussion with Mary before she died," he related, "about one of her husband's patients. This particular man had similar hostile traits, but not as bad as Harris or Clark. Doctor Sciaroni had noted the behavior pattern, the conduct, and his own personal perceptions of the patient.

"Mary told me the man ultimately took his anger out on himself. One day, after having waited over two hours for this patient to keep an appointment, Dr. Sciaroni went to his home and found him dead, hanging from a rafter in his room. Poor man, he was very unstable."

The conversation proceeded until Matthew pulled his horse to a halt in front of Gina's house. He encouraged Cody further with the words, "I'll have an answer for you soon, Deputy."

"Thanks, Doc, appreciate your help."

"*Grazie*, Matthew. *Ciao*! See you tomorrow," Gina said, as the doctor turned his pony back toward town.

Cody dismounted and tethered Sammy in a grassy area in front of the fence. Gina stopped at her gate and looked at Cody, wondering silently why he did not ride off.

He raised his arms over his head with his fingertips touching to mimic her description of the large bush and said with a grin, "I'm going to check out the bush."

With a condescending shake of her head and a large smile, Gina walked to the front door. Cody watched her walk, and he sighed deeply as he admired the natural sway of her hips.

Deputy Taylor and John investigated the oleander shrub. This particular oleander was nine to ten feet tall, large enough to hide a tall, big man. Cody stepped into the center of the bush and discovered broken branches and two different sized footprints.

One knee bent, his body resting on the other leg, Cody inspected the ground.

"Looks like someone was watching Gina's house," John declared, "maybe even spying on Myrtle and me. Have any idea who it might be, Cody?"

"No, John, but we need to find out who it was for the safety of you all."

Cody picked up a stone lying on the ground, turned it over and over in his hand, then stood up and faced Gina's house. "From in here, she could be watched during the day or night," he said, "especially when there are lights in the house. She must have sensed that someone was watching her, come outside and saw the branches moving." Cody paused. "I'll have to come back, John," he affirmed, "when Gina's at the doctor's office."

Suspicions gathering in his mind, he advised John of the precautions he should take and added, "Let me know if you see anyone."

John's face was somber when he answered. "Sure thing, Cody."

Pleasant aromas drifted from Gina's kitchen making the deputy realize he was hungry. The aromas suggested Gina was cooking something Italian.

"Gina," he called from the back porch.

She held the door open for him to enter combining Italian and English, "*Si*. Yes, Cody. *En'trare*. Come in."

Gina had changed from her uniform into a skirt, white blouse, and apron. She reached for a large bowl on the counter containing four beaten eggs and poured the contents into simmering herbs, onions, garlic and tomatoes. The aromatic odor was intoxicating.

"Hungry?" Gina asked. "*Mangiore*. You will eat and drink; I have wine, red Italian wine. *Sedere*, I want to give you a glass of wine with your food. It will be good for your blood. Sit, please."

While she completed the supper, the deputy told her what they found in the oleander bush.

"I am not surprised," she said, lifting the edges of the frittata to let the underside cook. "I knew someone was there. Rex and Butler knew someone was in that bush."

She put half of the *frittata* onto a plate and set the dish in front of him.

Cody pointed to his plate. "What is this?" he asked.

"A *frittata*. An Italian omelet. It has fresh eggs, herbs, tomatoes, and onions. *Mangiore tutto*. Eat, it is good." One hand on her hip, the other hand pointing in Cody's direction, she gave final orders, "Why do you ask so many questions? Are you hungry? Eat."

Placing homemade *focaccia* on the dish along with the frittata; Cody finished his helping of *frittata* and the homemade *focaccia*, handed it back to Gina, and requested more. "I'll have the rest."

"Are you sure, *Caro Mia?*"

"I'm sure. Gina, what does *Caro Mia* mean?"

"*Caro Mia?*" Gina tuned to look at Cody and questioned, "Why do you want to know what it means?"

"Because that's what you call Andrew, and you just called me *Caro Mia*."

She replied shyly, turning her face away, "I do not always realize what I say. It means 'my dear'."

She placed a second full plate before him, refilled his glass with wine, took off her apron, and sat down at the table. Dr. Sciaroni loved good homemade wine and had stocked a large supply in the cellar.

Swallowing the burgundy liquid in his second glass of wine, the deputy relaxed and asked Gina questions about New York and the tragedy that ultimately took both her parents lives. Gina answered his questions as he put them to her. She, in turn, asked Cody about Sheriff Taylor and his death.

He gazed into his wine and started the sad story concerning his father's death. "There was an argument in the saloon late one night. Two men, partners in a small gold claim, had a little too much whiskey and accused each other of stealing gold from the bags tied on their belts.

"The miners had already started to fight. One of the bartenders ran to get the sheriff. I wasn't the deputy then; Sheriff Sanders was the deputy. My father and Robert were at the jail. They had just finished the rounds. The bartender told my father what was happening, and both men went with him to the saloon."

Cody looked at Gina, her upper body arched slightly forward, listening intently. He now related the tragic part of the story. "Trying to calm the men, my father suggested that he would take their bags of gold and lock them in the safe at the jail until the next day. Then when they sobered up, he'd give them back, but they would have to leave town.

"Drunk and mean, they thought the sheriff meant to keep the gold for himself. One man pulled his revolver from his holster and as the sheriff tried to reason with him, it went off. My father took a bullet at close range in his stomach. The miner, the one who fired the shot, pointed the revolver at Robert, but the bartender aimed his rifle and killed the miner. So, the partner got all the gold, but my father was dead."

The deputy looked into his glass, swirling the burgundy liquid around and around.

"I am so sorry your father was killed, Cody," Gina said. "I only met him once, but I liked him very much. You remind me of Sheriff Taylor. You are strong like him."

While Cody spoke about his father's tragic death, Gina gazed closely at Cody's ruggedly handsome masculine features-the way his sandy-colored hair fell over the left side of his forehead, the two-day stubble on his face and neck, penetrating deep blue eyes, a strong jaw, and a well-proportioned nose.

She compared him to the young man she remembered five years ago. His mischievous, playful manner was the same, but at twenty-three years old, Cody had matured, and a steely strength and hardiness were visible in his shoulders, back, arms, hands, and chest.

Aunt Mary's cuckoo clock struck; it was time for Deputy Taylor to go home.

Cody stood up and announced, reluctantly, "I have to go now. It's getting late."

"I will walk you out to the gate," Gina replied.

Outside, when she looked up toward the heavens, a million stars were twinkling, and the moon was unusually big and bright.

"Guar'dare a Luna. Quanto Bello."

"What did you say, Gina?"

"I said to look at the moon; it is beautiful tonight. When the moon was big and brilliant like this in New York, my mother said it smiled at us."

He brought Sammy close to the gate and moved to the left side to mount.

Gina ran to Sammy and grabbed the bridle with both of her hands. "Wait, Cody," she said, "before you go, I want to feel his forehead and the side of his nose; it's so soft.

"You are so special, Sammy, and you know it. Someday, when I learn how to ride, we will fly, you and I at a gallop."

Desiring to prolong his departure, Cody put a suggestion to Gina. "I can show you tonight. Let's go for a ride now."

"Oh, no. It's too dark and too late."

"It's not late and Sammy's not blind," Cody reminded her. "He knows he has to stay on the path."

"You think we could, Cody?"

"I know we could, Gina."

Smiling her approval, she approached the stirrup and tried to mount Sammy in the normal way. But Gina was definitely a city girl and not in the habit of stepping up on a horse. Ultimately, Cody brought Sammy to a large rock. Gina climbed the rock, put her left foot in the stirrup and stretched her right leg over Sammy's back. If nothing else, she was finally sitting in the saddle.

"Gina," Cody suggested, "press your knees into Sammy's shoulders, the muscles here above his legs, and hold this; it's called the saddle horn."

Watching where Cody pointed, she muttered softly, puzzled, "Press my knees into Sammy's shoulders? But I cannot see where his shoulders are from up here."

"I'm going to ride with you. Don't move."

She squirmed and made an attempt to dismount. To sit in that position with a man directly behind her, embarrassed Gina. "I am sorry, Cody," Gina announced, "but I'm not going to ride Sammy tonight after all. It really is too late."

"You're going to ride tonight, Gina; sit still."

He swung up, sat on the skirt of the saddle, and reached with his right hand around Gina to take hold of the reins. She sat forward, as close to the saddle horn as possible, holding firmly.

But when his left arm went around her waist and pulled her back, Gina straightened into a rigid position. However, as Cody nudged Sammy into a walk, then into an easy cantor, Gina's thoughts turned quickly from impropriety to personal safety.

Well, Gina decided; sitting on a saddle and controlling a horse was definitely not as easy as it appeared. No matter how hard she tried to press her knees into Sammy's shoulders or hold the saddle horn, her incompetence as a rider was apparent. Gina gave up the effort and just had fun, sending out shrieks of laughter into the still night with every slip or bounce.

"Hold on, Gina, with your knees. Don't put your arms over your head or out to the side," Cody coached, again and again.

"*Si. Si.* Yes, I am trying. I promise to hold on," she answered between the giggles.

He listened with a smile when she apologized, mostly in Italian, for not being adept in sitting on a saddle. Clearly, Gina relied on the deputy's strength to keep her from falling.

In the last few years, Cody has pressed many women close to his body. But with his arm around this damsel, other women faded into hazy recollection.

He held Gina, his left hand below her midriff. He felt the incurve of a tiny waist and her rib bones, and he felt her stomach muscles tighten when she laughed. Fragrant, soft, long ringlets blew into his face as they rode together, but that didn't matter to him. She was definitely a pleasure to hold close, especially when she started to slip off the saddle.

While the soft breezes carried fragrance from the honeysuckle vines, and the moon radiated its magic on such a perfect evening, this light-hearted, carefree pair rode for thirty minutes after Sammy broke into a cantor. Then Cody pulled Sammy to a halt in front of Gina's gate. She was expected at the doctor's office the following morning, and he was leaving early the next day for Mariposa. Cody swung off the saddle; and waited for Gina to request his help, but she refused to dismount.

She looked at Cody and playfully tossed her head. "No, please, *Caro Mia*," she murmured, "can we not ride a little while longer? Sammy is not tired yet. I am not tired yet."

Cody looked at Gina long and hard. Her hair was loose; reflecting the moonlight as it spilled over soft delicate shoulders. Large, luminous eyes and full, pouting lips pleaded for his consent from a face that glowed with energy and pleasure. She captivated Cody with the beauty, both internal and external, that she radiated. The need to hold her again overpowered him.

Cody's strong hands extended toward her waist, and he voiced a command. "Gina, I want you to get down, now."

Miss Tufano was wiser than her years, and the look in Cody's eyes would suggest apprehension. Dr. Tufano had lectured her frequently about proper conduct and admonished her to uphold high moral standards, to behave in a proper way at all times.

Mama's words now rang in her ears. "You must be on your guard always, *Caro Mia*, when around any man, young or old. Often men will try to take advantage of you."

Cody's hands seized her waist and lifted her up. What was Gina supposed to do now?

He pulled her up and off the saddle and brought her down slowly near his body. When Gina's toes touched the ground, her hands left his shoulders, and her arms slowly circled his neck.

She knew better; it was time to push the deputy away. But Gina allowed Cody's arms to surround and pull her close to him. Strange though it seemed, she wanted to linger in those arms.

Cody's head drew near Gina's face. She looked into his searching blue eyes, and while her mouth formed the words, "No, Cody..." his lips pressed unrelentingly onto hers.

Gina had often wondered as she matured into a woman, how to react when a man wanted to hold and kiss her. She would wonder no more. Her eyes closed when Cody's lips covered hers; she melted into his chest, feeling the hardness of his body and the strong arms that held her captive. Sensations within her that Gina did not know existed now awakened.

Feeling the softness of her lips and firm breasts pressed against his chest, the deputy wanted to drink his fill from this lovely maiden, but checked the passion forming. "You better go inside now," he said, "it's getting late."

Collecting her wits, she backed away from Cody, stood a moment looking at him, and then walked toward Sammy.

"Thank you, Sammy," she whispered. "I had such a wonderful time tonight. I will never forget this night as long as I live."

Caressing the softness of Sammy's nostrils, then blowing a kiss to the moon, Gina started up her walkway, calling over her shoulder, "*Grazie*, Cody. It was a wonderful ride. *Ciao!*"

Cody spoke aloud after Gina had reached her porch. "Why did I stop, Sammy? I wanted to kiss her all night."

His boot in the stirrup, he swung up on the saddle. Cody watched as she closed the door, and the light from the oil lamp faded as she climbed the stairs. Slowly, grudgingly, he turned Sammy toward home.

$\mathcal{D}$eputy Taylor woke early, dressed, and went into the kitchen to make coffee. The Sheriff of Mariposa waited anxiously for his advice.

"The prisoner is not mean," the telegram read. "Steals anything not nailed down. Threatens people with pistol. Need help. Locked up. Don't know how long."

Cody sipped hot coffee; his thoughts went to Gina, not to the prisoner in Mariposa.

Millie interrupted his reflections by asking, "Cody, dear, why are you up so early?"

So absorbed in his thoughts that he had not been aware that his mother had come into the kitchen, he answered, "I'm riding to Mariposa today, Mom. I have to talk to the sheriff about a prisoner in their jail." Seeing the concern on her face he added, "They need my opinion, Mom that's all. I'll be gone two or three days."

"Son, you did not eat the supper I left for you."

"I was at Gina's last night. She fixed me something to eat. She wanted to ride Sammy. I had more trouble keeping her on that horse."

Millie went to the stove and poured the coffee, not at all happy Cody had spent the evening with Gina, alone.

She sat down to explain her dilemma. "Son, Gina is not an ordinary young woman. She is different, special, comes from a prominent family, but through no fault of her own, she is without family. She needs to be safeguarded by all of us, including you."

Cody was listening, but he did not acknowledge her entreaty. "You are a handsome man, son, in a rugged sort of way, and I know how you charm the single women in town. In fact, I know of several women that love for you to pay them more than the usual attention. You may think I am old-fashioned, but I know exactly what the young men of Sonora, including you, think of this maiden who is not experienced in the ways of men, especially Western men."

Millie continued with her admonition. "I want you to remember that Gina needs to be protected. Not compromised."

Cody looked into his cup of coffee, then lifted it to his lips. "I know that, Mom," he said, and swallowed the hot brew.

The discussion was over. Millie cooked breakfast and wrapped some food to send with him.

When Cody emptied his pockets of unnecessary papers and clutter, he found the arrowhead he had picked up from under the oleander shrub. Turning it over and over in his hands, this particular arrowhead looked familiar. He dropped it on the kitchen table; he would examine it further.

Kissing his mother on the cheek, he went out the back door to the stable and saddled up Sammy.

13

*A*ll morning, Andrew and Billy gathered pieces of wood and nails for their private treehouse. They didn't need rope. Cody had changed the rope on the swing, but they did need more scrap wood. Unsuccessful in scouring the town for used wood, they ended up sitting on the corral fence at Andrew's house, searching for a solution to their problem.

"I know," Billy shouted at Andrew. "Ted has old wood from the barn that was torn down. He's not using it; we can go get it and bring it back here."

"That's right," Andrew said. "Ted was going to burn the old wood anyway; he won't need it. No, that won't work. Mom doesn't want us to ride out to Ted's ranch alone. And, besides, once we got there, how would we bring it home?"

"I can ask Owen to help us," Billy offered. "He's always asking me to do things for him. Now he can help me."

"Why should we ask Owen?" Andrew questioned.

"Because he's my friend, that's why. He tells me all the time how much help I am to him. I always try to help him."

"Doing what, Billy?"

"Can you keep a secret, Andrew?"

"No."

"Promise, and I'll tell you the secret."

"Oh," Andrew said, disgusted, "what does he ask you to do?"

Billy disregarded the fact Andrew did not promise to keep the secret and started his story. "He told me to go to the old doctor's house, you know, where Gina lives now, and wait in the big bush behind her house and watch her. He wants to know who comes to visit her. He has me follow her around town and I tell him where she goes. He watches her too. I do all kinds of things like that."

Andrew turned with a glare. "You hid in the bush?" he demanded. "Did you, Billy? 'Cause that's spying."

"I know. But Owen wants to know who comes to visit Gina, if any men come to visit her. I think he wants to marry her."

"You better tell Cody about you spying on Gina. Because if you don't, I will." Andrew got down from the fence and headed into the house to eat lunch. He was disgusted with this conversation, disgusted with Owen, and close to being disgusted with Billy.

"Don't be mad, Andrew," Billy shouted after him. "I won't spy on Gina anymore if you don't want me too."

"I don't, so you can't do it. You hear me?" Andrew said.

The boys washed, got some food from the stove, and sat at the kitchen table to eat lunch.

Sitting quietly, Billy spotted the arrowhead lying by Andrew's plate. He picked it up, struggling to remember when he last had the arrowhead in his pocket. "I don't remember leaving my arrowhead here. How did it get here?" Billy inquired.

"I don't know how it landed on the table. You're always losing that arrowhead, Billy. I gave it to you after my dad died. All you do is lose it. Put it in your pocket and leave it there; otherwise, I will take it back and I will never give it to you again." Andrew's voice had risen to a crescendo.

Billy put the arrowhead into his pocket meekly and continued eating his lunch.

*U*p with the dawn, Gina tidied up the kitchen she had ignored the previous evening and reflected on her moonlight ride with Cody.

"Papa would never have approved," she said, wrapping her lunch in a towel. "He would have been furious knowing I was alone with Cody and on a horse. And Mama would have lectured me for days."

Miss Tufano had been highly incensed at Cody the first two times they met, but through all the aggravation he inflicted on her, Gina had never felt fear. Trust she did not give to many people, but she now trusted this deputy with her life. How could that be?

The doctor was at the gate ready to take her into town. She picked up her purse and lunch and locked the front door securely on the way out.

That morning the patients were steady. About midday, Matthew was summoned to treat an ailing guest at the Sonora Hotel. Gina watched him leave the office with his medical bag and stared at the work that waited on her desk. Matthew had asked her to total a few of the patient's accounts.

Head down, absorbed in the final charges, Gina did not see two men pass by the window. The bell pealed, and her voice stuck in her throat when she looked up. Owen Clark, an evil grin on his face, stood behind another man. Both were grimy, sweaty, and looked like they had worked all morning in the hot sun.

The man whose name she knew as Jed, took one step forward and spoke, "Can you help us nurse? Clark, here, tore his arm real bad."

$\mathcal{J}$ed and Owen had loaded the wagon with food, tools, and supplies as the first rays of the sun highlighted the hills of Sonora.

"We'll finish out there before noon, Jed; it's too damn hot to work after that. You dig postholes and I'll pull wire. Then we gotta ride back to the ranch soon as we get done 'cause old man Martin wants us to finish the work we started yesterday in the barn."

Owen kicked the dust and said, "I'm sick of this damn place. Tired of getting bossed around. I wanna get out of here."

"A cowboy came ridin' through town last Sunday," Jed said as he hitched the horse to the wagon, pleased that Owen was thinking of leaving Sonora, "and told me about a horse ranch in Mariposa. They need hands for ropin' and brandin' their herd."

"Oh yeah? I'll head for Mariposa. Can't work here no more."

The sun had reached its peak in the heavens. Jed and Owen had eaten little at breakfast and had toiled steadily for the last four hours.

"Jed," Owen shouted to his companion, "I'm hungry. After I stretch this wire, I'm gonna eat. Rest of the damn wire can wait."

Jed waved and laid down his tools. Owen stepped forward, stretched, and pulled the barbwire with all his strength. His foot stuck fast in a squirrel hole. He stumbled, reached for support, and fell against the taut wire. Blood spurted from a deep tear in his right forearm.

"Damn it! Knew I was getting tired."

Owen reached for his dirty, sweaty shirt in the back of the wagon and wrapped his arm. He would not be eating lunch anytime soon; the jagged tear needed medical attention immediately.

"Look at this arm," Owen shouted at Jed. "I tore it bad. Get your ass over here. You gotta take me to town. Hurry up! Let's get going!"

By the time Jed turned the wagon onto Washington Street, Owen's arm throbbed, but the bleeding had almost stopped.

A wicked smile broke across Owen's face, exposing filthy, tobacco-stained teeth. "I been wantin' to see that nurse," he confided. "Hope the Doc's gone. She's *I'Talian*. If the old man's gone, she'll have to patch my arm.

"First time I seen her, when old man Martin sent me into town for supplies, she'd just got into town. Followed her back to the old hospital. When the old Doc got in his buggy and rode out, I cut my arm with my knife. Walked into the doctor's office actin' like it was hurtin'. She was alone, felt sorry for me, held my arm, and washed it. I wanted to feel her close, you know, real close."

"Clark, you're always talkin' about that nurse. I seen how you stare at her. Other people seen it, too. They don't like it. I don't like it."

"I don't give a damn what you don't like. I seen her talk to you. She don't never talk to me," Owen complained. "She goes right by me."

"That's cause you stare at her like you're hungry. She ain't like that."

Two weeks before, Gina had cleaned and disinfected an open sore on Jed's hand that had taken its time about healing. Jed thought Gina to be a fine lady. He was no match for Owen's massive bulk, but if Owen was dead set on getting Gina alone, somehow Jed had to stop him.

"I don't care if she don't like me none," Owen shouted. "One night alone with her, that's all I need. Almost got into her house once. Then those damn dogs started barkin' and John saw me. She was alone, walkin' home and I was waitin'. I tell you I'm gonna be the first and last man she knows."

"You crazy, Clark? You'll never get near her," Jed said, as he stepped down from the wagon and tied off the reins. "The deputy will find out. He'll stop you."

"I'll kill you if you ever say anything. 'Sides, Deputy don't bother me none. Better not get in my way when I go after that nurse."

"Deputy's tougher than he looks. I seen him bring down two men at the parade and take their pistols. They was so bloody he brung 'em to the Doc to get patched up 'fore he could lock 'em up. He took your cousin, Harris, to Sacramento. He was hung. Remember?"

"Harris got whiskey in him. Bragged how he killed that miner. Should've kept his mouth shut. I'm ain't like him. No one's gonna get in my way. No one, ya hear?"

But Owen was thinking about the deputy. Before he got Gina alone, he was going to kill Cody. With that thought, he smiled.

Jed stood in front of Owen and spoke to Gina. "Clark here tore his arm on barbwire. I brought him to town to see the Doc. Can you get the doctor, nurse? It looks pretty bad."

At the examination table, Owen sat as the nurse removed the blood-soaked shirt he had used to bind the wound. The deep, jagged gash would require stitching after she cleaned the opening. But she had one little problem. Matthew forbid any patient to be left alone in the hospital. She had to send Jed to fetch the doctor.

"The doctor is at the Sonora Hotel," she said, facing Jed. "You must go there and tell him Owen Clark is waiting at the hospital. Be sure to tell him I need him to come quickly."

Jed had not closed the front door when Owen began undressing Gina with his eyes. Her degree of concern for a patient, no matter who that patient was, outweighed Gina's revulsion. She washed the injured arm and wrapped it with a clean towel.

"Sit in this chair," she said, as she picked up the pan of bloody water, "and do not move your arm or it will start to bleed again. Wait here, I'll be right back."

She walked to the back room where a large built-in cabinet, used as the dispensary, was located. Two glass doors allowed the medicine to be kept under lock and key, and three drawers on the bottom half of the cabinet held extra linen. A deep sink with a pump was also in this room. Gina put the pan in the sink, removed antiseptic, needles and thread from the dispensary, and set them onto a tray.

Owen ignored Gina's command, held his injured arm, slipped his massive bulk into the back room silently, and stood behind Gina. When she locked the dispensary door, picked up the tray, and turned around, Owen's left arm was just about to touch her hair.

Alarmed and infuriated, she shouted at him, " I told you not to move. Go back and sit in that chair."

His gaze exuded lust. She stepped back quickly, but the heel of her shoe touched the bottom of the cabinet and pinned her between him and the dispensary doors. He leaned forward, his body pressed against her, as he gripped the edge of the cabinet with his massive left hand. She turned her face away from his lecherous stare and offensive breath; escape was out of the question.

"I'm sorry," he apologized, insincerely. "Did I scare you nurse? I only wanna talk to you."

Outrage consumed Gina, but before she spit out her disgust and revulsion at this obnoxious man, the bell clanged. Someone had entered the office. Matthew called out her name, then immediately advanced into the back room. Doctor Gibbs shuddered to see Gina forced against the dispensary cabinet doors by Owen's massive bulk, a towel on his arm and a sickening smile on his lips.

"Clark, get away from the nurse. Now!" Matthew roared.

Owen turned and glared at the doctor. Gina wriggled away from the cabinet and quickly left the back room.

Matthew's face reddened with fury. "Go into the examination room, Clark, and sit in the chair. Don't get up again until I tell you to get up."

· · · · · · · · ·

"You are to return in ten days so we can remove the stitches," Doctor Gibbs said when the stitching and bandaging of Owen's arm was finished, "not sooner, not later, ten days. Clark, are you listening to me?"

"Yeah, I'm listening."

"On this paper I have written time and date for removal of the stitches. Take it so you'll remember."

When Owen and Jed left the office, Matthew approached Gina with a worried look, "Sit down, Gina," he said. "I want to talk to you. We cannot be sure what Clark will do from this point forward. I don't trust him. He went to your house once before in the dead of night, and I don't want him to try that again. I'm concerned for your safety. We can't take any chances with him. I'm going to talk to the deputy when he returns from Mariposa."

"I understand what you are telling me, Matthew," she replied. "I agree with you."

"Cody should be back tomorrow, or at the latest, the day after. In the meantime, young lady, you'll stay at Millie's house. I'm going to tell John to watch your house night and day. I just don't trust Clark."

The doctor walked to his bookcase and pulled out Vincente Sciaroni's medical volume. What little information doctors possessed about the science of the mind and what they had observed in certain patients was written in this book. Matthew needed answers in a hurry.

Gina watched him. It was not like Matthew to be so worried.

16

*W*hen the last patient for the day walked out the front door, Matthew asked Gina, "Are you ready for me to take you home?"

"Yes, Doctor."

"You'll get some clean clothes, then I'll take you to Millie's house." He turned and went into his office.

Gina followed protesting, "Matthew, I cannot stay at Millie's house forever waiting for Owen to turn up when I least expect him. I want to stay at my own home."

Unlike Doctor Gibbs, he raised his voice to her. "You can't stay home alone, Gina. I won't permit it. Don't you understand? Clark would kill just for the satisfaction of it, because something takes over his mind. Why it happens, I can't say. No, I won't let you stay home alone. You'll sleep at Millie's house, and I'll sleep better knowing you're safe."

"But, Matthew," Gina pleaded, "John and Myrtle live behind me. John protects me. He watches me leave with you in the morning and makes sure I come home safe in the evening.

"Rex and Butler are never out of my yard. I can bring Rex in during the night. The dogs will never let a stranger near my house."

Not swayed, almost angry with her, Matthew retorted, "Gina, listen to me, that man has serious problems and one of his problems is you. His actions can be erratic. He's a big man; if he overpowers you, there's no chance for your escape."

Matthew's pleas were to no avail; he left Gina at her gate and allowed her stay home for one week only.

She called Rex into the house, put a blanket on the floor, and set water beside it. Rex was free to move about the house and alert her if he heard a prowler.

Rex had fiercely protected Mary Sciaroni, especially after her husband died. With Mary gone, Rex had shifted his protection to Gina. He was a mixture of different breeds, not much of any one kind, and not the largest of dogs, but he was powerful. If provoked, Rex was downright mean and not to be trusted. His temperament was unpredictable, except when it came to Gina; then he was docile as a kitten.

While both dogs were on duty in and around Gina's house, no one dare harm her. At least not as long as Rex and Butler were alive.

17

*C*ody dismounted in front of the jail, tied Sammy's reins to the hitching post, and grabbed his saddlebags. In the jail, he pulled out papers from the sheriff in Mariposa and handed them to Robert.

"So, tell me," Robert said as he reached for the papers, "what happened with the prisoner in Mariposa? Did you find out why the sheriff arrested him?"

Cody leaned against Robert's desk and crossed his long legs at the ankles. "Yeah," he said, "we found out his wife had left him and he was acting like a crazy man wondering what she was doing when he wasn't with her. He thought she was chasing after other men."

"His wife? They didn't tell me he had a wife. How'd you find out?"

"A man that knew the prisoner came in the first night I got to Mariposa and talked to him. The deputy and I listened to their conversation."

"Did she chase after other men?" Robert questioned.

"No, she was a good woman. He was always accusing her of cheating on him, so she left him because he was so damn jealous and wouldn't let her out of his sight. She worked as a maid in the house of an old lady. Deputy Cole and I met her and brought her back to the jail. We let them talk; they made up, and the deputy told them to go home."

"Why was he stealing?"

"He didn't have any money to buy her nice things. He would steal, then save what he stole to give to his wife when he saw her again. I think he was crazy about her, but he thought he wasn't good enough. We ended up feeling sorry for the guy. The sheriff let him off with a warning. He wasn't mean, but he sure was jealous."

"Now I've heard everything. Well, deputy, some women can drive a man nuts. You get a good wife, Cody, mark my words, you'll be happy. If you get one that causes you problems, you might as well hang yourself on your wedding day."

Cody grinned at Sheriff Sanders, straightened up, and started for the front door. The doctor surprised him by walking into the jail.

Leaning back against the wall, arms folded across his chest, the deputy listened to Matthew.

"I'm concerned about her, Cody. Remember when she told us she thought it was Clark who had come in to be treated after she first arrived in Sonora? Well, she was right. On his left arm was a long cut about two months old. He must have waited until I left the office, presumably cut himself with his own knife. Gina was alone, so she had to treat him."

Cody stiffened visibly, but Matthew calmly continued to express his theory and carefully choose his words. "Clark wants Gina. He's obsessed with a lustful, overpowering desire for her. From what I've been reading, I know he's capable of sadistically harming her, possibly permanently, as an expression of his presumed love."

Deputy Taylor drew a deep breath, straightened up, dropped his arms to his side, and turned to face the doctor. "You're saying Clark won't stop until he's got her cornered, with no way out," Cody asked. "But that ain't going to happen. I'll make sure of that."

Outrage gained mastery over the deputy's cool exterior. With long strides, he crossed the street with the doctor trailing three steps behind.

Gina heard the bell peal as she locked the dispensary. When she saw the deputy, her heart leaped into her throat. All she could mutter was, "Hello, Cody."

He pushed his hat back from his forehead. "I hear we've another problem with Clark."

At this moment, Deputy Taylor seemed a different man. This usually calm, cool man now sent a message to Gina through the beads of perspiration on his forehead, the irritated, incensed demeanor. The man standing before her was the lawman, not the man on the horse who had kissed her first tenderly, then with passion.

"Yes," she said, "he came in two days ago when the doctor was with a patient at the Sonora Hotel."

"I want you to tell me what he did, said, how he looked, everything. Tell me now, Gina."

Gina did not embellish or understate her story. "When Jed had left to get the doctor, Owen stared obsessively at me whenever I looked up to speak to him and as I cleaned and washed the injury. When I walked to the dispensary to get thread and needles, he followed me. When I locked the dispensary and turned around, he was reaching for my hair. I was trapped between him and the cabinet."

As Gina spoke, Cody was livid with indignation and it showed in his behavior. Gina wished with all her heart that she had not spoken one word.

Before the deputy walked out of the doctor's office, he pulled Matthew aside and gave him a briefing of his immediate plans. It was clear that Owen wanted to get Gina alone to satisfy his perverted desires. As a lawman, Cody would stop Owen as long as he was alive. Not to mention his own emotional reasons for doing so.

*T*he back of the house looked different in the early morning hours, before the full light from the morning sun filtered into the kitchen. It was dark, shadowy, and suited Cody's temperament.

His mission today would not be easy. He sat at the table holding a cup of steaming coffee, and contemplated what Owen's reaction would be when he told him to stay away from Gina or face dire consequences.

Millie entered, struck a match, put it to the oil lamp, and placed it on the kitchen table. It was apparent her son did not want to talk, as he did not acknowledge her company.

She cracked three eggs and dropped each of them into a bowl. Today of all days, Cody needed nourishment for the crucial task ahead. Millie poured the mixture into a hot pan, and sympathetically watched her brooding son. Finally, she broke the silence. "What are you going to tell him, Cody? Are you going to tell him to leave town?"

To spare his Mother pain, Cody answered with silence. He would have to take whatever measures were needed to prevent this madman from getting Gina alone, and he realized those measures might need to be violent ones.

Andrew stumbled into the kitchen, not yet fully awake, and sat down across the table from Cody. On this day when Cody wanted to be alone to think, his mother and brother had crowded in the kitchen.

Cody gave up his contemplation and asked, brusquely, "What are you doing up so early, half-pint?"

Andrew leveled a look at his brother. "Cody," he said, "Owen Clark wants to marry Gina."

Whatever Cody had expected Andrew to say, it was not what he had just heard, and he swallowed the burning hot coffee unintentionally. Sputtering, he coughed out his question, "Andrew, who told you Clark wants to marry Gina?"

Millie walked to the table with Cody's breakfast and demanded an answer from her youngest son. "With whom have you been talking, Andrew Taylor? And, it better not be that filthy Owen."

"Billy's been talking to Owen, Mom. I talked to Billy. Owen asks Billy to do things for him, like spy on Gina from the bush behind her house. I told him he better not spy on her again." He looked at Cody and said with pride, "I told him I was going to tell you."

"When did you talk to Billy about Clark?" Cody asked.

"The day you went to Mariposa."

Ignoring his breakfast, Cody bolted down the remainder of his coffee and reached for his hat.

At the back door, he suddenly remembered the arrowhead, and turned back to look at the kitchen table.

Cody quizzed his mother, "Where's that arrowhead I left on the table?"

Andrew answered in place of Millie. "It was my arrowhead. The one dad found for me. Remember? I gave it to Billy last summer. He left it here one day. I told him to take it back and not lose it anymore."

In a hurry to get to Ted's ranch, Cody gave free rein to Sammy and a cloud of dust exploded when he leaped from his horse in front of the barn.

Before he asked the question, Ted told him the answer. "I knew you would be coming, Deputy. Clark's gone. He packed up two nights ago, no good-bye, nothing. I owed him some wages, but he left without getting paid. I don't understand why he'd leave in the middle of the night. Do you?"

"Did anyone know he was leaving?"

"He told Jed," Ted admitted, "on the way back to the ranch after Doctor Gibbs patched his arm. Jed said Clark wanted to work in Mariposa. There's a ranch hiring men to rope and brand. I don't know, Cody, but my guess is Clark could get a job quick and didn't need the money."

"Did he take his bedroll and saddlebags?"

"He took everything he owned. Even some of my stuff. Another funny thing, Billy's gone; I missed him about the same time as Clark. I knew Billy hung around Clark. I told Billy to stay away from him, but he thought Clark was his friend." Ted shook his head sadly in frustration and worry.

"I need to see his bunk, Ted."

Sammy trotted behind Cody as the men walked to the bunkhouse in silence. The bunks were cloaked with blankets and lined up against the wall, four on each side. Due to Owen's size, he had occupied a bottom bunk.

Ted stooped and pulled back the blanket "There wasn't much left here, Deputy. We straightened up his bunk after we found out he'd gone, and put clean bed covers on it. Clark was dirty. We had to burn his blankets, couldn't clean them. I need another ranch hand to take his place, because I don't think he's coming back. Do you?"

"I don't know, Ted. I just don't know."

Cody threw back the clean blankets and picked up the mattress, looking for cuts or tears. As he was about to replace the mattress, a small piece of white paper caught his eye. It was stuck between the ropes of the bunk and the wood rails. The paper was folded in half, then folded in half again. When Cody opened the folds and saw the pencil drawing, he burst into expletives.

Stretched out on a divan was a naked woman. Loose, long dark hair was draped over the side of the couch. Full, perfectly shaped breasts, a tiny waist, and round hips suggested a maiden. Presumably dead, a large knife lay beside her body and blood flowed freely from the neck area.

Cody knew without question, this was a likeness of Gina.

19

Three patients scheduled late in the afternoon cancelled their appointments. The doctor and his nurse left the office at a decent hour.

Matthew decided to show Gina the progress of the new hospital. Private contributions from the town had multiplied. The townspeople were eager to have an up-to-date medical facility by the coming summer.

"We are ordering all new medical instruments," Matthew explained. "The latest equipment that doctors now use in New York will be in this hospital."

Cody had cautioned Matthew not to tell Gina about Owen's disappearance. She had no idea he had left Ted's ranch and was perhaps lurking, unobtrusively, somewhere in Sonora. Matthew hoped the ride out to the new hospital would divert Gina's never-ending concern about Owen and his intentions.

"I am impressed by how much work has been done in the last month, Matthew. It is going to be such a beautiful building."

"I'm going to put your office right next to mine, connected by a small door," the doctor explained. "If I am out of the hospital, you will have access to my desk and papers."

"So much has happened in such a short time. Sometimes it is hard to believe that I am really living in Sonora and we are building a new hospital.

"I remember when I rode into Sonora on the stagecoach last April, Robert and William were so kind to me when they told me Aunt Mary had died. Do you remember when you came to my aunt's house with Millie and Andrew the first night I arrived and found me crying? I didn't have any idea what I was going to do next."

Matthew turned toward Gina. "Yes, I do," he replied. "Millie and I felt sorry that you were experiencing such loneliness. Remember what Andrew did when he saw you again? And, do you remember the day you saw Cody again?"

"I felt so much better after Andrew ran and hugged me. He was so happy to see me again. I was surprised he even remembered me.

"But please, do not remind me about the day that I saw Cody. I was so embarrassed. He scared me. And I had to drop everything, twice. Cody just stood there, smiling."

The doctor winked at Gina and said, "I think he liked you instantly. I know he liked the way you kissed him."

"What kiss, Matthew?"

"The only one I know about, at the restaurant. He took us to the Sonora Hotel with you protesting all the way. You kissed him on the cheek after lunch."

"Oh. That kiss."

"I think it was that small gesture of affection you showed that started him thinking about you."

"Really? He thinks about me?"

"Yes, he does, Miss Tufano, worries about you is more like it."

"That is comforting," Gina said, "but I had to take care of myself after Mama and Papa died. It was dangerous in New York. I feel like everyone is trying to protect me here."

"That's very true, Gina; we do protect you. In New York you had street lamps to light your way. There were always people on the streets, even police on the streets to protect people. We do not have that here. So we all have to work together."

A fatherly smile showed on Matthew's face. "So hush up, child," he said. "You are precious to all of us."

As Matthew halted the wagon at the side of Gina's house, John stood in front of his cottage, speaking to a man on horseback. The man dismounted and walked into the cottage.

John came over to the wagon. "That man is the neighbor of Myrtle's sister, Louise. She's sick and we have to ride over to Mather and bring her back to Sonora. Louise thinks she's dying and wants you to examine her, Doc. We'll be gone at least two days, maybe longer."

Unsure whether to stay or leave, John needed confirmation from the doctor.

Gina climbed down from the wagon and walked toward the cottage. "You must go, John," she said. "I will be fine. Please do not worry. You must go to Mather and bring Louise back so Matthew can examine her."

The doctor raised his voice, "Gina, get your clothes. You will not stay here alone while John and Myrtle are gone."

"Matthew, we have talked about my staying alone. I will be safe. I have Rex and Butler to protect me until John comes home." Ignoring Matthew's request, she continued, "Thank you, doctor, for showing me the new hospital. I will see you tomorrow morning. *Ciao.*"

Frustrated, Matthew turned the buggy around, but announced as he snapped the reins over the horse's rump, "I'll let you stay home tonight, but tomorrow after John and Myrtle leave for Mather, I'm going to talk to the deputy. You should not stay here alone. Maybe Cody can talk some sense into you."

John and Myrtle left early the next morning, but concerned for her safety, John made Gina give her word. "Promise me, young lady, you will stay at Millie's house until we come home."

"I promise if I see anything wrong, I will run to Millie's house as fast as I can run."

Blowing a kiss to them both, she watched as they rode in a southeast direction toward Mather.

Although Gina had never been one to be afraid when alone, somehow the comfort she felt when John and Myrtle were in their cottage gradually faded away, and she became increasingly apprehensive as time passed.

Rex was quiet, standing by her protectively. Butler was checking the grounds. She called Butler to her and patted the head of both dogs. "Good boy, Rex," Gina said, "and, Butler, you're a good boy too. You will protect me, will you not?"

The dogs went on duty outside the house. Gina sat on the entry hall chair ready and waiting for Matthew, but her thoughts went to Cody.

Lately, whenever she saw him, he was buried in his work at the sheriff's office, riding into town or riding out of town. He did not acknowledge her at all. She reminisced about the night, not to long ago, when they had ridden Sammy together.

Matthew's buggy approached. They were going to be late today. Gina remembered that the doctor had planned to look in on a patient before he picked her up. Once again, she made sure the back door was secured, took a final check on Rex and Butler, went out the front door, listened for the click of the lock, and started down the walkway to Matthew's waiting buggy.

20

When the doctor pulled the horse to a halt at eight o'clock in the morning, patients were lined up outside the hospital. A full schedule kept Matthew and Gina working steady until after five o'clock in the afternoon.

"Doctor," she said, as he climbed into the buggy, "it's a burden for you to constantly pick me up and take me home. I'll walk to town tomorrow."

Matthew's stern glance made Gina turn the conversation into a new direction. "Have you spoken with Cody?"

"No. He has other duties, Gina. Sometimes he is gone for a few days."

"I know, I was just wondering if you had seen him today. When I saw him yesterday, he looked worried."

Gina realized the doctor had passed the road that led to Mrs. Humphrey's house. "Doctor," she said, "you were supposed to be at Mrs. Humphrey's home tonight. You passed the road to her house."

"I'll take you home and then I'll go back to the Humphrey home."

"Matthew," Gina argued, "it will take me just ten minutes to walk home. The sun is still bright and I can see my fence. You know Mrs. Humphrey. You'll be there all night. She loves to talk and she'll make you stay for supper."

"Yes, you're right."

Matthew stopped the buggy; Gina waved good-bye as she started down the path to her house. The day was slowly slipping into evening, and Gina knew she would enjoy the brief walk home.

When Gina lived in New York, she walked on pavement, without the fragrance of honeysuckle and wild roses or the songs of birds. The beauty of the West, especially Sonora, with its majestic oak trees, green valleys with a multitude of colorful flowers, and lush hillsides was the reason her uncle and aunt chose to live the rest of their lives in Sonora.

Today, Gina played her quiet game. She stepped only on tuffs of grass, dancing over or around the gravel and stones that littered the path. Before she realized, she stood in front of her gate.

For the past few days, the dogs had anticipated her arrival and were waiting for her by the fence. But tonight she did not see or hear Rex and Butler.

She reached out, quietly opened the latch, stepped lightly around the gate, and left it open. When Gina rounded the corner of her house to the backyard, she stopped dead in her tracks. Terror gripped every bone of her body. On the ground by the porch, she saw the dogs lying in a pool of blood.

Forcing her body to respond, Gina dropped her tote and purse and ran with every ounce of stamina in her. Through the front gate she flew, down the path toward Millie's house, not daring to look back.

For five agonizing minutes she ran blindly until the fire in her lungs stopped her. She hid behind a large oak tree, drawing air deeply into her lungs. As Gina was beginning to breathe normally again, she heard the gait of a horse coming closer and closer.

Gina crouched lower behind the trunk of the tree and watched in terror. Relief flooded through her when she saw that it was the deputy on Sammy. She cupped her hands to her mouth and shouted Cody's name, but no sound came. She stepped from behind the tree, shaking fiercely, and Cody reined up.

"Gina," he asked, as he ran toward her, "what the hell are you doing out here alone?"

Gina's words came now, in a surge. "Rex and Butler are dead. They are lying in the backyard by the porch. John left for Mather today. I was alone without Rex and Butler. Somebody killed them, Cody."

Her eyes filled with tears, but Cody gave her no time to cry. "You're not going with me back to the house," he said, "I'm taking you to Mom's house where you'll be safe, and then I'll go back. If Clark's there, I'll find him."

"Please take me with you. I must be with you," Gina begged.

Cody looked at her. Expose Gina to that madman? Never!

Again came the desperate pleading. "Please, Cody. I must be with you."

Tears flowed from her eyes when she realized the danger that lurked this night for her and the deputy when they went back to her house and faced Owen Clark.

How could she fight off this giant if Owen killed Cody? Gina would never be able to defend herself from this ape. No matter how hard she tried to prevent the ultimate outcome, in the end, she would die a humiliating and painful death.

Cody held her tightly to his chest as she pleaded desperately, between sobs, to take her with him. He knew exactly what Owen wanted from Gina, and what Owen would do to her if he got the chance to kill Cody.

How could he release her from his arms? Gina was safe now. He tightened his hold around her. How could he take her with him while he confronted Owen? Holding her in his arms now, made him realize he did not want to be parted from her. If Owen waited for Gina, they would face him together.

Cody lifted Gina into the saddle. The last time they had ridden Sammy together, Gina was laughing joyously. They had nothing to laugh at now.

His left arm around her waist, Gina held onto his arm with both her hands. Cody's face was next to her right cheek, his shoulders folded around her.

"Cody, John, and Myrtle left this morning," Gina said. "They went to Mather."

"I know, I watched them leave. Then I rode out to Ted's ranch to see if Owen was there."

"Did Owen leave Ted's ranch?"

"Yeah. A few days ago. I've been to your house a hundred times to see if Clark would turn up."

"If the dogs saw you," Gina asked, "why did they not bark and alert me?"

"They know me, Gina."

At the front gate, Cody dismounted and helped Gina from the saddle. Gina stood behind Cody while he removed his heavy Walker Colt from his pommel holster. As she handed him the key to the front door, Gina noticed it stood slightly ajar.

"I locked that door this morning; I'm sure of it," Gina said in horror.

Putting a finger to his lips to quiet her, he swung the door open. When Cody stepped inside, she followed him into the large entry hall.

Open double mahogany doors to the left of the center stairs led into an elegant living room. To the right side of the living room was Doctor Sciaroni's study, sometimes used as a parlor. Located in the area behind the stairs was a guest bedroom.

A dining room, with a massive mahogany table over an Oriental rug, stood in the center of the room with ten matching chairs around the table. An ornately carved mahogany sideboard that matched the table, and filled one long wall, was located to the right side of the center stairs. A swinging door, always kept closed, led into the kitchen from the dining area.

The silence seemed to thunder in Gina's ears. She could hear the blood pulsing in her brain.

Cody beckoned Gina. "I'm going to search the top floor," he whispered. "You stay here." He pointed to the landing of the stairs. "Don't move. After I'm through searching upstairs, you and I will check the other rooms."

The thick Persian carpet on the staircase hushed Cody's steps. Gina followed him mentally into each room. He opened one bedroom door, searched it, and then walked to the other bedroom across the hall. A large linen closet located at the end of the hallway held Dr. Sciaroni's medical instruments, bandages, and dressings, along with bed linens and towels, but it concealed no intruder. Cody closed the door and started toward the stairs.

Gina was listening so intently to Cody's muffled footsteps that she did not notice the door to the kitchen open. Nor did she notice the huge man slip quietly into the entry hall. She reacted only when long arms reached out and locked Gina to his sweat reeking body. She opened her mouth to scream, but a huge filthy hand sealed her face from the bottom of her nostrils to her chin. She squirmed and twisted to wrench herself from this crushing grip, but she was held completely off the floor. Despite her most frantic efforts, Gina was a captive.

Owen Clark waited for the deputy to appear. When Cody reached the top of the stairs, he saw Gina kicking and struggling to free herself. Cody controlled the rage that bubbled within quickly and considered how to rescue Gina from this maniac.

Owen's right hand released Gina's mouth. However, his massive biceps kept her arms pinned to her side. With his right arm, Owen reached into his boot and slid out a Bowie knife, which he placed at Gina's throat.

In Cody's right hand was his Walker Colt, but if he shot Owen the bullet would penetrate Gina's body.

Cody's booming voice covered Owen, "Let her go, Clark! We can settle this by ourselves."

"I got plans for Gina and me," Owen roared, "later, after you're dead. And I ain't plannin' to let her go."

Overcome by his lust, Owen dropped the knife to the floor and moved his hand slowly over Gina's breasts. Cody saw the hate Gina felt for Owen blazing from her eyes.

As a nurse, Gina knew a man's sensitive body parts. This defense was foremost in her mind, but she had to free herself from Owen's grasp before she could inflict the blow that would disable him.

Without lifting his gaze from the deputy, Owen removed his revolver and targeted the left side of Cody's chest.

Straining to get free, Gina's one thought was how to incapacitate this fiend. "*Sudici'ume*," Gina screamed, "you filth! My fingers will dig out your eyes and rip off your face before you touch me. I will never let you touch me. Never!"

The smile left Owen's face, he glared at Cody with malevolence in his eyes. "She won't never get away," he lisped, "I like it when women fight me. You ain't gonna stop me 'cause you're gonna die."

Owen drew back the hammer. "Drop the Walker, Deputy," he snarled, "and start down them stairs. Slowlike. I want her to watch you die."

Cautiously, holding his revolver steady, Cody started down the stairs. Gina felt Owen's body tense, as he readied himself to shoot the deputy. As Cody reached the bottom of the stairs, his anger for Owen escalated, devouring him.

"I told you, Deputy," Owen's voice dripped with hate. "Drop that Walker. Now!"

As the sole of Cody's boot touched the last step before the landing, the swinging door separating the kitchen from the dinning room was thrust open with full force and crashed against the opposite wall.

Billy stumbled clumsily into the entry hall with his arms and hands waving frantically, screaming, "No, Owen! Don't shoot Cody!"

Owen's intense concentration was diverted from the deputy by Billy's sudden entrance. He turned his head toward Billy. Gina felt his grip relax. In that split second she wrenched free, dropped to the floor, and rolled away.

It was the opening Cody needed, he raised his revolver, but Owen pulled the trigger first. The bullet missed Cody's heart, but ripped through his flesh and burst out the back of his left shoulder.

Deputy Taylor's Walker Colt exploded an instant after Owen's bullet had pierced his shoulder, and the slug tore into Owen's leg just above the knee. He dropped to the floor squealing in pain.

Owen reached for the knife he dropped earlier, and pulled it back to hurl at Cody. Gina crawled toward him, her arms extended to block the throw. At that moment, Owen felt an overwhelming hatred for Gina and instinctively raised the knife to plunge it into her body.

The deputy, his left arm held at his side, aimed and fired two shots in rapid succession. Blood squirted from a gaping hole as the first bullet exploded into Owen's monstrous chest. The second bullet killed him instantly when it penetrated his thick neck.

Gina scrambled to her feet; the deputy's consciousness waned as he grabbed the banister to keep from falling. She steadied him with her shoulder and held him firmly around the waist with both of her arms.

Billy gaped; he was afraid for Cody, but did not know how to help.

"Billy, come here," Gina screamed. "Help me get Cody to the bedroom. I have to stop this bleeding. Come! Quickly."

Billy obeyed unconsciously as if in a dream and used his strength to walk Cody to the guest bedroom. When they laid him down, a loud groan slipped involuntarily from his lips.

"Gina, what are we going to do?" Billy asked. "He's losing a lot of blood. He's going to die."

Gina held Billy by his arms, and centered him to look squarely at her. "You are going to ride Sammy to Mrs. Humphrey's house," she answered. "The doctor's there. Tell him Cody has been shot and I need him here immediately. Send Mr. Humphrey for Millie and Andrew. And get the sheriff. Go at once, Billy, we have no time to lose."

"I can't ride Sammy, Gina; he won't let me ride him. I'll find Owen's horse. He tied it up somewhere around here. I think it's behind John's house."

Gina was losing patience. She had much to do and Billy was not cooperating.

"Billy," she said, pointing to Cody, "look at him. The doctor must stitch the wounds, but I have to stop the bleeding."

She pulled Billy to the front door. Sammy scraped the ground by the front porch with his hoof. "No, Sammy," she spoke softly to calm him. "Stay, Sammy. Billy, talk to him. Tell him he needs to help Cody. Sammy will do what you tell him. He already knows Cody is in great danger. Now, go, quickly."

Billy grabbed the reins and spoke frantically, "You gotta help Cody, Sammy. You gotta to take me to town. Hurry, Sammy."

Clutching the saddle horn, he swung up onto Sammy's back. A quick nudge, and horse and rider were off, on their way to the Humphrey home.

21

Gina removed Cody's shirt and examined the back wound. The bullet had ripped through the left shoulder, and blood flowed over dangling strips of muscle and flesh. Using her fingers, she pressed the mass into the opening and covered it with a thick wad of dressing.

Dark bloody matter oozed from the opening under the clavicle on the front of his shoulder. Warm water, infused with herbs, would clean the black powder and blood. Shock had caused Cody to shake, so Gina tucked blankets under his body.

In the kitchen, she stuffed the stove with wood and kindling and struck a match. When the fire ignited, Gina place a pan with water on the burner.

From the pantry she pulled out the apothecary jars with Aunt Mary's healing herbs, then ran upstairs for extra dressings, bandages, and blankets.

There was no time to lift her skirt every time she raced from room to room and up and down the stairs. She reached between her legs, grabbed the back of her skirt, pulled the fabric up through her legs, and fastened the material inside the waistband. A trick she had learned in Bellevue Hospital where nurses often needed to run, not walk, from floor to floor and room to room. Gina was now free to move quickly from the linen closet on the second floor to the kitchen and back to the guest bedroom.

She set a shallow pan with a small amount of warm water on the sink, and began tearing towels into small pieces. A buried memory tried to urge itself from out of the dim recesses of her mind, a persistent feeling that she had the means to stop his bleeding and prevent infection, but it remained elusive.

Back at Cody's side, Gina cleaned black power from the front wound. She bathed his face, neck, and chest with lavender, rosemary, and comfrey water. If too much time passed, infection could reach his heart. But what could she possibly use to prevent it? There was no antiseptic anywhere in this house.

"You will be better soon, Cody," Gina soothed. "I am taking care of you."

Back in the kitchen, Gina grabbed a cup. Again the same nagging feeling beat in her head. "I know there is a way to stop the infection. What is it? Please, God, tell me," she prayed.

Holding the cup, she sprinkled in herbs, added hot water, and reached for a spoon to stir the mixture. Suddenly, the memory flared in her brain.

Gina's thoughts flashed back to New York City, when she had been a little girl only seven years old standing by a lake with her parents and a group of Italian friends. A small boy was taken from the water, crying, as blood gushed from two deep cuts on the side of his foot.

The boy's grandmother took charge. She poured some wine into a cup, spooned in sugar, and stirred the mixture continually while she walked to her grandson's side. Her command that someone hold his leg securely was obeyed and she poured the entire contents of the cup directly onto his foot.

Gina shuddered as she recalled the boy's heart wrenching screams as the liquid saturated the cuts. But within minutes the bleeding had stopped.

Four weeks later, Dr. Tufano had taken the opportunity to examine the boy. Tony was amazed; the cuts had healed without stitching and without infection, leaving visible only two small, clean scars.

"I can use wine and sugar," she shouted. "Wine and sugar will prevent infection and slow the bleeding."

Draping towels around and under Cody's left shoulder, Gina supported him with a pillow. "Cody," she said, "I must stop infection from starting and halt the bleeding. But you will feel pain when I pour the antiseptic over your shoulder. Cody, do you hear me?"

He opened his eyes, but made no sound.

"It will help you," she comforted. "I promise."

Standing in front of the counter, Gina poured wine into a cup, added sugar, and stirred. At his side, she enclosed him with her left arm, uttered a silent prayer and watched half the contents of the cup spill over the back wound. She had to use both her arms to hold him as his body twisted and distorted from excruciating pain.

"One more time, *Caro Mia*," Gina said as she poured the last of the wine and sugar onto the front wound. "I am so sorry to hurt you."

Cody's teeth clenched from the pain as the liquid dripped inside the opening and ran down his chest. Gina blotted the front and back wounds with a towel and covered the area on both sides with thick, clean dressings. Then she wrapped bandages around his left side to hold the dressings in place.

Blood and perspiration soaked into towels and mattress as the fever raged through his body. She bathed his face, arms, and chest with warm herbal water. From a separate cup, the nurse spooned herbal tea into his mouth, a few drops at a time.

Time and again she replaced the sweaty, blood soaked towels and sheets with fresh ones. The litany ran through her mind: Stay by his side; keep him as comfortable as possible, and wait for the doctor. And, she prayed that the bleeding would stop and infection would not start. Waiting was the hardest part.

She had disinfected the wounds to the best of her ability. It was now up to his strong, healthy body to work with the wine and sugar to cleanse the area of infection.

Finally, about an hour after she had applied the homemade mixture, the flow of blood began to slacken.

From the moment Owen had shot Cody to the sounds of wagons approaching her house, almost two hours had elapsed.

She was in the entry hall when Millie burst through the front door. "He is in the guest bedroom, Millie," Gina said, "I think he is out of danger."

Ignoring Owen's body lying in a heap on the floor, Millie charged into the bedroom, Andrew following. Treading on the heels of Andrew was Matthew, carrying his medical bag and extra supplies.

Sheriff Sanders, Mr. Humphrey, and Billy entered through the front door, "How's Cody doing, Gina?" Sheriff Sanders asked, hesitantly. "Will he live?"

"The bullet missed his heart. Once Matthew says he is out of danger, I will feel better. He had to kill Owen, Robert. Owen was going to kill me."

An unpleasant, urgent necessity caused Gina to plead, "Please remove Owen from my floor, Robert, and take the rug with you. I need to assist the doctor now."

Robert, Mr. Humphrey, along with Billy, picked up Owen's dead body and carried it to the wagon while Gina raced back to Cody's side.

Flesh and muscle were trimmed from the back of Cody's shoulder. Gina supplied the doctor with surgery items as he needed them. Fortunately, the chloroform that Matthew gave to Cody made it possible for him to slip into unconsciousness. Finally, Doctor Gibbs wrapped his shoulder and chest with bandages. A relieved nurse covered the deputy with a clean sheet and blanket.

Matthew stood up and stretched his back. "I didn't see infection starting, Gina, thank God," he said, "but I did smell wine. Did you give him wine to drink?"

He waited patiently for an explanation; Gina mulled over what to tell him. After some deliberation, she spoke out, "I mixed wine and sugar together, then poured it over his wounds. It helps prevent infection, but causes a great deal of pain."

"Well, well. Imagine. Wine and sugar. I've never thought of using that method. Come to think of it, I've never heard of using that method. You probably saved Cody's life, young lady. I'll try and remember that cure-all."

The ladies again carefully shifted Cody from one side of the bed to the other and exchanged the bloody sheets for clean ones. They also bathed his arms and chest with herbal water to remove dried blood that clung to his flesh. Cody remained asleep; under the effects of the doctor's chloroform, but any movement caused him to cry aloud in pain.

Andrew sat in a chair close to Cody's bed, worry and exhaustion lining his face.

Gina held him gently. "You can sleep in the room across from my room, Andrew," she said. "You need to rest. Cody will be awake in the morning. He needs quiet now."

Gina suggested Matthew sleep in her room, but the doctor suggested an alternative. "You need to sleep, Gina, and Millie too. It will be a busy day for both of you tomorrow. Where are you ladies going to sleep?"

The ladies stared at Matthew and said nothing. It was clear that neither Millie, nor Gina, would leave Cody's side, not until he was completely out of danger.

*A*s Gina watched Cody's rhythmic breathing, her mind relived every second of terror from the moment Owen's apelike arms confined her. Owen had planned to kill Cody first, then inflict a slow and degrading death upon her.

She felt Cody's face with the palm of her hand. He appeared to have a fever, but it was not raging.

"Cody," she said, bending close to his ear, "swallow this tea, please."

Not fully awake, but conscious of Gina's voice, he tried to lift his head. "One more spoonful, Cody," Gina said. "I will make you broth later."

On her knees beside the bed, Gina listened to his heartbeat with Matthew's stethoscope. She patted his chest and whispered, "Steady and strong, you will be awake soon. Now, I can make your broth."

In the morning light that filtered its way into the house as she made her way to the kitchen, Gina noticed dried blood splattered everywhere. The entry hall staircase had large stains on the Persian carpet, mostly on the lower steps. Cody's blood had also spotted and smeared the banister. Blood had soaked through the entry hall carpet and stained the hardwood floor from Owen's body.

"I will clean later," Gina muttered. "The rug must be removed from the staircase another day. Today, I will ignore my work; the deputy saved my life, and he needs my attention."

Bright orange, red, and golden rays of sunrise greeted her as she stepped outside the back door. The beautiful hills of Sonora had awakened. The weight of a mountain had been lifted from Gina's shoulders. She was once again free to go and come as she pleased without fear that Owen was stalking, lurking, waiting.

Rex and Butler lay unburied by the back porch steps. While she picked zucchini, summer squash, carrots, and fresh herbs for Cody's broth, she shed buckets of warm tears. The dogs had given their lives to protect her. Gina would miss them dreadfully. On her way back to the kitchen, she gathered fresh eggs from the chicken coup for breakfast.

While Cody's broth simmered, for the first time Gina felt fatigue overwhelm her. She sat at the kitchen table and laid her head onto her folded arms. Within seconds, she was in a deep sleep.

In the guest bedroom, Cody stirred. When he started to raise himself, intense pain throbbed through his shoulder, and he shouted in anguish.

Millie woke from her sleep and kneeled by his side. "Son," she murmured softly, "Cody, I'm here, right beside you. You're in Gina's house. Owen shot you last night. Can you remember what happened? How do you feel, dear?"

Recalling the previous night, Cody went deathly pale. He remembered Owen with a revolver, Gina struggling to get free, and torturous pain when a bullet blasted through his shoulder.

Millie put her head in her hands, and thinking that the son she had nursed and nurtured had almost been killed the previous night, gave way to tears.

"I am sorry I cry, dear," she said finally, wiping her eyes. "I know you do not want me to worry."

"Don't cry, Mom; I'll be all right," he whispered. "Where's Gina? I want to see her."

"She's in the kitchen, I think, making you broth. I'll find her. Rest; we'll be right back."

The nurse had not been asleep long when someone called to her from far away, "Gina, Gina. Wake up Gina."

She tried to focus on the face close to hers. "Is it you, Millie?" But seeing Millie's red and swollen eyes, Gina asked fearfully, "What has happened to Cody? Has infection started? Why have you been crying?"

Not waiting for Millie's answers, she flew out of the kitchen. Cody lay motionless and as white as the sheets he lay on. In Gina's mind, he was dying. But when she felt him, there was fever, but it was not burning fever. The bleeding was minimal, no abnormal swelling existed around the wounds, and infection had not set in.

Gina looked at Millie and asked again, "Millie, why have you been crying?"

Cody opened his eyes. "She's happy Owen didn't kill me, that's all," he said, just above a whisper.

Gina and Millie sat together on the floor, and they shed happy tears and beamed on Millie's son.

Matthew walked into Cody's room. "What's going on?" he asked, looking at Millie and Gina. He leaned over the deputy and felt the area that surrounded the wounds. "He's doing well, considering he lost a lot of blood, and he has a large hole in the front and back of his shoulder."

"Gina thought Cody was dying, Matthew," Millie answered. "She saw I had been crying. I'm sorry, Gina; I should have explained that he only wanted to see you."

Millie stood up and tidied her hair. "Gina dear," she announced, "I'm going to fix breakfast now. Andrew will be hungry when he wakes up. I know Matthew is hungry. Aren't you, Matthew?" Not waiting for the doctor's answer, she mumbled as she headed toward the kitchen, "I'll make myself at home, Gina dear; don't worry about me."

The nurse sat in the chair watching Matthew while he listened to Cody's heartbeats. He put the stethoscope back into his medical bag, somewhat dubious about asking delicate questions, but he asked anyway. "Gina, what caused you to pour the wine and sugar mixture on an open wound? You knew it would cause intense pain, but how did you know it would help?"

She related the story of the little boy in New York City. "The way the foot healed with no stitching, leaving two barely visible scars, amazed my father. He brought up the story many times at his medical meetings."

"I can't believe that mixture would prevent infection," Matthew said.

"It sure worked for the little boy. Dr. Sciaroni kept his supply of homemade Italian wine in his wine cellar. I fixed supper for Cody a few nights ago, so I had moved two bottles of wine into the pantry.

"Father claimed that wine is a natural antiseptic. They had used it in Italy, and it was also used in Bible times to heal open wounds. I prayed it would help him. Do you think it helped, Matthew? He was in agony when I poured it over his shoulder."

"Other than pain it didn't seem to cause a problem, my dear. I think it probably saved him from infection that would have caused very serious problems."

Matthew held his watch to his ear to make sure it was ticking. "I'm going into the kitchen to help Millie and fetch a cup of coffee," he said, "then I'm going to the hospital."

Gina started to rise from the chair. Matthew anticipated her actions. "Oh, no. You're not going anywhere, young lady. I'll go to the hospital alone. I need you to stay here and take care of the deputy."

Matthew knelt beside Gina, voicing one or two additional questions. "Gina," he said, speaking softly, "what happened? How did you manage to get away from Clark? How did Cody prevent Clark from killing you both?"

"It was Billy. He flew into the entry hall from the kitchen, waving his arms and hands, screaming, 'No Owen, don't shoot Cody.'"

The doctor listened intently as Gina continued. "Owen held me above the floor. Billy distracted Owen by pushing open the swinging door with so much force that the door banged against the wall, and when Billy started screaming, Owen turned toward him and relaxed his hold on me. I dropped to the floor and rolled away. It was the chance Cody needed, but Owen shot first. He aimed for Cody's heart, but the bullet went through his shoulder instead."

"So, it was Billy that saved you both?"

"Yes. After Cody shot Owen in the leg, Owen dropped to the floor. He saw his knife on the floor in front of him and reached to pick it up. At first, I think he wanted to throw it at Cody. I crawled toward him to yank the knife away, but Owen grabbed it and raised it over my body. He wanted to kill me. That's when Cody killed Owen. He had no choice."

Matthew stared at Gina and mumbled in disbelief, "Who would have thought that Billy, always underfoot and in the way, would end up being the one to save Cody's life?"

"I told Billy to ride Sammy, fetch you and the sheriff. Then I cleaned Cody's wounds with warm comfrey, lavender, and rosemary water. Cody swallowed the comfrey and lavender tea I offered him, but he did not like the taste."

Matthew laughed and remarked, "No, I don't think he would. Our Cody does not like fancy stuff like herbs."

"Finally, I remembered the time Mrs. Spano used wine and sugar on her grandson's foot, and I was desperate so I tried the old-fashioned home remedy."

Andrew walked into the room and asked in a loud voice, "Isn't he awake yet?"

"I am now," Cody replied.

"You lost a lot of blood, Cody." Andrew said, rapidly. "Billy rode your horse to town to get the sheriff and doctor. Sammy let Billy ride him. Billy kept telling Sammy how he needed to bring the doctor to you."

"Where's Billy?" Cody said in a soft voice. "I want to talk to him."

"He's standing outside the door; he's afraid to come in. Billy thinks everyone's going to blame him because he was friends with Owen."

Andrew went to the door and beckoned to Billy. He entered the room sheepishly, walked to Cody's bedside with his hands in his pockets, and averted his gaze from the deputy's face.

"Thanks, Billy," Cody said, "for saving my life and Gina's life. Gina got away and Clark didn't kill me."

"You mean it, Cody? I really did? I saved your life? I've always wanted to do something brave," Billy answered, busting with pride and disbelief, "but I didn't know that running into a room could be brave, until now."

The doctor watched Cody's color fade. "Boys," he advised, "I think you better go into the kitchen and eat your breakfast. Andrew, you speak to your brother later; he's tired and he needs to sleep."

When Gina positioned the pillow under Cody's head, he asked, "Gina, what was that stuff you poured on my shoulder?"

"Close your eyes and go to sleep. You need rest."

"What was it?"

"An Old Italian remedy. You ask too many questions. Go to sleep. I will tell you some other time."

For the remainder of the day, Millie and Gina nursed Cody, gave him broth to drink, and tried to keep him quiet. The combination of weakness from the surgery and laudanum to lessen the pain would bring Cody sleep.

23

*I*n the days following the shooting, Cody directed anyone within hearing range at Gina's house to do his bidding. They brought him water, food, fluffed his pillows, and changed sheets. Anything he asked of them, they did with pleasure.

Two days after Cody was shot, John returned home and brought Myrtle's sister, Louise Carlton.

John was informed of what had happened during his absence. "I should have been here to help you, Cody," John said. "Clark never would have shot you as long as I was alive."

The deputy corrected John's reasoning. "You could not be in two places at the same time. Clark's dead. He won't hurt anyone again."

Gina put Andrew and Billy to use getting floors scrubbed and walls cleaned. Mattresses and pillows, permanently stained with Cody's blood, were burned. Aunt Mary's extra Oriental rug was brought from the attic and placed on the entry hall floor. On the stairs, a new Persian carpet was installed.

Sheriff Sanders came by daily to brief Cody on affairs around Sonora that would need to be looked into at a later date.

It was a full six days after Cody was shot before Matthew allowed him to be moved to his own bed. Ten days after the shooting, Cody's color had returned, he was requesting seconds at meals and he had regained some strength.

After twelve full days at home, Cody, his arm in a sling, commenced his duties as deputy at the sheriff's office. Always the lawman, he needed action.

Cody accepted praise from the townspeople for saving Gina's life and relieving the town of scum like Owen Clark. It was a job well done.

24

T he doctor's office overflowed with patients all day. At five o'clock in the afternoon, Gina finally tackled the cleanup before Matthew locked up for the evening.

The bell sounded as a familiar voice called out, "Gina, Gina. Where are you?"

The nurse ran from the back room, "I'm here, Sara. What's all the excitement?"

Sara Jones was the postmistress. She stormed into the room waving a parcel. "This came from New York City," she said. "I have been so busy today I didn't have time to bring it to you."

She waited, filled with curiosity for Gina to open the package.

"I'll open it later, Sara," Gina said. "I'm too busy now. Thank you for bringing it to me."

Amazed at Gina's own lack of curiosity, Sara blurted, "Aren't you going to open it now?"

"I have to finish my cleaning, Sara. I will let you know what is in the package when I leave the doctor's office."

Shaking her head and mumbling to herself, Sara walked out the front door.

But, on second thought, Gina was curious. The letter was from James Nathan, her solicitor. He must have news about the sale of her parent's house and property.

"Matthew, can you come in here, please?" Gina called.

She opened the box with trembling fingers and lifted out a train ticket and an envelope. "It is a one-way ticket to New York City, Matthew," Gina said. "I am scheduled to arrive in New York by the middle of July according to this ticket. I will have to board the train in just four days."

"What's in the envelope, Gina, a letter? Who sent it?"

"Aaron Levi, the house agent. Sit down, Matthew, I'll read the letter aloud."

Gina read, the concern growing in her voice as she proceeded.

"Dear Miss Tufano:

"We have sold the house and property as you have instructed. The new owners would like to take occupancy as quickly as possible.

"Mr. Nathan sends you a one-way train ticket, and we need your prompt arrival in New York City to finalize the sale. I do hope the date meets with your approval.

"We will purchase you a return ticket after documents are executed, and if you still choose to return to California.

"After the sale of the property is completed, all papers finalized, your solicitor, James Nathan, will meet with you at his office in regards to the Last Will and Testament your parents entrusted to him.

"Please wire me your intentions.

"I remain, yours truly,

"Aaron Levi"

Gina placed the letter and the ticket onto her desk. Dropping her head, she muttered to herself, "What am I going to do?"

Matthew helped her decide. "You have to go, Gina. We can get by here at the hospital. Millie can help while you're gone. You have to go to New York and by the date on this ticket, you have to go soon. The trip will do you good. But I hope you won't be gone too long."

"Matthew, it will take me a full seven days traveling on the train to reach New York. Then, with the reading of the will and the sale of my parent's property, it could be several weeks before I return to California. What will you do? How will you get along?"

"You, young lady, have to sign papers and you must listen to the reading of the will. Wire back to the solicitor and the house agent that you'll arrive on the date they suggest. Then, make arrangements to return to New York. You really don't have any choice, Gina. You are the only living heir."

"I will miss you all so much." Holding her head in her hands, Gina stared at the letter sadly.

Matthew pulled his chair closer to hers. "Gina," he said, "I want you to go back to New York and finalize your business there, but I want you to leave New York and come back home to Sonora."

Sara interrupted their conversation by bursting into the office once again, waving another envelope. "I'm sorry, Gina," Sara announced, breathless. "This was in the wrong box; I just found it." Seeing the sadness on Gina's face, she turned to Matthew. "Not bad news, I hope?"

"No, Sara, Gina has to leave Sonora for a few weeks. I think our New York Lady is sad about leaving us."

Pleased that Gina liked Sonora and the people, Sara smiled and nodded, then closed the door quietly and returned to the post office.

The second envelope was from Dr. and Mrs. Eric Mueller. Doctor Mueller and Doctor Tufano had attended medical school together in New Hampshire and had graduated at the same time.

Later, in New York, they had been close friends and colleagues.

She pulled the letter from the envelope and again read aloud.

"Gina Dear:

"I wanted to let you know of Eric's recent health problems. I felt sure you would want to be notified.

"Eric is having heart problems lately. His health has taken a downward swing, and we do not think he has much longer to live. You would not recognize him, he has gotten so frail.

"The problem is that he gets so very tired, even reading exhausts him. So he sits idle all day. If his heart does not kill him, surely the monotony will. You know how he always hated to be idle.

"I do wish he could see you again, but with you in California, I know it would be almost impossible. Eric has been thinking and speaking of your father lately.

"If you can come back home, hopefully, permanently, at least for an extended stay, please telegraph me the date and approximate time of your arrival. I will be at the train station to meet you.

"You will be most welcome at our home. If you want to return to California, so be it. But if you choose to stay with your dear friends in New York, who miss you so very much, you can live with us as long as you wish.

"Miss and Love You,

"Gertrude Mueller"

Doctor Gibbs realized that Gina was both wanted and needed in New York. However, he wondered how would Gina react once she returned to New York City. Would she want to remain in her birthplace, her former home?

There was always the possibility that Gina's sad memories might not haunt her any longer. Once she saw her home and all the friends she left in New York City, she may want to stay permanently.

Matthew was skeptical; he did not want Gina to leave Sonora, and he did not think she would come back.

"Doctor," she said, once her cleaning was finished, "I want to go home now. Do you mind? I'll stop by the telegraph office, have Cecil send my acceptance to Aaron Levi and Gertrude. I promised to let Sara know what I received in the package, so I need to stop by the post office."

"I'll go with you, Gina. I'll take you home in my buggy."

"No, thank you, Matthew. Not today. I really want to walk."

Tonight the walk home was not going to be long enough. Gina needed time to think. She was so wrapped up in the pondering of this new problem that she did not hear a rider approach. The horse snorted behind her and Gina jumped in fright. When she turned and looked up, Ken Thorton, the Mayor's youngest son stared down at her, smiling.

The oldest of Mayor Thorton's four sons was Edward. He lived in San Francisco and worked for the United States Government. David Thorton, second son, was a brilliant young lawyer who resided in Sacramento, California. Wesley, the Mayor's third son, was the local pharmacist. He lived with his lovely wife, Juanita, and two children in Sonora.

The youngest, Ken, was twenty-two years old. He was keenly interested in the breeding of horses. He lived and worked on a horse ranch in Coulterville, gaining experience toward the time he would become the owner of his own spread.

Ken was on a three-month holiday from the farmstead in Coulterville. He had been home for two weeks and had noticed a pretty young woman at the doctor's office.

Of all Mayor Thorton's four sons, Ken was the most handsome. Well over six feet tall, he was ruggedly built, with honey-colored hair and a winning smile, in addition to possessing a charming personality. However, these qualities also caused Ken's weakness. Ken knew he was handsome and charming.

Intrigued by Gina's striking good looks and personality, Ken had made frequent visits to the doctor's office, often hanging around until she finished her work.

"Gina," Ken said, "I've been riding behind you for five minutes. You didn't even hear me. What's wrong?"

"Nothing. I was thinking about something."

"Give me your hand. I'll pull you up onto the saddle. You can ride back to your house. You look tired."

"No. I do not want to ride, Ken," Gina bristled. "I want to walk. It helps me think."

Undeterred, Ken dismounted and walked with her. "What's on your mind?" he asked. "Are you sad for some reason? Someone sick?"

"No, Ken. I need to think out a problem. It's something I do not want to do, but I must."

Puzzled, Ken looked at her.

Gina felt that Ken was entitled to know that her problem had nothing to do with him. "I have to leave Sonora and go back to New York. I'll be leaving in four days and I do not know when I will return. I'll miss the whole month of July. I hear it is the most beautiful time of the year."

Gina's voice cracked and her eyes filled with tears. Ken draped his arm across her back and held onto her shoulder as they walked. She felt no need for Ken to remove his arm; he was only trying to console her.

A lone rider watched them as they walked closely together. This man knew nothing about the train ticket or Gina's upcoming journey. Thus, Sheriff Robert Sanders was completely unaware of the reason Ken Thorton had his arm around the nurse.

26

*O*ne tear replaced another in a never-ending flow. Gina detested good-byes. This trek back to New York might be her final. She feared in her heart that she would never see Sonora or her dear friends again.

Gina would ride to the Milton-Sonora Road Station by stagecoach, and after an overnight stay, she would board a train for Sacramento, California. Then, a Pullman Car and the Wagner Palace Car would carry her across the country to New York City.

"I will do the best I can to help Matthew, Gina dear," Millie said, "but come home soon. He will be overjoyed when you return."

Andrew put his arms around her waist and held her tight. He did not want Gina to leave him and go back to New York. It had taken her five years to come back the last time. Gina reluctantly released Andrew, hugged Billy, and kissed Millie. The doctor lowered his head as Gina kissed his cheek.

Matthew closed the door to the stagecoach. "Be careful," he said. "Wire us if we can help in any way. Come back to Sonora as soon as you can, Gina. We will all be waiting for your return."

"If everything goes smoothly, I will be back in four weeks. I don't think it will take more than ten days to sign the papers, arrange my parent's remaining property, and listen to their will. If I am detained for some reason, I will get word to you."

The day Gina received the ticket from the house agent, and the letter from Gertrude Mueller, Cody had been on his way to Fresno, California, searching for the murderer of a miner. He had no knowledge of Gina's sudden departure from Sonora.

· · · · · · · · · · · · ·

Miners were constantly assaulted and killed when they staked a large claim. One young miner uncovered a vein of gold in Jackson, a town some miles to the north of Sonora, where mines run deep. Before he made his way home to Mariposa, to his wife and small daughter, the miner stopped at the assessor's office in Columbia to weigh his gold nuggets. His fortune totaled $10,000.00 on the assessors' scales, and he was now a happy, wealthy man. He left Columbia early the next morning and rode to Sonora to visit with his aunt, Mrs. Mildred Tabor, who ran a boarding house.

What one man had acquired with backbreaking work and sacrifice, another man would take freely, if he were desperate for gold.

Every evening about eight o'clock, Charlie Green would reach for his cane, being a little more than seventy years old, and he would walk to the boarding house. Mrs. Tabor always saved him dessert and Charlie's mouth was watering for a piece of her excellent apple pie. Except for a hoot owl, and the wind rustling the leaves in the trees that lined the street, Charlie was alone, no other person was out and about on this moonless night, or so Charlie thought.

When he was passing a dark, narrow alley, he heard a scuffle and a cry of pain. Charlie was suddenly jostled when a man carrying two saddle-bags shuffled out of the alley. The man limped to a tethered pinto pony in the front of the boarding house, mounted with difficulty, and galloped off.

Charlie Green found the young miner bleeding profusely from three stab wounds in his chest, the bloody knife lay beside him, and he was in death's throes. Charlie hurried to the boarding house to get Mildred.

The man that killed the miner and jostled past Charlie, was Adam Wells. Charlie recognized Adam by his unique limp.

Through no fault of his own, Adam Wells seemed to acquire nothing but a long series of hard knocks. Trouble started for Adam when he was working the sluice boxes seven years earlier and had suffered a fall, which resulted in a compound fracture in his right leg.

The men working with Adam, Charlie Green being one of the men, aligned the separated bones. But without the care of a doctor, infection commenced and ran its course. Adam's leg finally healed, but it was now several inches shorter than the left leg, and he would walk with a painful limp for the rest of his life.

Adam had family that owned a small ranch in Fresno, California, and Charlie told Cody that Adam would probably take shelter there and hide out for a bit. Cody was determined to apprehend this killer, eager to return the gold and pinto pony to the miner's wife and daughter.

. . . .

Gina leaned out the window of the stagecoach, crying and waving her handkerchief. The beginning of her return journey commenced.

_27_

The same train that conveyed Gina to California was home-
ward bound for New York City. If she felt depressed now, she would be
even more heartsick when she neared New York State.

Wonderful aromas drifted from the dining car, and most of the passengers left their seats for a hot, delicious lunch. But Gina did not feel
hungry. All she felt was miserable.

"I wonder what Millie, Andrew, Billy, and Matthew are doing at
this moment," she asked herself, as the train rolled through the San Joaquin
Valley. "I wonder if Cody will miss me when he finds I have gone back
to New York."

Memories of her parent's death and the home where she was raised
intruded into her thoughts. "How will I react when I walk though my
house for the last time? Someone else will sleep in my room. Another
family will build happy memories in my parent's home.

"My friends may beg me to stay in New York and tell me that I
should never return to California. What if they convince me to stay in
New York? I will never see Millie, Matthew, and Andrew. I will never
again see Cody's smile. Oh, what am I going to do?"

Tears gushed and not a soul sat near Gina to wipe them away or
comfort her. But as woeful recollections intruded into her inmost thoughts,
a feeling of contentment surfaced, as memories of the last four months in
Sonora flooded her mind.

In her memory she saw Millie standing at her stove and command-
ing everyone to sit at the table. Matthew tending to a young patient's
broken arm and comforting him as he gently wiped his tears away. Smiles
filled the faces of Andrew and Billy as they came galloping up the path

to Gina's house. Sheriff Sanders sitting at his desk in the jail, reading the *Sonora Herald*. And above all, Deputy Taylor, with his crooked, mischievous grin, smiling at her.

Gina wiped away her own tears. "I may not be able to return to Sonora today," she murmured aloud, "but I will return to California in one month, so help me."

She settled back into her seat. No matter what, nothing would keep her away from Sonora. Gina would meet with the house agent, sign the papers, and listen to the will. Then, she would buy a one-way train ticket from New York Central Station to Sonora, California.

*I*t took Gina eight fatiguing days to arrive in New York City. After being in California for almost four months, she had returned to the city of her birth.

Gertrude was the first to greet Gina as she stepped from the train, speaking a mile a minute in unending sentences. "It has been ages since I have seen you, Gina. You look thinner. I knew you would hate it there. I do not want you to ever return to that uncivilized place. You are staying with us. Eric has practically commanded it. He looks like he has perked up a little since you wired us that you were coming."

As they walked to the waiting carriage, Gertrude did not let Gina get a nod or a word in edgewise to confirm or deny any of the conversation.

When Gina put her satchel into the waiting buggy, she felt a pressure around her waist. James Nathan, her solicitor, thirty-three years old, and a handsome and wealthy bachelor suddenly lifted her into the carriage.

On several occasions, James had expressed his love for her. The last instance Mr. Nathan told Gina he loved her was shortly after her mother's funeral. At that time, he also asked for her hand in marriage. She refused, but said that she would think about becoming his wife.

The week before Gina's departure from New York City, he tried to prevent her from leaving with eloquent words. "I understand that you want to help your aunt now that her husband is dead. But she can sell her house in California. You can go to Sonora when her house is sold, help her pack, and move her back to New York.

"Your home would not have to be sold, Gina," James continued. "It is large enough for both of you to live in together until her death. If she lived here, you could hire a nurse to watch her while you are at the hospital working. Mrs. Sciaroni knows most of the doctors in New York. Any one of them would gladly look in on her daily."

James was a lawyer, successful in his profession. What he recommended was true. Aunt Mary had lived in New York once, and she might agree to leave California.

But Gina had not listened to his logic. For some reason, California beckoned. She had felt that she must follow the dictates of her heart.

Doctor Tufano had hired James to complete his Last Will and Testament the year before Tony's death. However, the many visits James made to the Tufano home were merely excuses to see Gina.

When James had confirmed that Gina was on her way back to New York City, he searched and found the most beautiful engagement ring to suit his beloved. It now rested in his breast pocket for the moment when he would assure her of his deep love and again propose marriage. James would then dazzle her with luxuries. When she agreed to marry him, and he slipped the ring on her finger, Gina would be his and would never return to California.

Gertrude spoke of all the events that had been planned in Gina's honor and the appointments that had been scheduled with the dressmaker and cobbler. "Gina, dear," she said, "when you wear your new dresses, you will be a fashion testimony as you walk along the Avenues. Melissa will make any style you desire. When you receive your inheritance, you can buy practically anything your little heart desires."

However, attending dinner parties and having dresses and shoes made was certainly not foremost on Gina's mind. No, it was definitely something else. When could she sign the final papers to complete the sale of her home? When would James read her parent's Last Will and Testament? And, most of all: When could she make arrangements to return to California?

Gertrude and James were dear to Gina's heart, old and good friends, but Gina realized that she could never tell them when she stepped off the train at New York Central Station how much she wanted to turn around and go right back to California. No, they would never understand her need to leave New York. Especially Gertrude would not understand.

_29_

Over a week had passed since Gertrude and James had met Gina at the train station. During that time she had seen the dressmaker and the cobbler three times. She looked at hats, undergarments, umbrellas, purses, and gloves in every emporium in New York City. But Gina had not signed papers, she had not listened to the will, nor had she taken the final walk through her parents' house.

On Wednesday morning, a particularly hectic day seeing friends in Brooklyn, and being pressured by Gertrude to pick out material later, for an elegant gown to wear at the opera, Gina lost all control. Her Italian temper blazed. "I do not want an elegant gown for the opera," she retorted. "The opera is not for one month. I did not know I was going to the opera. Two dresses that is all I will buy, one for the ballroom dance, and another to wear to the dinner party with my school chums. _CAPISCE?_"

Clearly, the intention of all her friends was to make Gina see what she had missed by living in a primitive country like California.

Back at the Mueller home, she climbed the stairs to seek solace in the comfort and privacy of her room, desperate to leave New York.

There was a soft knock on her door. "_En'trare_," she called out.

Eric entered, "I heard you talking to yourself in Italian, Gina," he said, "all the way up the stairs. You remind me of your mother. What is the matter?"

Gina's thoughts were like a whirlpool swirling around and around. The words spilled out in torrents. "Eric, I want to go back to California. I want to sign all the papers I need to sign and listen to the will. If I need to make repairs to the house, I will do it. In fact, if I must make concessions in order to have all the papers signed, I will do that too. Then I want to leave New York and return to California."

Dr. Mueller lowered his head; saddened Gina wanted to leave New York.

Ironically, she tried to comfort him. "Eric, I am so happy to be with you and Gertrude again. I love you both very much, and you know that, but I am not happy in New York. I was happy living in Sonora."

"I know you are not happy here in New York. I knew it the first time I saw you, when you walked through the front door. I have told Gertrude you want to go back to California and I have also told James."

"You told James? Then, why has he not read to me my parents' will? He knew I wanted to get all that behind me. Why?"

"Because James is in love with you, Gina. He thinks you will leave New York and he will never see you again. So, he prolongs the reading of the will until it is absolutely necessary. James wants you to be his wife. Did you realize that?"

"Yes. I know he wants to marry me. He told my father. After my mother's funeral, he formally proposed. I told him I would think about it. Then Aunt Mary wrote asking for my help in Sonora. I moved to Sonora because I wanted to be with family again. I was lonely, Eric, I missed having family around me. But I love it in California. I am sorry Aunt Mary died before I arrived, but I am happy I listened to her."

Gina ambled to the window. Eric observed her silently. She looked out at broad avenues, the busy sidewalks, and the women in fancy dresses. Men walked the streets in top hat and tails and carried umbrellas although no rain was imminent. Positioned on the walkways were huge pots containing small trees, and sick-looking flowers drooped in the dirt around the trees.

No soft breezes were gently blowing; no flowers kissed the air with their fragrance. There were no stately or gnarled oak trees that reined proudly in green valleys or on majestic hills. Gina was many, many miles away from the place she now considered home.

"I will tell James to bring you to his office to read your parents' will," Eric announced, sadly. "Then I will have him contact Aaron Levi to finalize the signing of the papers for the house. However, since she knew you were coming to New York, Gertrude has been anticipating your homecoming dance for this coming Saturday, and also looking forward to the special dinner she has planned with all your friends on Sunday. I want you stay in New York long enough to be at those two events. Then you can return to your beloved Sonora."

Gina ran to Eric and hugged him. "Oh," she said, "will you? You promise? I will stay for the dinner and the dance, Eric, I will. When can I buy my return train ticket?"

"James can purchase the return train ticket," Eric said. "He knows better then to go against my wishes. Now, remember that the dance in our ballroom will be on Saturday and the special dinner will be on Sunday. You will be on your way to Sonora by the middle of next week."

"Who is going to tell Gertrude that I am leaving?" Gina questioned Eric. "What if she resists my leaving?"

"I'll tell her, Gina. Of course, she'll not want you to leave New York or us. Gertrude cannot imagine anyone living in a town that is not New York City. Sit down Gina; I want to tell you something."

Eric and Gina sat down on the settee in Gina's room. "Do you remember five years ago when you, Tony, and Tina went to Sonora for a visit?" he asked kindly. "Your father told me the same things you just told me. Tony stared out the window at his office while I visited, about a week after all three of you had come back to New York. He spoke of the beauty of California, especially the beauty of Sonora. Your Father and Mary loved the West."

"You know me as well as you knew my father, Eric."

"Gina, remember that I was the doctor that brought you into the world."

"There is not enough green here, Eric." Reproaching herself for not being grateful for all the kindness shown her, she attempted to explain. "I am so sorry, it is just so…so…"

"So lonely here?" Eric answered. "I personally think that if you, Tony and Tina had moved to California five years ago, your mother and father would be alive today. We will all miss you Gina, but I think your life awaits you in California."

"There is a doctor in Sonora that I assist. His name is Matthew Gibbs. He reminds me so much of you; he is so kind and all knowing. I love you, Eric."

Eric stood up from the settee; an unpleasant task awaited him. Eric had to tell Gertrude that Gina would leave New York.

With his hand on the doorknob, he turned to Gina. "Is there someone in California?" he asked. "Some young man that might be special to you?"

"No," she said, "but I am very fond of the Taylor family. We met them five years ago. They were neighbors of Aunt Mary.

"Millie Taylor's husband, Andrew Benjamin Taylor, was the sheriff of Sonora when we visited five years ago. He was killed shortly after we came back to New York. Sheriff and Millie Taylor had two sons, Cody Benjamin Taylor and Andrew Michael Taylor. Cody is the deputy Sheriff of Sonora. He saved my life last month."

Why she used their full Christian names, Gina would never know. Millie had showed her the Taylor family Bible and all the birthdates of the Taylor family members born in the last one hundred years. Sheriff Taylor's full name, along with Cody and Andrew's full Christian names, were the last three listed in the family Bible.

Eric sat down on the settee again, eager to hear about this heroic young man who had saved Gina's life. "Tell me what happened," he said. "How did you come to be in such danger that the deputy had to save your life?"

Gina gave the account, smoothing over some of the events, because she did not want to upset Eric. The last thing she related was using the wine and sugar mixture to sterilize the bullet wound in Cody's shoulder.

"I remember Tony relating that story of the little boy and how his foot healed without stitching and developed no infection," Eric commented. "How is the deputy's shoulder healing?"

"The last time the doctor and I examined his shoulder," Gina answered, "it was almost healed. Cody does not know I am here in New York. He went to Fresno, a town to the south of Sonora, searching for a murderer. He left the day before I got your letter and the train ticket from James."

"Fascinating and very frightful events, Gina. Well, this only confirms that you must return to these good people and the deputy who saved your life. By now, they all must miss you terribly, possibly as much as we will."

Eric started for the door. "About tonight," he said, "just before you and Gertrude returned home from Brooklyn, I had Francisco take a note to James at his office, and I asked him to join Gertrude, you, and I for dinner tonight. He has papers ready for me that I must sign. I will send Francisco again with a note to James, and ask him to buy your return train ticket and bring it with him when he comes for dinner. I want you, young lady, to freshen up and look happy when James arrives. After next week, he probably will never see you again."

"I will, Eric. But I cannot tell you how happy I am to finally be going back to California."

Eric set out to find Mrs. Mueller. His wife could be a bit difficult and hard to handle at times. He decided to begin by telling her the story of how the young deputy had saved Gina's life. It might impress Gertrude.

"What do you mean she wants to go back to California? Eric, she can't! James wants to marry Gina. Her friends want to see her on a regular basis. If she goes back to Sonora, who knows when she will return. If ever!"

Gertrude was an excitable person; at this moment she was close to hysteria. "Eric, I cannot let her throw her life away in Sonora," she asserted. "California is filled with savages and is a very uncivilized place. How can I agree that she leave New York to take up life again in such a barbaric town? We must talk some sense into her. You and I must do it, and James, tonight!"

She paced from a chair to the window. Finally she sat down. Her elbow on the arm of the chair and her chin resting firmly on her closed hand. Gertrude felt that she had to think of a way to prevent Gina from forsaking New York City in favor of Sonora.

Eric led his wife to a secluded area of their home, well away from the servants' quarters. The staff did not need to overhear what promised to be a heated conversation.

Doctor Mueller leaned against the edge of an old mahogany desk, his feet crossed at the ankles. He watched his wife intently; a slight smile curled his lips.

Concerned that she had alarmed him, Gertrude attempted to explain. "I am sorry, dear. I do not know what to say to you. I hope you are not unhappy with me. I cannot believe Gina actually wants to leave New York and us. What is wrong with her?"

She settled back into her chair, this time with her hands in her lap and looked placidly at Eric. He had always known the ways to explain complicated matters to his wife.

"Gina's life was saved last month by the deputy of Sonora, Gertrude. Obviously, a mentally deranged man had been stalking Gina. He was eventually going to kill her, but the deputy protected her and killed him."

For emphasis he added, "Gina is lonely for California. She misses the Taylor family that befriended her there, and she also helps a doctor on a daily basis. I personally think she has special feelings for this young deputy, but she may not know, as yet, how much she cares for him."

"You mean she may be in love with him? A deputy? Oh, no, Eric, that would be disastrous."

"Gertrude, you have not met him. How do you know it would be disastrous?"

"Oh, never mind, I just know. It's too dangerous in California anyway. She would be much safer here in New York with her friends."

"My dear," Eric said, exasperated, "Gina must make that choice to stay or to leave. We can't do it for her. She doesn't want to hurt our feelings. She loves us, but she has to return to California.

"Gina is not in love with James; she will not accept his proposal of marriage no matter how many times he asks her. But she doesn't want to destroy their friendship."

Hoping that his wife would appreciate how Gina felt, Dr. Mueller continued. "Gertrude, if Gina does not return to Sonora because she wants to please you and me, her friends, and James, then, we will all make her a sad and lonely young lady.

"I have asked her to stay for the ballroom dance and the special dinner you have arranged. She has agreed to my request. You, my dear wife, must encourage her to return to California."

Gertrude stood before her husband with pleading eyes. "What? I cannot do that. I will not encourage her to leave New York. Eric do not make me do it."

Dr. Mueller looked at his wife, as he always had, with love in his eyes.

"Oh, all right," Gertrude agreed, reluctantly. "I'll do it. But I do not want her to live in California. I thought the longer she stayed in New York and saw what she was missing, the more apt Gina would be to agree to live here permanently.

"Eric, did you know James asked her what she was going to do with the profit she would receive from the sale of her house?"

Knowing Gina's reply, Eric asked Gertrude the question anyway, "And what did she tell him, my dear?"

"She told him that with some of the money she was going to help build a hospital in Sonora. Can you imagine that? However, after what you told me about Gina's experience last month, that town no doubt needs a large hospital. With many, many beds."

He leaned against the desk and watched Gertrude pace from the window to the chair. They both dreaded the day that Gina would leave for California, but it must be her choice.

31

*T*rue to Charlie's words, Adam Wells rode to his family's ranch in Fresno, California. Discreet inquiries from the deputy of Sonora after his arrival revealed the whereabouts of a man with a unique limp seen on a ranch north of Fresno.

Justin Fulton, the sheriff of Fresno, in company with the deputy of Sonora, took turns around the clock and observed the farmstead.

The month of July is always uncomfortably hot, dusty, and dry in Fresno, but the lawmen's vigilance paid off. On Wednesday, mid-morning, after one whole week of surveying the ranch from a mesa with an outcrop, which kept the lawmen out of view, Adam Wells limped out of the barn holding the rein to a beautiful pinto pony. He mounted and rode off the ranch into the direction of Fresno.

When the sheriff and deputy apprehended Adam, as he was crossing a dry steam bed, he was completely taken by surprise learning that he had been recognized leaving the scene of the crime. And, after further questioning by the lawmen, he admitted to killing the young miner in utter desperation, and taking his gold.

The death of the miner and the trial of the killer would cause disorder in Sonora. The evidence could legally be heard and examined in the Fresno Superior Court. If sufficient reason to proceed were discovered, a trial date would be set. And, whatever the outcome of the trial the miner's wife could claim the gold and the pinto pony.

The stagecoach deposited Cody in front of the Sonora Hotel and rolled out of sight. He had been away from Sonora for three long weeks.

Robert stood up from his desk. "Good to see you again, Cody," he said. "Did you find and arrest the man that killed the miner?"

Cody sat on his desk chair and put his satchel on the floor. "We found him," he answered, handing Robert the papers that documented the apprehension. "Sheriff Fulton has him in jail awaiting trial. I'll be needed in Fresno to hear the evidence since the killing took place in Sonora."

"I'll show these papers to William. Cody, you get settled. If the Mayor needs to ask you questions, I'll come for you."

Robert stopped at the front door. "Are you tired?" he asked. "Hungry? Do you want me to take you home?"

"No, it's almost time for the Doc to lock up. He usually goes to our house for supper; I'll hitch a ride with him."

Cody looked across the street to the window in the doctor's office. He saw his mother at Gina's desk.

"What's Mom doing in the doctor's office?" he asked, perplexed. "Is Gina sick or something?"

"That's right. You haven't heard, have you? Gina left Sonora and went back to New York."

Struck by those words, Cody was not able to speak. He sat staring blankly at Robert.

Finally, he heard his own voice. "What did you say?"

"Gina received a letter and a one-way train ticket back to New York over three weeks ago. It came the day after you left for Fresno. Gina's home was sold; she had to sign papers and listen to the will. After she read one letter, another letter came telling her that an old friend of her father was sick and he wanted to see Gina. She decided to leave Sonora and go back to New York."

This sounded far to final to Cody. If anyone knew if Gina was coming back, it would be his mother and the doctor. "I'm going to the doctor's office, sheriff."

"One more thing, Cody. While you were gone, Ken Thorton and Gina were getting serious with each other."

Cody frowned. "What makes you think that? I saw him going into the doctor's office before I left for Fresno, but it didn't seem like much to me."

"The day she got the letters and the ticket, they walked to her house together, and he was holding her. I sat on my pony not twenty-five feet away from them. They were so wrapped up with each other they didn't even see me."

The deputy stood up and reached for his hat. "I'll be back, Robert," he said. "I'm going to talk to the Doc."

Millie saw Cody stride across the street. She stood to greet him as he walked through the door. "I'm so glad to see you, Son. Did you have a good trip? Are you hungry?"

Cody cut her words with his own. "Mom, when is Gina coming back?"

"So you heard. Who told you she has left Sonora?"

Again the finality of the words struck Cody.

"Robert." Cody answered. "When did she leave and when is she coming back?"

Millie stammered, unsure what to tell her son. "She left over three weeks ago. I don't know if she is coming back to Sonora."

Impatient and exasperated at his mother's answer, Cody rapped at the examination door. "Doc, its Cody. I need to talk to you."

When Matthew opened the door, he saw that Cody was very disturbed. "Millie," he said, dismissing her, "would you go into the examination room with Jeffrey? See if you can keep him comfortable for a few minutes while I talk to Cody."

Deputy Taylor wasted no time in getting to the point. "Doc, explain to me why Gina left Sonora."

Matthew closed the door to the examination room and repeated what Cody had learned from the sheriff.

However, there was one detail that only the doctor knew. "And, after she concluded her business in New York, the letter said she could buy a return train ticket to Sonora, if she wanted to come back."

"What did she say? Doesn't she want to come back to Sonora?"

Matthew rubbed his forehead with his fingers. "Honestly, Cody," he said, "I don't know. At first Gina didn't want to leave; she was worried about me. We talked about the trip for a few minutes, then she walked to the telegraph office and sent two wires, one to her house agent and one to a Mrs. Mueller. She left four days later. Gina has been gone over three weeks. I need an assistant here. I may have to find someone else."

Deputy Taylor's hat was pushed back, his fingers shoved deep down into his pockets. He paced from Gina's desk back to the doctor.

"Cody, she was born in New York City," Doctor Gibbs said calmly, "and she lived there for most of her life. No doubt the sale of her parents' home left her with some money. New York has many luxuries to offer someone like Gina. Now that she has money, she might have proposals of marriage. If she accepts one of them, she'll never come back to Sonora."

Matthew wanted the deputy to know there was a strong possibility that the nurse might choose to stay in New York permanently.

"What I am trying to say, Cody," the doctor continued, "pressure can be put on Gina. An opportunity to assist well-established, well-known doctors may tempt her. She comes from a family that has worked in hospitals for most of their lives. Above all, Gina will be with the people she has grown up with, colleagues of her father and mother, school chums."

Cody still sought an answer to his question. "When will we know if she's not coming back?"

"Gina told me when she left Sonora that if she were delayed more than four weeks, she would send us a telegram. If she decides to come back, she may arrive sooner. But until we hear from her one way or the other, I just don't know if or when she'll come back to Sonora."

Matthew knew Cody wanted positive words. "I wish I could tell you more, son. Believe me, I hope she is on her way back to California at this moment."

The deputy walked out the front door of the doctor's office. Robert had gone to meet with Mayor Thorton, and the sheriff's office was empty.

Cody sat back in the chair with one leg bent and rested his ankle on the opposite knee. "Gina left Sonora over three weeks ago," he said in an undertone, "and Matthew's right. She'll have money now. There's far more to do in New York than in Sonora. Will she want luxuries? Will she want to marry someone she knew before she left New York?"

He recalled all that had happened in the past four months since her arrival. The way they stood together against Owen. How she poured that crazy homemade remedy on his wounds and nursed him devotedly for a week in her own home.

"No," Cody answered one of his own questions. "She doesn't give a damn about luxuries and money."

The deputy would never forget the night they had ridden Sammy, never forget her laughter when she had slipped and bounced all over the saddle. Nor could he ever forget his need to hold and kiss her. Sitting in his chair now, he remembered clearly how Gina felt in his arms, pressed so close to his body.

"I never thought that Gina would leave this town," Cody said, sadly. "What am I going to do if she never comes back?"

Robert left the Mayor's office and headed back to the jail at break neck speed, something was definitely weighing upon his mind. He threw the door open, interrupting Cody's meditations and wasted no time speaking. "Deputy, I need to talk to you. I told you about Ken holding onto Gina the night she received the letters and the ticket, didn't I?"

"Yeah. They didn't see you sitting on your horse."

"Ken told me what really happened." Robert's words were not leaving his mouth fast enough. "I just talked to him at the Mayor's office. I didn't tell you the whole story because I didn't know the whole story.

"Gina was upset; she didn't want to leave Sonora. But she felt that she had to return to New York, Cody. Ken was trying to cheer her up when I saw them walking together. That's why his arm was around her shoulder. He tried to make her feel better.

"After she did everything she had to do, she planned to come back to Sonora. And, listen to this; she told Ken that when she had the money from the sale of her house, she was going to help build the hospital here in Sonora. She told Ken her aunt and uncle wanted this town to have a hospital that was up-to-date, whatever the hell that means. That sure doesn't sound to me like someone who was going to stay in New York."

Sheriff Sanders paced around the room, agitated and restless. He had a few more things to tell Cody but he was hesitant to speak.

"Oh, what the hell, I might as well tell you what I think. Cody, you ought to marry Gina. Keep her here in Sonora permanently. Now, what do you think about that?"

Cody directed a broad grin to Robert and stood up. "I'll be back sheriff," he said, and walked away as Robert stood looking bewildered.

Deputy Taylor crossed the street and headed toward the telegraph office.

Cecil Mott came to the counter as Cody entered. "Good to see you back, Deputy. What can I do for you?"

"The nurse sent a wire a few weeks ago. Do you still have the address?"

"You know I never throw away an address, Cody. I keep them right here." Cecil pushed papers around in an old worn-out box until he found what he was looking for. "Gina sent two telegrams," he said, "one to a Mrs. Gertrude Mueller and one to Aaron Levi. Which address do you want?"

"The lady's."

A slow smile spread across Cecil's face when he read the deputy's telegram. His remark was typical of how many people felt about the nurse in Sonora. "Good for you, Deputy. I don't think she'd have left if you'd been here."

"How much do I owe you, Cecil?"

"This one's on me, Deputy."

Cecil grinned, showing all the gold in his teeth. Deputy Taylor did not remember Cecil ever smiling. He looked ten years younger.

The telegram was sent; Cody thanked Cecil and went back to the sheriff's office. Robert was sitting at his desk reviewing papers he needed to show the deputy.

"I'm going home, Sheriff," Cody said. "Do you need me to stay?"

"No, I don't need you to stick around. I can show you these papers tomorrow. I'll be leaving for supper myself soon. You wanna hitch a ride with me? I can take you home."

"No, today I want to walk. I'll see you tomorrow."

Sheriff Sanders watched the deputy shut the door to the jail. "I sure hope Cody thinks about what I told him," he muttered quietly.

As he walked up to the gate of his home, Cody whistled. Sammy neighed from the corral, pawed at the ground, and shook his beautiful mane.

Andrew called out from the back yard as Cody walked through the gate, "Hi, Cody. I'm glad you're back."

"What are you doing sitting out here on the swing?"

"Because. That's why. I just wanna sit here."

"Where's Billy?"

"At Ted's ranch. He's helping with some work they needed to get done."

Cody reached out to feel Andrew's forehead. "What's up? You look like you lost your best friend. Are you sick?"

Andrew jerked his head away. "I'm feeling fine."

"What's wrong Andrew?"

"Gina left Sonora and went back to New York City."

"I know," Cody admitted.

"Do you think she'll come back to Sonora, Cody? I miss her. I don't think she's ever coming back. Sonora isn't the same since Gina left. Matthew says she has a lot of friends in New York. But they can't miss her as much as we miss her."

"I know, Andrew. Gina might come back. I think she likes Sonora. I know she likes you, Mom, and Matthew."

"And you too, Cody."

"And me, too."

Cody stared at the swing, then turned and looked toward the barn. He left his satchel and coat on the ground. "Come on, half-pint," he said, "let's take Sammy for a run. You can help me saddle him up."

Cody pulled Andrew off the swing and carried him to the fence. Andrew was distracted and distant. While his brother saddled Sammy, Andrew took out his pocketknife and carved notches in the corral fence.

"You really miss Gina, Andrew?"

"Uh-huh. It isn't the same since she left. She always yelled at me in Italian and got mad at Billy and me. I liked the way she always made me laugh. I didn't want her to leave me. I never want her to leave me."

Cody shook his head. "I wish I'd been here when she got those letters."

He threw the saddle over Sammy's blanket, cinched the belt tight, secured the bridle, mounted, and reached out to help Andrew, "Come on up half-pint," he said, "Sammy's ready for a run."

Cody moved his boot from the stirrup; Andrew climbed up and sat on the skirt of the saddle, his arms around the deputy's middle. Sammy was almost to the road when they saw Matthew and Millie coming home from the hospital. Cody waved, then nudged Sammy into a gallop, leaving behind a cloud of dust.

Millie was flabbergasted at the way her sons had departed so suddenly. "Now just where do you think they were going?" she demanded. "Those boys are always so hungry this time of the day, and they didn't even ask if supper was ready. Matthew, where could they be riding off to? Cody just got home."

The doctor pulled the horse to a halt in front of Millie's house. "If I know your boys, Millie," he stated, "I would guess they are headed to Gina's house."

"Why? They know she's not there."

"Why, Millie? Because Andrew misses her. And Cody is afraid she'll never come back to Sonora. Your boys wonder if they'll ever see Gina again."

Matthew and Millie stared toward the horizon, following the dust cloud Sammy made as the boys rode away. If Gina decided to stay in New York, the doctor would have to find another nurse, and that would not be an easy thing to do.

What would Millie think if Gina married someone in New York? The doctor knew Millie wanted Gina to marry Cody. They listened to the sound of Sammy's gait on the road until it disappeared completely.

Millie spoke quietly. "She has to come back to Sonora, Matthew. Gina has to come back to this town. What are we going to do if she decides to live in New York City?"

32

Francisco, the butler, was dispatched with a message to James to purchase a return train ticket for Gina. He was instructed to bring it to the Mueller house that evening.

"Eric gave me orders, and when Eric speaks, I listen." James told Gina. "It was 'buy the ticket' or he would find another solicitor."

James was quite gallant when he placed the ticket in her hand. "I have always known that I loved you far more than you ever loved me. I will miss you, Gina."

A woman married to James Nathan would never want or need anything; her every wish would be his command. Gina knew this, but James was also imposing, he had grandeur. Gina felt she would never measure up to that standard. She was always talking in Italian, no matter who heard her, and she had a terrible temper. She also had a habit of slamming doors or cupboards when her temper got the best of her-definitely not the ideal wife for James Nathan.

"Thank you, James, for being so understanding," Gina said. "I will never forget you. Ever."

Holding her return train ticket tightly in her hand, Gina knew her days in New York were numbered. She will be returning to Sonora soon.

Comforted that James held no bitterness, she enjoyed the evening. During this informal dinner with James, Eric and Gertrude, and later when the four of them sat together in the living room for coffee, she felt herself drift away from the conversation. Gina envisioned herself with her friends, Millie, Matthew, Andrew, Billy, Sheriff Sanders, and with the young deputy of Sonora.

33

The emerald green, elegant taffeta evening gown had been approved at the final fitting. Gina looked exquisite in it.

The bodice hugged Gina's waist and flowed into a long full skirt. Material pulled from the bodice cascaded into folds, creating balloon sleeves that draped over her arms and drooped loosely at the elbows.

The style exposed the top of her breasts and left Gina's shoulders bare. To Miss Tufano this vogue was immodest. She expressed her concern at the final fitting, but Gertrude was not swayed, Gina would look perfect in that gown.

"The dress is lovely on Gina. And, in New York, beautiful breasts should be admired, not pushed down as they are with other women in the world. Ignore Gina, and leave it just that way, Melissa. It's a perfect fit."

Gertrude had always endorsed modesty. Why was she changing her mind now?

"Melissa," Gina interrupted, "I will wear the gown to the dance. But please, make me a wrap from the same material to put around my shoulders in case I get a chill."

The same skillful hand made a Gina a second dress, this would be worn the next day to the special dinner party. A style suitable to Miss Tufano's upbringing. Fine gray wool, a tight fitted bodice with small covered buttons from the waist to the bottom of her chin, long sleeves, and a flowing skirt.

The cobbler made shoes that matched each dress. Gertrude put pressure on Melissa and the shoemaker to have everything ready within ten days.

She intimidated to Melissa, "You have been making my dresses for many years and I have really never complained." This was not exactly true, but Gertrude continued, "I really do not want to seek any other dressmaker, so Gina's dresses must be done by next week. By next week. Is that clear Melissa?"

Gina was embarrassed when Gertrude pressed the cobbler in the same way she had put pressure on the dressmaker, but tried on the shoes to go with the green taffeta and the gray wool dresses. As Gina walked around the room, first in the shoes to go with the green taffeta, and then the shoes to match the gray wool, Gertrude finally expressed pleasure, and gave well-deserved complements.

Dressed in the evening gown before the dance, Gina stared at her reflection. The bodice caused her some concern. "Can we not pull it up higher, Maggie?" she asked. "All my bosom shows."

When Miss Tufano had arrived back in New York City, Gertrude had assigned Margaret McLeod to be Gina's personal maid. And, being a whole five years older than Gina, Margaret knew *haute couture*.

Maggie tugged the bodice down to fit Gina's figure and chided her. "You cannot hide your breasts, girl. You have to let part of them show in this dress, it was made that way."

. . . .

Margaret McLeod was of Scottish descent, from aristocratic lineage. Raised in Scotland, she was the picture of a pure Scottish lady, lovely red hair, blue eyes, creamy white skin, and a ready smile.

The McLeod castle had been her birthplace and home, and only the clan members of McLeod had lived in the castle from the eleventh century. Maids had waited on Maggie and did her bidding from birth onward. Consequently, her manner of speaking was always aloof and a bit superior.

A disagreement between family heads had ended in a heated argument that left Margaret's father dead. His wife Keren, his daughter Margaret, and his son Terence had been forced to leave the castle when another descendant of McLeod clan took residency.

Devastated at the death of her husband, Keren immigrated to New York. When the little money they had saved was depleted, Maggie took work as a maid. For someone who had always given orders, taking orders was definitely not Maggie's style. She spoke out frequently whether or not her superiors asked for an opinion. Maggie's disposition caused her to lose one position after another.

After Keren's funeral, Miss McLeod was left destitute. Laura, Gertrude's maid, entreated Mrs. Mueller to hire Maggie. Gertrude reluctantly agreed to Laura's request, and for the last eighteen months Maggie had worked and taken orders from Mrs. Mueller, but not necessarily without complications.

· · · · · · · · · · · · ·

"Now, leave the bodice alone; do not pull it up anymore," Maggie ordered, "I have to go downstairs to help serve the guests. Promise you will not pull it up?"

"Wait, Maggie. Where is the wrap? Melissa was supposed to have it delivered tonight before the dance."

"I have it right here, Miss," she said, and held the wrap up in front of Gina. "You always worry. Leave that dress the way it is. Do you hear me? And, do not wear the wrap."

Out the door she went, as Gina called out, "*Grazie*, Maggie."

Ignoring Maggie's instructions, Gina put the wrap around the top of her chest and shoulders, hung her mother's cloth evening purse, with exquisite silk needlework and jewels on the frame and clasp, on her arm, and walked out of the room. The musicians were positioned; the dance would soon be underway.

James entered through the front door as Gina descended the stairs. In tails for the evening, he looked handsome and stately, but it was Gina's appearance that captivated him.

"Gina," he said, surveying her from top to toe, "you look absolutely breathtaking. You are truly beautiful in that gown."

"Thank you, James. Gertrude picked out the style of the gown; I liked the material and the color. I think it should be higher."

As no skin was visible, James looked at the hem of her dress and asked, puzzled, "Higher, Gina? It looks fine to me. You look ravishing."

Everyone was assembled in the main hall when James and Gina entered. The music started into a waltz.

Smiling, he said, "Shall we?"

Once around the dance floor was all it took. The wrap had slipped and was hanging on Gina's arms. James stared at the top of Gina's chest.

Vexed and embarrassed, she was about to pick up her skirts and run when the gentleman in James emerged. "Do you remember Dr. and Mrs. Franklin? There, standing by Dr. Paonessa. Mrs. Franklin was the lady that always copied your mother's hats."

He had deflected Gina's embarrassment and had acted the gentleman to the highest degree. For this Gina would be forever grateful.

The dance ended and friends surrounded Gina. Maggie was passing a tray of tiny tea sandwiches among the guests. She stopped in front of Gina and offered her a sandwich.

Gina refused, but Maggie spoke out in front of everyone. "Will you take off that thing! Enjoy the dress and the dance. Please!"

Gina gasped. Maggie winked and walked away to offer sandwiches to other guests. Miss Tufano took Maggie's suggestion and removed the wrap. Tonight she was the Belle of the Ball and might as well enjoy the dance.

A large, green flowering plant hid Gina as she sat and rubbed her swollen toes after dancing the better part of an hour. Someone sounded an "Ahem" above her head and Gina sat up quickly and replaced her shoes. Francisco the butler, had urgent news. "Miss Gina, a telegram has just arrived for you. Mr. Mueller is in the library, waiting along with Mrs. Mueller. Can you follow me at once, please?"

"Yes, surely, Francisco. When was it delivered?"

"Only now, Miss Gina. I gave it to Mr. Mueller straight away. He wants you to read it immediately."

Francisco knocked at the library door, then opened it to allow Gina to pass through. When Gina entered, Eric was anxious. "This telegram just arrived for you," he said. "I thought you should read it at once."

Gina took it from Eric. "It is from Sonora," she muttered.

Fearing the worst, she opened it quickly, read it through, smiled, sat down on the brown leather, high-back wing chair and read it through again. She handed it back to Eric and relaxed in the chair to hear the words repeated again.

Eric read the telegram silently, smiled and then read aloud:

"Gina Tufano:

"Sonora says come home.

"We miss you very much.

"I want you to come home.

"I miss you even more.

"Cody"

Gertrude asked, "Who is it from Gina? Who is Cody?"

Eric provided the answer for his wife. "Cody is the deputy of Sonora, my dear. The deputy who saved Gina's life last month. Obviously, he wants her to come back to California because he misses her, more than very much. Wouldn't you say so, Gina?"

Eric savored the expression on her face as Gina sighed and said dreamily, "Cody misses me. He says he misses me, even more."

The rest of the evening, Gina's feet did not touch the floor; she floated in the arms of all her dance partners. Oh, she nodded in agreement and smiled to them as she danced, but she did not retain one word spoken by anyone during a waltz or polka. She would read Cody's telegram, now tucked safely in her purse, later to her hearts content. By the middle of next week, she would be on her way to California. On her way home.

34

In the early morning hours, the last guest was bid a goodnight. Gertrude and Gina collapsed into their beds and slept until almost eleven o'clock the next morning.

"How did it happen you scheduled the dance and the dinner so closely together?" Gina asked at coffee.

"When I dispatched the invitations, this person could not attend on this day, or that day, and so it goes. This particular Sunday seem to fit everyone's schedule. I was worried about Eric, but he promised me that he would not tire himself out on either day. It worked out well for you, dear. Now you can be on your way to California by the middle of next week. I will miss you so, Gina."

"I will miss you and Eric, Gertrude. But by the time I get back to Sonora, it will be over four weeks since I left. I often wonder how the doctor is getting along without me."

"That telegram you received last night impressed me, Gina. You obviously know the deputy well enough for him to tell you he missed you and wanted you to come home. Most impressive."

"The message meant a great deal to me," Gina admitted.

"He is the one who saved your life, isn't he? My, it must have been frightening for you. How brave of him."

With her mind revisiting each scene of that horrible night, she answered Gertrude. "Yes, he was very brave. Owen was desperate to kill Cody, but Cody only wanted to disable Owen. When Owen raised his knife to kill me, the deputy had no choice; he had to kill Owen."

Gertrude listened to Gina's story, eyes wide open and staring, her coffee cup halfway between her mouth and the table.

"I cannot believe such danger exits in California," she remarked. "It is a good thing your poor dear mother and father are not alive to know what you have been through." Draining her coffee cup, Gertrude stood up and announced, "Gina, I must talk to the cook and the servants about dinner this evening. Please eat your breakfast, dear; take your time."

"Yes," Gina said in a soft voice when Gertrude left the room, "you go talk to the servants about dinner. I will take my time with my coffee and think about the people that I have missed because I have been in New York City for three never ending weeks."

$\mathcal{M}$aggie helped Gina dress for the special dinner. Ten young couples were invited, including James.

"What's for dinner, Maggie?" Gina asked. "The smell is making my mouth water. My dress seems tight since I tried it on last week. What do you think?"

"Beef roast. I hope it fits tighter; you are far too skinny. No, it fits the same."

"Oh, it is lovely, and I can bend over without worrying about the top of my dress showing all my chest."

Never one to let words stay in her head when she wanted to blurt them out, Maggie spoke to Gina nose to nose. "Listen to me, girl, if you wear that evening gown to another dance, you carry that wrap. Do you hear me? Do not wear it. It hid all of your shoulders and neck. What is the difference if it shows a little of your chest? All the women I know have breasts. You worry too much."

Maggie was right. Gina was modest. She turned away from the mirror. "Most of the women of Sonora make their own clothes, Maggie," she said. "It's not important to have the latest fashions. It's much easier living in California.

"I want you to see Sonora someday; it's so beautiful. Trees line the board walkways. We do not walk on pavement. Flowers are everywhere and their fragrance is divine. The hills and mountains are so green, they are literally covered with huge oak and pine trees."

Maggie sat on Gina's bed in deep thought. When she came out of her dreams, she spoke. "Scotland is green on the hills and in the valleys. The houses are old and made of stone. Fences are built with different colored rock; they separate one property from the neighbor's property. Scotland is so beautiful. A beautiful place to live."

Heaving a sigh, Maggie stood up to adjust Gina's dress and add a reminder, "Dinner is at six o'clock, girl. You look special tonight."

"It is because I am so happy."

Maggie smiled, and closed the door on her way downstairs.

During the last three weeks, Gina and Maggie had become like sisters. It was true Maggie spoke out of her place and ignored people if she did not like them, but her work was excellent. Gina wondered if Gertrude appreciated Margaret McLeod. Never did Maggie have to be told when or what to clean; she cleaned anything with pleasure. But, alas, there was little resemblance to a genuine, docile maid.

A knock at the door interrupted her meditation. "Please come in." Gina said.

"I must dismiss Margaret." Gertrude said as she walked to the settee.

"Maggie? Why?"

"Margaret is entirely too outspoken. At the dance last night, she told the one of the servants that Dr. Neilsen was too miserly, that he should have insisted Mrs. Neilsen wear a new dress. I hadn't noticed, but according to Margaret, Mrs. Neilsen wore the same dress to a party I had last year about this same time.

"You and your mother couldn't come to the party, Gina, because your Mother was too ill then. Anyway, Mrs. Neilsen overheard Maggie telling Laura that Mr. Neilsen was miserly. I am so embarrassed. How I will smooth over this matter with Mrs. Neilsen, I cannot say. I know in the end, I will have to agree to dismiss Margaret."

"But what will she do? Does she have family living in New York?"

"I hired Margaret because she was quite destitute. It was Laura who convinced me to hire her. Margaret is a good worker, excellent at cleaning wood floors and walls. But I cannot keep her any longer. I have spoken to her many times about her manners. It's that fiery red hair, makes her too outspoken. I am sorry I must burden you, Gina dear. Whatever shall I say to Mrs. Neilsen?"

Gertrude walked to the door, heavy of heart. As she closed the door she murmured, "Our guests will be arriving soon, Gina, for the special dinner I planned in your honor. I was hoping it would not be the last dinner I held in your honor. But no matter, now. Don't be late coming down to dinner, dear."

When Gertrude went into the study and closed the door to inform Eric of Maggie's imminent dismissal, Gina raced downstairs. Laura was in the kitchen preparing a tray of canapés.

Gina asked pointedly, "Does Maggie have family living here in New York?"

"Maggie? No, Miss. She came from Scotland five years ago. She had a mother, but she died. She has no one, Miss, except a brother who still lives in Scotland."

"Thank you, Laura. I was only curious."

Gina smiled to herself. The way Maggie spoke, her vitality, the way she worked, these were qualities she would need if Miss Margaret McLeod were to live in Sonora.

At the first opportunity, Gina would suggest to Maggie that when it came time for her to board the train at New York Central Station, Miss Margaret McLeod should board with her. They would return to California together.

36

The dinner was a terrible strain. Gina's friends held her close and cried. James held her hands in his, then kissed her tenderly on the cheek.

Alone in her room, Gina removed the telegram from her purse. The words, "I miss you even more," were special. She looked forward to seeing Cody again.

A soft tap at the door woke Gina the next morning. Maggie averted her face as she entered, and proceeded to open the curtains and the window.

"Mrs. Mueller says I must pack the things you will be taking back to California," she said finally, staring into the open wardrobe with her back to Gina. "What dress will you be wearing on the train? I will box all the other dresses, shoes, and personal items, Miss."

"Maggie, please turn around; I want to speak with you."

Maggie's eyes were red, her nose was red, and she had obviously been crying most of her morning. She turned to Gina, "I have been dismissed. Again!" she said tearfully.

"I know all about it; Gertrude told me. What are your plans? Do you have family or friends you can stay with until you find another position?"

"No, no more family, at least not in America. I will find something. Do not worry yourself now, girl. Just tell me what I must pack."

"Maggie, when I left New York and moved to Sonora, I went because my Aunt Mary encouraged me to go. She said I would be happy in Sonora. I did not believe her, but I went anyway, and I have never regretted my decision to move away from New York.

"When I got to California, Aunt Mary had died. I was completely alone. But the townspeople welcomed me and helped me adjust to the West; it was so different from New York. The people that helped me became like family to me.

"I live in my aunt and uncle's house; it's a big house. There are caretakers for the acreage of the property, but no one to help with the housework or cooking. I want you to move to Sonora. I know you will want to work; that is the way you are. If you would like to, you can work for me."

"Move away from New York? No. I could never do that. But, to be near green hills and meadows again, oh, now that would be lovely. Yet, I don't think California is the place for me. You really would want me work for you?"

Gina sat up in bed. "I can use the help, Maggie, and I think you will love Sonora, and I know you would be happy there. I will pay for your first-class train fare," she said, "and the sleeping accommodations. You can pay for your food when we eat in the dining car. It will take seven or eight days to reach California, I will start your wages when we get to Sonora."

Maggie sat down on the bed beside Gina, "I do have some money, Miss," she answered. "The Scottish people are not known for spending their money freely. I have two hundred dollars saved, which should be enough money for train fare and extra. And, I guess there is nothing to keep me in New York anymore. But what am I saying; I cannot travel to California with you. It's so unexpected."

"Think it over, Maggie. You do not have to tell me this minute. I want you to be happy, and like I said, I think you will be happy in Sonora, but this move must be your own decision. I will not attempt to influence you further."

Maggie walked back to the wardrobe. "I have to give you my answer, Miss; my wages are paid through today," she said sadly.

"I am sorry, Maggie. Gertrude is not always the most compassionate person."

"New York is where my mother died, but that is no reason to stay in New York," she muttered. "Actually, I was thinking of returning to Scotland to live with my brother." She stood for a moment staring into the wardrobe, then turned to Gina with determination in her voice. "I will earn my wages, Miss, if I work for you. I will move to Sonora. Why not? What keeps me here? If I do not like California, or it does not like me, I'll go to Scotland."

"Good for you, Maggie. I hoped that would be your answer. But from now on, I am Gina, not Miss. Do you hear me?"

37

$\mathcal{B}$efore the train rolled out of New York, Gina sent a telegram to the deputy:

"Cody Taylor:

"Will arrive in seven days.

"Bringing a surprise.

"I missed you, too.

"Gina"

When she embraced Eric and Gertrude, Gina's heart was aching, knowing she might never see Eric again.

James chose not to see Gina depart. He had a short note delivered to New York Central Station:

"Gina:

"I hope you will always be happy.

"I will always love you.

"James"

Legal issues at the reading of the will had been difficult for Gina; James' advice helped her decide how to distribute monies from the sale of the property. She knew the final walk through her parents' home would be a painful experience. James went with her. He would always be her good friend. For twenty years she had lived in New York City. Precious memories and dear friends had etched a place in her heart. Gina would never forget any of them.

She thought how true was the old saying, "Enduring hardships ensures the best outcome."

Traveling from New York to Sonora four months previously, Miss Tufano's heart had been heavy, laden with doubt and apprehension about her future. One month ago, on the return journey to New York, anxious concerns invaded Gina's mind again. But traveling back to California with Margaret McLeod was an experience all its own.

When Gina and Maggie met they had been strangers. Different heritages, schooling, and ambitions made them unlikely friends. But being sensitive and compassionate to the genuine grief each had suffered broke down all barriers. These young women became more than friends, they had become like sisters.

Meekness not being one of Miss McLeod's virtues, however, two days into their journey, she corrected the chamberman's mistakes after he had tidied their room. Maggie's irritation did not end there; she found and dragged him back to point out all his errors.

Closer to California, Gina sat red-faced while Maggie chastised the waiter for his ineptness, as the rest of the patrons of the dinning car listened.

But through all of the embarrassment, not once did Miss Tufano feel, on the return journey to California, apprehensive or heavy of heart. Before the ladies realized, they were on their last transfer of conveyance. A few more miles and Sonora would bloom in front of them.

As the stagecoach turned onto Washington Street, Gina's anticipation mounted. In a matter of minutes she would alight in front of the Sonora Hotel. Would everyone she had longed to see in the last four weeks be waiting for her return? She particularly hoped that one person would be waiting, Cody Taylor, the deputy of Sonora.

Andrew and Billy were in front of the crowd of people when the stagecoach stopped, waving their arms. Matthew, Millie, John, Myrtle, and Louise waited behind the boys, everyone wearing broad smiles.

Jovial, giddy, able to once again see the town with her own two eyes instead of closing them to fall back into her memory, Gina took in the people and place she had grown to love.

When Gina opened the door to the stagecoach, Andrew and Billy ran to help her step down. "Gina, Gina," Andrew bellowed, holding her around the waist. "I missed you so much. Don't ever leave again. Promise you'll never leave?"

"Yeah, Gina," Billy chimed, his arms encircling both Gina and Andrew, "promise you'll never leave us again?"

"Mi bambinos. Mi bambinos. I love you both. I hope I never have to leave Sonora," Gina cried as she held them tightly.

Matthew and Millie waited patiently for Gina's hugs and kisses.

She sobbed when she held them and did not want to let them go. For Matthew and Millie, having Gina back in Sonora, finally, was an answer to their prayers.

Louise stepped in front of Myrtle as the nurse approached. "I am so glad you are back, Gina," she said, "I have to fill you in on everything that has happened to me. Why, do you know…"

"Not now, Louise," Myrtle said, pushing Louise out of her way, "Gina just got home. You'll have to wait. Welcome back, Gina. We missed you so much."

"You were needed here, young lady. We wanted our nurse," said John. "I hope you are not planning to leave us again any time soon."

"John, as soon as I got off the train in New York," Gina said, stretching her arms out to the side to show the depth of her sadness, "I wanted to get back onto the train and return. I had barely left California and I was longing to come back."

"Gina."

She whirled around when she heard the familiar deep, masculine voice. Her heart heaved in her chest as she saw Cody standing looking down at her, smiling. Gina swallowed hard to calm the palpitations of her heart, and gazed into Cody's intense blue eyes.

He came closer, reached out, and grabbed her by the upper part of her arms. He pulled her to him and bent to kiss her cheek. "I'm glad you're finally home," he said, his lips close to her ear. "I missed you."

"Thank you, Cody," Gina whispered, breathless, "and I missed you."

She stood on her toes and kissed his cheek, enjoying the touch of his unshaven face on her lips, and she held onto his strong arms with her hands. Gina realized from that moment when her lips brushed Deputy Taylor's face, she never wanted to be away from Cody's side again.

It was the sheriff's turn to greet Gina. "It's about time you got back to Sonora, young lady. Welcome home, Gina."

"Thank you, Robert," Gina said as she kissed his cheek. "Thank you all for being here."

"Oh, *mi a smemorato*. I am so forgetful," Gina said, patting her forehead with her hand. "I want all of you to meet someone I know you will like when you get to know her. I am so sorry, Maggie, please step down from the stagecoach."

Miss McLeod had witnessed Gina's happy homecoming with a big smile. Cody and Robert helped Maggie alight.

"Everyone," Gina said, "this is Margaret McLeod, originally from Scotland, and a short while ago from New York City. She is thinking of making Sonora her home. Please, everyone, welcome her."

Shouts of welcome went out; the men and boys shook Maggie's hand; she was grabbed and hugged by the women. Gina stood by Cody, his arm around her waist, while residents of Sonora welcomed and introduced themselves to the woman with the beautiful smile and flaming red hair.

"I'm glad you're finally back," Cody confessed to Gina. He was pleased that Gina had not been in the least bit tempted to stay in New York City. Living in opulence with many luxuries was not Miss Tufano's style.

Robert watched Maggie as she addressed Matthew, Millie, Andrew, Billy, John, Myrtle, and Louise, calling them by their names, as if she knew them.

Approaching Cody, she announced with dry humor, "I know you most of all, Deputy. Gina never stopped talking about you."

Sheriff Sanders had been married once, early in his youth. He had loved his wife very much; she was a beautiful, caring young woman. But she died of consumption a few years after they were married and Robert had never remarried; he knew his wife was irreplaceable.

However, Maggie's flashing smile, creamy white skin, exquisite blue eyes, and flaming red hair dazzled Sheriff Sanders the moment he set eyes on her. She seemed thoroughly unlike any woman he had ever met.

"Sheriff Robert Sanders, I presume," Maggie said as she reached out to shake his hand. "I am pleased to meet you."

"How do you do, Miss McLeod?" he said, eager to finally speak to her. "Welcome to Sonora. What do you think of California, Sonora, and its people so far?"

"So far I like California, what I have seen, anyway. As for the town and people, I can't say yet," Maggie chimed, "but time will tell, will it not."

"Yes, it will," Sheriff Sanders agreed.

To welcome newcomers, to provide assistance if it was needed, this was the sheriff's duty and pleasure. Yes, this was one lady Robert would be happy to assist. He'd make it a point to keep tabs on Margaret McLeod.

"**N**o, I don't want you to come to the hospital tomorrow. You just got back today," Matthew scolded. "You can start Thursday morning."

"I know you need my assistance, Matthew. It has been over four weeks."

"The work waited this long and it can wait another day. You can catch up on all the patients' accidents and sicknesses when you get to the office."

Maggie suggested a good thorough housecleaning before Gina went back to work. She said tartly, "The house surely needs cleaning; it hasn't been cleaned in over four weeks. It could do with my touch."

Gina agreed, because it was useless to disagree. "You want to start upstairs or downstairs, Maggie?"

"Downstairs. Dust is everywhere. Must be the dirt roads. Roads should be covered with rocks like the roads in New York. It would keep everything cleaner. Maybe I will speak to Sheriff Sanders about it."

"You most certainly will not speak to Robert," Gina reproved, strongly, "Ignore the dust and dirt, Maggie. Besides, how can a person plant trees and flowers along the road if rocks are in the way? It cannot be done, therefore, you will just have to adjust your thinking and put up with the dirt. And, with more dirt and dust around, you can do what you do best. Clean whatever is dusty."

Anything Maggie found out of place, she put right, with or without direction. If she saw a picture hanging crooked or anything that required washing, Miss McLeod took the task upon herself and corrected the error with eagerness.

The smell of turpentine and beeswax had invariably drifted through

Mrs. Mueller's house after Maggie cleaned the wood floors, sideboards, wardrobes, and furniture. Gina will need Miss McLeod's assistance. It was always a pleasure to come home to a clean, spotless house.

Maggie tapped at Gina's bedroom door while the house aired after cleaning. "I have put away my lot," Maggie said, "both dresses, my two uniforms, my coat, hat, underskirts, and, oh yes, my second pair of shoes. Not extensive, but adequate. Do you need any help with your trunk? I'm supposed to take John the crate I used for my clothes."

"I think I will keep the crate, Maggie. I'll fold my new dresses and store them in the attic. I know I will never need them in Sonora."

"You will not leave them in a box, girl. Hang them in the wardrobe. Who knows when the town will hold a special event and you can wear one of the dresses. However, do pack the wrap. You will never wear that as long as I am around."

"Well, you might be right. Who knows? Maybe I will wear them both, someday. Yes, take the crate to John."

Maggie headed toward John's cottage. She liked to go to the cottage. Myrtle and Louise were fascinated with her tales of Scotland.

Gina rose early, anxious to start at the doctor's office after being away over four long weeks. Bird songs and the sound of leaves swaying in soft breezes greeted her as she stepped out the front door. It was still summer, but autumn was not far away.

Several past seasons in New York held bitter memories for Gina. But there will be no sadness today. The air was clean and fresh, the sky a sapphire blue; fragrances of different flowers lining the road welcomed her. Gina was at home, where her heart had remained, and once again she was walking to the doctor's office.

The sound of thunderous hooves broke into her meditation. The rider called out as he halted his pony. "Hi, stranger. Need a ride?" It was Cody and as usual, he was grinning.

The deputy had been in Gina's thoughts too much while she was in New York for her to deny his request now. He lifted his boot from the stirrup and reached down to grab her hands. "Put your left foot in the stirrup and hold my hand. I'll pull you up."

Easy directions from the deputy. But could she master these directions? Hardly. The art of swinging her weight up and over Sammy's back, once her foot was in the stirrup, did not come easily to this city girl. In addition, Gina was unable to stop her hysterical giggles at all the failed attempts.

Cody gave up, reached down, grabbed both of Gina's hands, pulled her up, and sat her in front of him on the saddle, holding her around the waist with his left arm. Once again, she shared the saddle with Cody and was not in the least embarrassed to be so close to him. She leaned back, secure, contented, and free from harm. The deputy nudged Sammy into a walk.

"Cody," Gina said, "I brought a present back for you from New York. I hope you like it."

"You came back. That's all I wanted." Pleased at her expression, he continued, "Mom's cooking Saturday. She's invited everyone, even Billy and Robert."

"It sounds wonderful. It has been such a long time since I was in your house. I have missed everyone so much."

Two weeks earlier, Gina had been in a state of despair not knowing when she would leave New York. Today, she sat on the saddle with the deputy in sheer ecstasy while Sammy transported them both to town.

Matthew was in the examination room with Paul, an accident-prone patient who had stepped on a nail early that morning. The doctor dabbed antiseptic on Paul's foot, and smiled broadly as the nurse entered the office.

Gina sat in her desk chair. Cody tethered Sammy at the hitching post, went into the jail, and looked out through his window at Gina. Contented to see her sitting at her desk again, smiling and waving to him, Deputy Taylor was ready to begin his day.

It was well past the noon hour when Matthew finally sat down to eat his lunch. While Gina cleaned and put away medical instruments, the doctor inquired about her trip to New York.

"Gertrude Mueller arranged so many things for me to see and do during my stay in New York. Visits with old friends, lunches with school chums, dinners with Father's associates. And, we trudged from emporium to emporium until I was exhausted. On the Saturday before I left New York, she even had a beautiful ball held in my honor, with musicians and many guests. I had a new gown made with shoes to match, and I was the 'Belle of the Ball'. The day after, Sunday, she had an elegant dinner inviting only my old friends. It was so lovely, and so very kind of her, Matthew."

She sat down in a chair beside the doctor. "All the friends I spoke with tried to convince me to stay in New York permanently. They said they missed me. I did not want to disappoint anyone, especially Eric and Gertrude, but I had to return to California.

"Maggie and I became friends the minute we met, just as if we had known each other all our lives. When Gertrude had to dismiss her, I asked Maggie if she wanted to leave New York and work for me in Sonora. It didn't take long for her to decide. She agreed and made arrangements. And here we are."

"I think she will be happy here, Gina. She has the temperament to live in the West."

There was one additional piece of information Gina had saved for last, and it meant a lot to her. "I have an allotment set aside, Matthew, from the sale of my parents' home. I want to contribute to the new hospital."

"That is very commendable of you, Gina. I am so proud of you."

"It is what my family would approve of, Doctor. You know how much Dr. Sciaroni wanted to have an up-to-date hospital in this town. I remember him talking to my father about a new hospital when we visited five years ago. My contribution can mean another wing, or a larger surgery room, or whatever the board of directors decide to add. Now, I feel I really belong here, that I really am part of the community."

"You are needed here, Gina, believe me. We all waited patiently for you to return."

"Hi," Maggie said, the bell clanged, and she stepped into the office. "I just left the grocery store. I thought I ought to look the town over and walk home with you. It is a nice walk from your house to town, Gina."

Looking around the room, she asked, "Is this the hospital, Doctor?"

"Temporarily, Maggie. We are in the process of building a new hospital on the edge of town."

"I worked at a hospital in New York for a time, mainly cleaning up after the patients, which was the reason I was hired, anyway. That was before my mother died. From what I was able to learn there, from the nurses, I cared for my mother at home until her death."

"I did not know you knew nursing, Maggie," said Gina.

"No, I did not have the money to learn to be a nurse, girl, but I helped the nurses by bathing patients and cleaning up after surgery, doing anything that needed doing. It did not bother me to see blood, parts of bodies, or intestines. I would clean or wash whatever was bloody, so the nurses began to request me by name. In return, they taught me how to care for the sick and I learned some of the tricks to nursing.

"I have always like to keep everything tidy. We had servants when I was growing up in Scotland, but I taught them how to clean properly."

"I can see why you brought her along, Gina."

"No one cleans like Miss Margaret McLeod, Doctor."

"I watched the nurses help the sick and I learned how to make patients comfortable. I wanted to learn how to care for the sick; I liked to help people get well. But I did not have extra money for schooling."

"Who knows, Maggie," Matthew said, "maybe we will need your help someday. Never enough nurses, I always say. We can always use more. It's good to know there is someone willing and able to help."

Gina waved to Cody from her window, as he stepped from the jail.

Maggie looked over Gina's shoulder to the sheriff's office. "Is that where they keep prisoners?" she asked, pointing to the jail. "I have heard stories of the West. I wonder if they are all true."

"Come with me, Maggie," Gina said, "and satisfy your curiosity."

Cody watched Maggie and Gina cross the street and approach the jail.

Gina said, "Maggie wants to see a real Western jail, Cody. She'll probably want to clean it. Well, go in, Maggie, I have to go back to the doctor's office."

Robert was at his desk when Maggie opened the front door. Surprise and pleasure showed on his face when she stepped inside the room and closed the door.

He stood up to greet her. "Miss McLeod, what a pleasant surprise. What brings you to the sheriff's office?"

"I was born Margaret McLeod, and I was called Margaret in Scotland, but everyone calls me Maggie in America. I just wanted to see what a jail looks like."

She looked into the first two cells. But the constant rasping sound from the dirt and sand on the floor evidently grated upon her. Surveying the room, she asked pointedly, "Do you not think it could use a bit of cleaning? If you have a bucket and a brush, I'll scrub the floor. I have nothing to do this afternoon."

"What did you say?" Robert asked in disbelief.

"I said, do you have a bucket and brush? I will scrub the floor."

"Yes, we do. There is a brush in a bucket," Robert answered, "there in the corner. They don't get much use. This isn't the doctor's office, you know, and most of our guests aren't too clean."

"Yes, I can see," she replied, scanning the office and cells.

Emanating from the first cell was a horrible stench. Maggie held her nose and announced, "I will start in this room."

"Are you sure, Maggie? That's the cell where we put prisoners when we arrest them for being drunk and causing a ruckus. We let them sleep it off in there. It hasn't been cleaned in a long time."

Ignoring Robert's question, Maggie walked to the bucket and picked it up. As she turned to face the sheriff, she asked, "Where will I find water for the bucket?"

"There's a pump in the back. Are you sure you want to clean that cell?"

"Yes, I cannot stand anything dirty and this place is filthy. Someone needs to clean and I am offering. Do you not want me to clean it?"

Robert grabbed the bucket, fetched water, and carried it into the cell before she changed her mind. Maggie pushed by him to add shavings of lye soap.

When she began her scrubbing, another problem developed. "The floor has too much sand," she announced, "I must sweep it first. Do you have a broom?"

Robert was a kind man, but not known for his patience. However, he reminded himself that the room did need to be cleaned and went off to fetch the broom.

As he handed it to Maggie, he offered a suggestion. "Would it be better if I waited outside? I could sit in front of the office until you're finished in here."

"Please do, but I will come back early tomorrow morning to finish. There is not enough time today to do a satisfactory job. This place is much too dirty. How anyone can work in filth such as this, well, it is unconceivable to me."

As he looked around, the sheriff agreed that the jail did reek and it had the appearance of being neglected for some time. Robert left the room in Maggie's capable hands and went outside to sit with Cody.

"Sheriff, did you take care of everything inside?" Cody asked, snickering.

"That's quite a woman," Robert apprised. "She wants to clean the jail and she didn't ask for money. She's sweeping the floor in the first cell and then she's going to scrub it. She wants to come back tomorrow morning and finish cleaning. What should I tell her?"

The deputy had a simple solution. "Let her clean it."

"But she wants to come back tomorrow. She might stay all day."

"All she wants to do is make it look like a fancy hotel. Let her do it, Sheriff. Who knows, maybe we'll arrest somebody important."

The men sat in front of the jail. From time to time, they heard loud noises and Maggie mumbled words which they did not understand.

"What's she saying in there?"

"Can't make it out, Sheriff."

"She don't sound happy, Deputy."

"Nope, she sure don't. You think our jail was a mite too dirty for her, Sheriff?"

"Yep, I think so."

$\mathcal{M}$aggie was at the sheriff's office all morning and into the afternoon. Millie had been pressed into her service and the ladies were busy cleaning every table, chair, cot, and desk.

Maggie directed orders to Millie, Robert, and Cody. The sheriff and deputy rearranged cots and furniture, brought new bedding and linen from the dry goods store, and burned the soiled, smelly mattresses and pillows.

Vinegar and water were mixed to clean the difficult problems. Everyone toiled, but the combined effort showed. The sheriff's office and cells looked and smelled healthier.

Matthew wandered around the jail after Millie left and looked over Maggie's work. "We could almost have surgery in here now, Maggie," he praised. "It looks so clean. Yes, I would say one hundred percent better than it did yesterday. You did an excellent job."

"Thank you, Doctor," Maggie said and turned to the nurse. "Gina, I am going to the grocery store. I promised Millie I would make Scottish shortbread for dessert on Saturday. We are low on flour and sugar, and we need yeast. I will buy the supplies; you can meet me there when you leave the hospital."

"So much energy, Doctor," Gina remarked as Maggie closed the front door. "That lady does like to keep busy."

Matthew smiled, removed a medical volume from the bookshelf by his desk, and turned the pages slowly in hopes of finding a treatment for one of their patients.

However, the melancholy, somber feeling that Gina had awoke with that morning was back and it distracted her. She was not able to concentrate on her work.

Gina had the same dismal feeling one morning when Dr. Tufano kissed his wife and daughter before he walked out their front door to the hospital. It was December 1873; the snow had fallen steadily for most of the week and was piled high in the streets of New York City.

Pneumonia patients filled the hospital and died at an alarming rate. After hours at the hospital, Tony finally came home that December evening, dead tired, his shoes wet, and he was feverish. Gina recognized that night how her father had started to neglect his own body's need for rest and food.

Over three months, Tony's healthy body took a beating as he pummeled it day and night. Tina and Gina begged him to rest.

"My patients need me at the hospital," he replied. "The beds are still full. People are dying, and some we even have to turn away. By the time I start to treat my patients, pneumonia has taken hold.

"I have to sleep at the hospital again, my dears. Mrs. Gimbarti struggles to take air into her lungs with her every breath. Death will be soon. I want to make her as comfortable as possible until her battle ends."

In April of 1874, after spending days and nights at the hospital, it was Dr. Tufano who contracted pneumonia. One month later, Tony was dead. Six months later, his wife died while mourning the loss of her beloved husband.

As the afternoon concluded and the last patient left the doctor's office, Gina stared across the street to the jail. The deputy appeared suddenly, mounted, and nudged Sammy into a gallop.

Cody was a lawman; it was his job to keep the townspeople safe. But like Dr. Tufano, the deputy's concern was for the safety and welfare of others, not his own.

What was this apprehension within her? Was something going to happen to the deputy?

She shook the premonition from her mind. Work waited on her desk; the quiet warnings that had commenced were ignored.

Heaving a sigh, Gina disciplined herself. "You worry too much," she murmured.

$\mathcal{M}$aggie sat between Myrtle and Louise in the back of the buggy on the way to Millie's house. The ladies listened with mouths gaping as Maggie expounded on the dangerous exploits between the clans of Scotland.

Before supper was consumed, Gina passed out gifts from New York. Gold watches and chains for Matthew, Robert, and John. A musical jewelry container, each different in design and melody, went to Millie, Myrtle, and Louise. Andrew and Billy received identical brown leather vests, and a black-tooled leather vest with pockets in the lining was Cody's gift. The only time Gina enjoyed having Gertrude lead her from emporium to emporium was when she selected keepsakes for her special friends in Sonora.

While the ladies were washing and putting away dishes, a young Mexican woman, wiping away her tears, walked into the kitchen. Her husband, Luis Serrano, followed her. They led Cody and Robert into the living room. One half-hour later, when all emerged, the Mexican couple showed concern, Sheriff Sanders was worried, and the deputy looked troubled.

Millie greeted her unexpected guests. "Luis, Maria, how good to see you. Please, sit down and eat, and you must meet Maggie. She is from New York City."

Luis was a handsome Mexican man. He and the deputy were about the same age, and they were close friends. Luis Serrano was the type of friend that appeared the moment his presence was needed. Born and reared in Sonora, he was the son of a prominent rancher.

Because of Luis' extensive knowledge in the breeding of horses,

Ken Thorton relied on Luis to care for his valuable herd of prime Appaloosa ponies when he was in Coulterville.

Loyal, brave, unswerving, and a firm promoter of justice and equality among all residents in Sonora, Luis had come to alert Cody and Robert to a serious problem.

Before Millie went outside to join the others, she heaped food on Maria and Luis' plates. Maria picked at her food, but Luis was hungry and enjoyed every mouthful.

Robert sat beside Maria at the kitchen table and questioned her. "Tell me what happened at the North Star Mine. When did Arnoldo tell you that Jose had been shot?"

Maria was learning English, but pronunciation was still difficult for her. "One month ago, he go to dig," Maria said. "Three day ago, he see Jose die."

Maria's seventeen-year-old brother, Arnoldo, had witnessed a disturbance at the North Star Mine. Their cousin, Jose, had been shot and killed during a confrontation between Mexican miners and American miners, presumably in cold blood.

A small number of Sonora residents had always tacked the name "Greasers" to the Mexican population. Sheriff Sanders and Deputy Taylor did not tolerate this type of remark. It was a cruel and heartless name that lowered the dignity of these hardworking people.

A Mexican population originally settled in California, and they were the ones that gave the town of Sonora its name. But in spite of that fact, there was prejudice against the Mexican race. By 1875, it had cooled somewhat, although some American people still misjudged these people and tried to take advantage of them.

"There is an abandoned site," Luis began, "between Columbia and Sonora. Rumors were heard of a vast amount of gold still in the mine, although none had been found. About one month ago, Arnoldo and seven other Mexicans started working the mine again, hoping the rumors to be true and that the gold had been overlooked.

"They worked for two weeks. Out of frustration and desperation, four men climbed 200 feet above the river. Boulders prevented the men from digging into the rock. They pushed the boulders down the side of the mountain into the river below. Under the boulders they found gold. They continued working until they collected four thousand dollars worth of large gold nuggets."

Maria interrupted Luis. "American's hear," she said, "and they angry. They want gold."

"Yes, the American miners learned of the Mexican men finding gold at the abandoned mine," Luis continued, "how they found out we do not know. Perhaps they heard from someone that was at the assessor's office. About fifteen American men on horseback, fully armed, rode into the Mexican site early in the morning while the Mexicans were still sleeping.

"Their purpose was to intimidate, run the Mexicans off, claim the abandoned site, and keep all the gold that was found. The Mexicans gave no resistance; it was pointless to resist and would have resulted in a slaughter.

"Except for Maria's cousin, Jose. His anger was directed toward one man, the leader of the group and a man who had goaded the Mexican miners. Jose spoke excellent English, tried to reason with the leader, explaining the site had been abandoned for many years. When Jose defended their right to the claim, the leader ridiculed him and accused the Mexican men of stealing the site.

"It was all lies. Jose threw up his arms and walked toward his tent. Arnoldo thinks the American men thought he was going to get a weapon."

Luis stopped before he related the painful, tragic end of his story. Robert and Cody waited patiently until Luis could proceed. "Three men on horseback drew their revolvers, but William Johns, the leader of the group, also known as Rattlesnake, was the one who shot down an unarmed man.

"William Johns fired three bullets. One bullet went in Jose's right leg; Jose fell to the ground. Johns waited, watched Jose suffer, and then fired again, hitting Jose this time in the left shoulder. Proud and determined, Jose somehow got to his feet and turned around to stumble toward his tent. He did not have a weapon hidden there, but perhaps he wanted protection. Johns aimed once more. The final bullet went into Jose's back and killed him."

Luis consoled Maria as she wept quietly. Robert and Cody offered no words of defense for William Johns. How does one explain that people do unthinkable acts of cruelty to their fellow humans?

Robert patted Maria's back. "Tell Arnoldo that Cody and I will investigate the murder at the North Star Mine," he promised. "We'll find this human rattlesnake. Luis, does Arnoldo know where Rattlesnake may be hiding out?"

Luis shrugged. "Manuel, Jose's brother, knows of a man called Rattlesnake who has a dig north of Sonora, in the hills by Columbia, but he does not know the exact site, my friends. Arnoldo told the miners that you and the deputy would help them, for he trusts you. He knows you will find the man who killed Jose.

"Arnoldo will stay with Maria and I for a few days at the ranch. Since he witnessed the killing, he is afraid Rattlesnake will find and kill him."

The guests from the backyard filtered into the kitchen.

Seeing Maria wipe her eyes, Millie was concerned. "Maria," she questioned, "are you all right? Is there anything I can do for you?"

"No, thank you, *Senora* Millie."

Robert and Cody walked Maria and Luis to their waiting buggy. "We will start early tomorrow, Luis," Cody promised. "You take care of Maria and Arnoldo."

Luis pulled Cody to the side of the buggy and offered his assistance. "I want to go with you Cody," he said. "You will need help with the language, and the Mexican men know me. They will talk to me and you will know where to search for the Americans."

"Not tomorrow, Luis. The sheriff and I need to find Rattlesnake's campsite. But if I need your help, you know I'll ask."

42

Robert and Cody rode early the next morning, north into the hills between Sonora and Columbia, in search of William Johns' mine.

The lawmen did not possess a detailed description of the killer. During the fray at the North Star Mine, Arnoldo had stood near Johns' dapple-gray horse, but he had been afraid to look up when Rattlesnake was hurling threats and abuses to Jose.

When Arnoldo did look up, Johns' had turned the dapple-gray and was riding out of the camp. Arnoldo saw his face at a glance, but giving an accurate description in words was not possible. Nevertheless, he would never forget that face. It was etched indelibly in his brain. If Arnoldo ever saw William Johns again, he would know him.

Sheriff Sanders and Deputy Taylor asked questions of miners at each campsite they approached. About midday, they had spoken with miners at five different digs, but no one knew William Johns.

At the sixth campsite, Robert dismounted to speak with four miners who were hunched over a small stream panning for gold. They looked up suspiciously as Robert walked closer, but said nothing. One man had a long, white beard. Two other men, much younger than he in age, were identical in looks, and the fourth was still a boy, no more than eighteen-years old.

The badge on Robert's chest flashed in the sunlight as he stood facing the men, the stream between them.

The youngest, and obviously the most audacious of the four finally spoke. "What do you want, Sheriff? You here to arrest us? This is our dig and we ain't doin' nothing wrong."

"We're looking for information, that's all. The deputy and I are looking for a man called William Johns. Do any of you know where we can find him?"

"Never heard of him," the older man answered, not even raising his head to look at the sheriff.

Sheriff Sanders directed his question to the three other men. "Do any of you men know of a man named William Johns?"

"We told you, none of us heard of him," the youngest of the four said. "Now, go on, git out, Sheriff. We're working our dig and ain't doin' nothin' wrong. We don't know no one named Rattlesnake."

As soon as the youngest said the word "Rattlesnake," one of the twins dropped his pan into the steam and fell into the water trying to retrieve it. These four men knew William Johns; there was no question about it.

Sheriff Sanders decided to find out just how much these men knew and asked, weighing his words carefully, "Do any of you know anything about a killing at the North Star Mine last week? A Mexican man was shot in cold blood. Can you men tell me about the shooting?"

All four men were now standing by the side of the stream, but none of the four answered Robert's question.

He persisted, "If any of you know about this killing, you need to tell me. The deputy and I want to talk to the men that rode out to the North Star Mine that day. There were fifteen American men that witnessed the shooting."

"We don't know nothing," the youngest man said pugnaciously. "We told you that. I think it's time for you to leave, Sheriff, and take your deputy with you."

Hostility was mounting. Robert tried once more to reason with the four miners. "The Mexican man was shot three times. None of the other Mexican men were armed. This was a cold-blooded killing. They were not going to resist the Americans and they would have left the site peacefully. No reason to shoot or kill an unarmed man."

The old miner threw down his pan, crossed the stream, and stood defiantly in front of the sheriff. "You better git out of here, Sheriff," he growled. "We don't know this man. We don't know nothin' about that mine or the shootin'. Now git out."

He raised his hand, pointing the way out, but continued with his belligerent warning. "But you better stay away from them greasers. You are always sidin' with them over your own kind. You and that deputy of yours, you think of them, not us. Keep doing that and somethin' could happen to you. Now, git out."

"The deputy and I don't side with the Mexican people any more than we side with any other people. We only want to be fair. Whoever shot an unarmed man will be prosecuted. If he's found guilty, a jury will see that he hangs for his crime."

Sheriff Sanders turned from the angry men and mounted his pony. When they had put some distance between themselves and the dig, Robert pulled his horse to a halt. "I'll bet my last dollar those men know where Rattlesnake is, or at least where he stakes his claim," he said.

"They sure knew one of the names he goes by, Sheriff. You didn't mention it."

Glancing toward the hills in the distance, Robert summed up his plan. "Let's go up by those big pines, Cody, behind their camp. I want to see if any of the four ride out to visit another site."

Overlooking the stream where the four miners panned for gold, hidden by an area densely covered with trees and undergrowth, Cody and Robert watched the activity in the camp.

Four men stood in a circle leveling angry outbursts at one another. Within an hour, the youngest of the men jumped on his horse and left the dig, riding north toward Columbia. Robert and Cody waited. When the horse and rider were out of sight, they crept down the hill and followed him.

Trailing fresh horse tracks, they rode into a thicket flourishing with scrub oak, manzanita bushes, and massive old gnarled oak trees. The rider's tracks stopped in front of an immense boulder, which through the passage of time had separated, and somehow shifted from its original position.

Cody and Robert halted their horses, sat in their saddles, and looked around. It seemed as if they had ridden into a blind canyon with no way out. However, on closer examination, the rider's tracks went around the boulder and through the narrow separation, into a natural hidden opening or pathway. That pathway led onward into a spacious enclosure.

Robert and Cody backed away from the entrance, dismounted, and hid the horses behind large trees. Climbing a small hill, they inched closer and slid on their bellies to a position overlooking the camp. From their lookout, they could clearly hear the words spoken by the men below.

Eight men were in the campsite. There appeared to be six miners who milled about the area, the latest arrival who stood by his lathered horse, and a man who sat on an overturned box in front of a shack with tent material draped over the top. He rested his back against the weathered wood boards and stared, without speaking, at the man who had just ridden into the camp.

The man sitting on the box was young, about thirty-five years old, clean-shaven, with an unusual hat perched on his head. This hat boasted a small brim and showed most of his ears and his well-trimmed hair. He had on a brilliant white shirt with long sleeves, black trousers, and a matching black vest. Beyond any doubt, this man did not live or work at this campsite; his clean clothing witnessed that fact.

He finally spoke to the rider. "What brings you here, Kevin? Haven't I told you never to come to this camp in the daylight? So tell me. Why did you come?"

Kevin attempted an explanation of what had prompted his intrusion. "The sheriff and deputy was at our camp, asking questions about the North Star. I thought you'd want to know, that's all."

"So, you rode all the way out here to inform me. How kind of you. By any chance, were you followed, Kevin?"

"No! No one followed me. The sheriff asked if we knew William Johns. We told them we didn't know you. Pa told them to get out, so they left."

"I see. Well, well. So they have heard about the doings. We will have to keep an eye out for the sheriff and the deputy, will we not? We do not want them to find our mine, do we, Kevin?"

William Johns, alias Rattlesnake, was a lettered man, evidently a new arrival to the gold country, as neither Robert nor Cody, had seen him before. When he spoke the English language, his accent and style of speaking was different, almost pretentious. His literary form was uttered with perfect diction. He seemed out of place in the West. The sheriff and deputy knew that he was not indigenous to California.

"Kevin, go back to your own camp and stay there," he commanded. "I have told you before, have I not, that you do not come out here unless I tell you to come. Is that understandable?"

Kevin nodded, grunted something that was impossible to comprehend, mounted his horse, and rode out of the camp via the same secret way he entered.

Cody and Robert watched as William Johns removed his hat and wiped his brow and neck with a clean handkerchief. He beckoned to the miners toward him, and all walked where Johns' had tethered his horse. This was an unfortunate turn of events, as Cody and Robert were no longer able to hear the words spoken.

The sheriff and deputy watched as some men nodded, others shook their heads, but all seemed agitated at whatever Rattlesnake divulged. Finally, the miners signified agreement and Johns mounted his beautiful dapple gray pony.

Robert and Cody clearly heard the last chilling words William Johns spoke with a loud voice. "You men know what happens when someone disobeys me. Never hope to deceive me. You will not live long enough to experience regret. I will see you both in town later tonight."

The two men that Rattlesnake selected were the youngest of the six. Johns rode out of the camp heading north toward Columbia.

43

*R*obert and Cody waited until Johns was well out of range, and then they led their horses out of cover and walked a quarter of a mile before they mounted and rode away from Johns' mine.

They brought their horses up at a creek and let them drink and cool down. Cody walked into the stream up to his ankles, washed his face, and filled his canteen. Robert stood by his horse. There was much to say, but the men were not yet ready to speak.

Deputy Taylor finally broke the silence. "I'll check some of the wanted posters when we get back to town, Sheriff. He's foreign; somebody must have something on him."

"Wire Sacramento, Cody, and give them his description. Maybe something will turn up."

"No, I don't want to wire Sacramento yet, Sheriff. I don't want anyone to know we know what he looks like. I got a feeling he's trying to lay low."

"I'd go along with that, Deputy."

"What causes a man to shoot an unarmed man three times? The first two times to cripple him, the next one to kill him."

"I couldn't say. You don't turn your back on William Johns though, that's for sure."

"Sounds to me he's the type that enjoys shooting people in the back." Cody stood up, rubbed his unshaven chin with his fingers, and spoke in an undertone. "I didn't like the way that old miner threatened you, Sheriff." He clutched Sammy's rein. "It's getting late, we better head for home."

It was almost evening in Sonora when Robert and Cody finally rode into town. As they tethered their horses in front of the jail, a sultry feminine voice called out their names. Pretty widow Nancy had slicked up for the evening and was longing for masculine company.

She spoke as she sauntered toward the men with her come-hither walk. "Hi, Sheriff. Good evening, Deputy. Either of you boys want to enjoy supper at my house?"

The widow was bedecked in her latest expensive fashion, dark-blue velvet dress with a low neckline that exposed most of her lovely breasts, and, in addition, a tight bodice that accentuated all the right areas of her upper body. Completing the evening dress was a long flowing skirt and matching shoes.

Standing close to Cody, Nancy turned to look at the sheriff with her most enticing glance, then looking back at Cody, she extended the invitation once more. "I was wondering Deputy, how about coming to my house for supper tonight?"

Cody faced the widow and grinned. "Not tonight, Nancy," he said.

Nancy looked at Robert, smiled, and repeated the request. "How about it, Sheriff? Do you feel like having supper with me?"

"No, maybe some other time, Nancy." Robert had much on his mind and he was hungry and in a hurry to sit in the restaurant and eat Chef Madame Pamela Dumont's special steak supper. He nodded to Nancy and headed in the direction of the hotel.

Cody touched his hat and fell in stride with Robert. He glanced back over his shoulder at the lovely widow standing by the horses feeling rejected and annoyed.

With a snicker in his voice, he noted, "That was quite a dress she was wearing. Wouldn't you say, Sheriff?"

"Not at all bad, Deputy, not at all bad," Robert agreed with a chuckle.

The men walked down the street into the Sonora Hotel for a well-deserved rest and something to eat.

$\mathcal{P}$lates containing two gigantic steaks that still sizzled from the fire were placed onto the table. The sheriff and deputy picked up their knives and forks and devoured their suppers without speaking one word.

While Robert debated ordering a piece of the hotel's famous hot apple pie for dessert, Cody sat back in his chair and reminded the sheriff about a wanted poster that they had received from Auburn. "You remember, Robert, a few months ago, some rich Chinese man was shot and killed. He had three shots in him, one in the leg, one in the shoulder, but the shot that killed him was in his back."

"Yeah, I remember, Cody. But I can't remember if there was a drawing of the wanted man."

"No drawing, had a written description: 'Brown hair, wears dark clothes, clean-looking', something that fits two hundred men in Auburn alone. No, it's the way the Chinese man was killed. He had three shots in him, leg, shoulder, and back, the same way the Mexican man was killed."

Cody leaned forward and spoke softly. "Rattlesnake's too clean; he sure doesn't stay at that camp day and night. He's got to live close by so he can wash and change clothes."

Sheriff Sanders passed on the apple pie. "Johns rode north," he mumbled as the dessert cart rolled by, "toward Columbia. Maybe he lives in Columbia."

"Somebody's seen him around Sonora or Columbia; somebody had too. He talks different, and remember that hat." The deputy stopped in the middle of his sentence, thought for a minute, then proceeded. "You know, Sheriff, there's one lady in town might've seen him. Pretty widow Nancy lived in Columbia before she and her husband moved to Sonora.

"Sheriff, I think we better take Nancy up on her invitation for supper tonight," Cody said. He stood up and pulled money out of his vest pocket. "We don't want to hurt her feelings, do we? She might think we don't like her anymore."

"What? We just ate supper. And I don't think you need to visit Nancy, Cody. Gina's back in town. You know what I mean."

"Come on, Sheriff."

As he swung up into the saddle, Robert again voiced his disapproval. "Cody, we don't need to be at Nancy's house this time of night."

"You know Nancy, Sheriff. If there's a man she doesn't know within a radius of fifty miles, she'll find out who he is. It's possible she's already met William Johns. If we ask her nice, maybe she can tell us something about him."

"Don't ask her too nice, Deputy," Robert cautioned. "She might get other ideas."

The deputy rapped on the widow's magnificent stained glass and solid tiger-oak front door. Nancy opened it wide, wearing a large inviting smile, but the look of surprise on her face told Cody she expected someone else.

Looking most alluring in her dark-blue velvet dress, she declared, "Well, Deputy, you decided to come over after all." Then, seeing Robert standing beyond Cody on the top step of her porch, she called out. "I see you both came by for supper. Aren't you going to come in, Sheriff?"

"I'll wait here, Nancy. The deputy wants to ask you some questions."

Cody passed through the entrance and stood in the entry hall, but he held onto the knob of the door and kept it open.

Nancy had a way of distracting a man from his original intentions. She moved close to Deputy Taylor and stroked the leather of his vest with her soft fingers. As she gazed deep into his blue eyes, the widow leaned against him provocatively.

"What can I do for you, Deputy?" she inquired. "Are you sure I can only answer your questions? Isn't there anything else I can do for you?"

"Not tonight, Nancy." The lawman proceeded with his questions. "Have you ever heard of a William Johns? Or maybe a man called Rattlesnake?"

Nancy let go of his vest, walked over to a chair, and sat down. She took offense at Cody's indifference, but answered his questions anyway.

"William Johns?" she repeated. "No, I don't know anyone by that name and I have never heard of anyone called Rattlesnake. Who would have such a disgusting name anyway."

Whatever Nancy was, she was also a woman with a kind heart. She regretted her sudden irritation toward Cody and asked, "What does this Rattlesnake look like? Is there anything noticeable about him? Scars? Is he young? Fat? How old is he? Does he walk with a limp? Anything?"

"He's young, middle thirties. No hair on his face. Don't think he has scars. Wears city clothes, clean. He's got a funny-looking hat that sits above his ears. Doesn't look like he works much. Foreign, talks with an accent."

Cody waited as Nancy deliberated. Men were pleased to admire Nancy, a woman of stunning natural beauty, marked by long brown hair, brown eyes, dark eyelashes and full red lips. Nancy was also blessed with a figure that made most men stop dead in their tracks when she passed them, and made most women jealous.

She had slipped into a becoming pout, her chin resting on the fingers of her closed hand, elbow on the arm of the chair.

She looked up and announced with a large smile, "Yes, I do believe I have seen this man."

Robert stood by Cody as Nancy struggled to remember when and where she had seen William Johns.

After a full minute, the widow rattled off the incident. "I don't know this man's name. I mean we were never formally introduced, but your description of William Johns fits a man I saw recently, actually last month.

"I was in Columbia visiting the sister of my late husband. She's not young and can't even wash her own clothes. Since my friend was driving my buggy, my sister-in-law asked us to take her to the Chinese laundry in Columbia.

"They waited in the buggy while I paid for whatever needed to be claimed. She sure had a lot of laundry; I don't think she had washed anything for six months. But as I was leaving with all the packages, I dropped a small bundle on the floor.

"A man suddenly appeared at my side, kneeled down, and picked up the bundle. I was grateful and thanked him. He said, 'You are most welcome, my lady. It is my pleasure to assist you.'

"He spoke funny, but very nice. He even took off his hat when I thanked him, and I believe it was the same hat you described.

"In fact, he kept the package, walked me out to the buggy, and helped me into the carriage. I must say, he was a charmer, a real gentleman."

Sheriff Sanders walked forward, stood behind Cody, and asked, "Have you seen him since that time, Nancy? In Sonora?"

"No, never in Sonora, and I have not been back to see my sister-in-law in Columbia lately."

The conversation was interrupted by a scraping sound coming from the porch. Orville Browne, a local gambler, young and handsome, with money in his pocket on occasion, stood in the doorway, wondering why the sheriff and deputy were talking to Nancy.

"Come in, Orville. They were just leaving."

"Appreciate your help, Nancy." The deputy touched his hat, turned, and walked with the sheriff to their waiting horses.

45

fter a long day of riding, mounting and dismounting, Cody's left shoulder ached and burned. When he stepped down from the saddle, he stretched his shoulder in large circles, then rubbed it.

Robert blocked Cody's way into the jail and asserted his authority. "Deputy, I want you to go home and get some rest. That's an order. Early tomorrow morning is soon enough for you to start looking through the wanted posters. We'll talk about wiring Sacramento then. I know your shoulder is bothering you. Go home."

"I'll stick around a little longer, Sheriff, make the rounds. You check the posters."

"No. I'll check the posters and do the rounds. I want you to go home. I'll see you tomorrow."

Relieved that Cody was on his way home, Robert opened the door to the sheriff's office. He put a match to the oil lamp, sat it on his desk, and pulled out all the wanted posters that had been received in the last six months.

After three long hours and no closer to finding information on a man named William Johns, or his alias, Rattlesnake, it was time to do the rounds. He strapped his holster to his hip, and made sure the chambers in his Colt single action .45, Sheriff's model were full. Robert left the lamp burning on the desk near the window to light the entrance to the sheriff's office.

Except for feminine laughter coming from the saloon across from the jail, the main street of Sonora was quiet. Music and muffled voices trailed from a saloon into the next block, but few people were out and about at this time of night.

The shades were pulled on all the trade shops; no lamplight came from any of those buildings. Dark alleys, doorways, and empty spaces between buildings made the sheriff feel nervous. At least the saloon shined its light out past the board porch, better than no light at all.

He started the rounds in front of the saloon across from the jail. In the past, Cody walked on one side of the street, and Robert walked on the other side. For some reason, tonight Sheriff Sanders felt apprehensive and uneasy.

"Must be what that old miner said to me," Robert grumbled, as he hoisted his Colt to make sure it was riding free and easy in the holster.

Two men exited through the bat-wing doors of the saloon. Robert watched them try to direct their unsteady steps toward the hotel, but his attention was unexpectedly interrupted.

He heard the sound of a horse snorting and stamping his hooves. Robert gauged the sound and reckoned it came from the middle of a building that had recently been gutted by fire. It was located two doors away from the jail, directly across from the saloon, and it was in the process of being cleaned of debris. Wooden planks, river rocks, and bricks were stacked to a man's height in different spots, waiting to be reused.

Sheriff Sanders listened intently for additional sounds, but hearing nothing, he moved along the front of the building, stepped inside the ruins, and searched. He retraced his steps, quietly dodging debris, stepped away from the ruins, then paused again and strained his ears. He leaned forward, with his back slightly arched as he peered into the darkness. No sounds were heard, no movement was seen.

"I know there was a horse in that building," Robert said to himself. "After I finish the rounds, I'll search again."

An instant later Robert heard the blast from a revolver. A burning pain ripped through his right upper thigh. Warm blood streamed down his leg and saturated his trousers as his left hand pulled his Colt from the holster. Another explosion followed the first. Robert dropped his Colt and grabbed at his lower back.

The second shot had hurled him to the ground in excruciating, torturous pain. Unable to move, he tried to call for help, but no sound emanated from his throat. His ability to reason diminished rapidly, but before he drifted into unconsciousness, Robert forced his mind to record every sound, every motion, around him. He realized that the shots had come from the location of the saloon directly behind him.

Barely conscious, Sheriff Sanders heard heavy footsteps stop beside him, heard words muttered above his body, heard the sound of footsteps fade away, and finally heard several horses breaking into a gallop.

Before he lapsed into the darkness of oblivion, Sheriff Sanders felt a hand reach under his head and heard someone shout, "Quick, somebody! Get Doctor Gibbs!"

Cecil Mott, the telegraph operator, had heard two shots. But by the time he arrived in front of the ruins, Sheriff Sanders was lying on the ground, motionless.

"Hold on, sheriff," Cecil spoke into Robert's ear. "I'll take care of you." Two men ran out of the saloon toward Cecil, who shouted to them, "Jack, Thomas, help me get him to the jail."

The three men carried Robert, blood gushing from two bullet holes, into the jail and laid him on the cot in the nearest cell. Fear reached panic dimensions and for an instant the men stood silent, staring at Robert's dying body.

"I'm going for the deputy," Jack said as he ran to the front door. "Thomas, you go get the doctor."

Thomas jumped into his wagon, whipped his mule to attention, and rode off. Jack mounted his horse and galloped toward the Taylor home. Cecil cooled Robert's face with water to keep him conscious and wrapped his leg in a blanket.

Matthew's house was near the edge of town, and within a quarter of an hour, Thomas had the doctor attending to Robert's injuries.

The bullet wound in the thigh was not serious; it had passed through the hamstring and had not broken any bones as it exited. But the wound in the lower back was serious. The bullet had torn into the flesh and lodged deeply in the lower back muscle that surrounds and compresses the abdominal contents. It was far too risky to move the sheriff to the hospital; Matthew would have to perform the surgery in the jail.

"Someone get my nurse," Doctor Gibbs said impatiently. "Tell her I want towels, sheets, bandages, everything. Hurry, there's no time to waste."

Cody entered the jail as Thomas flew passed him, "How bad is it, Doc?" he asked, apprehensively. Not waiting for Matthew's answer, he dropped onto one knee close to Robert's cot. "Sheriff, did you see anyone? Do you know who shot you?"

Robert heard Cody's voice, and his lips attempted to form words, but he had no power to utter them.

Matthew, Cecil, and Jack removed Robert's clothing and covered him with a clean blanket. His right leg was dressed and the packing would slow the bleeding. This wound would have to wait until the doctor finished extracting the bullet in Robert's back. That wound was of primary importance and could not wait; Doctor Gibbs must perform surgery immediately.

"As soon as Gina gets here," Matthew said, "we will need to start the operation. Where is my nurse?"

"Thomas went to get Gina, Doctor," Jack said. "He had the wagon. They should be back any time now."

"Deputy, I heard two shots fired," Cecil said as he approached the deputy who was standing silently by Robert's bed. "One came right after the other. It didn't sound like bullets from a Colt. Sounded different."

"Did you see anyone, Cecil?"

"No. No one. Didn't hear nothin' but the shots fired. The sheriff was in front of the gutted building when I walked out of the saloon. I heard the first shot, then another. I should've left the saloon when I heard the first shot. Maybe I could've seen who shot him."

"Don't worry, Cecil. If you think of anything else let me know. Don't let anyone near the center of that burned out building. Until we search the area around the saloon, keep everybody away from it, too. As soon as it gets light, I'm riding out. I'll need to form a posse, but I'll be back. Mayor Thorton will have to deputize the men riding with me."

"I won't be leaving either until it grows light, Deputy."

Cecil looked at Sheriff Sanders lying unconscious, ashen in color, and barely breathing.

46

*C*arrying towels, dressings, and herbs in apothecary jars, Gina and Maggie pushed through the front door of the jail and went directly to Matthew's side.

Maggie stood behind the nurse as Doctor Gibbs detailed Robert's injuries. "He has a bullet lodged in his back, on the left side under the kidney. A bullet passed through his right thigh, but that wound can wait. I've bandaged it and I think the bleeding is controlled."

Gina now knew what was needed for surgery. "Cody, Thomas, Jack, we will need plenty of hot water, soap, and extra lamps from the hotel. I'll need help bringing dressings, bandages, antiseptic, and chloroform from the hospital."

Cody followed Gina to the door, giving additional orders. "Thomas, you and Jack get what you need from the hotel and saloon, and I'll help Gina with supplies from the hospital."

"Jack, Thomas, we need extra oil for the lamps," Gina interjected. "The doctor will need a lot of light to operate in the cell."

Following Gina's instructions, Jack headed to the Sonora Hotel and Thomas ran to the saloon across the street from the jail. Cody led Gina to the hospital. Once they had opened the door and entered, he struck a match and lit another lamp in the front office. In case more supplies were needed during the surgery, this lamp will be left burning.

Cody's arms were loaded with extra blankets, sheets, and dressings. Gina carried the lamp, antiseptic, chloroform, and cloth bandages.

Maggie emptied most of the hot water into a pan for Matthew to wash, then helped Cecil turn Robert onto his side and supported his body with pillows. The doctor and nurse examined the wound and prepared Sheriff Sanders for surgery.

Matthew used the chloroform to send Robert into a deep sleep. Well over an hour elapsed before the doctor was able to find the bullet and dig it from Robert's body.

After Matthew removed the bullet and dropped it into a pan, Cody reached into the pan and put the slug into his pocket.

Maggie and Gina carefully cleaned the surgical opening with rags dipped in comfrey and rosemary water, packed the wound with wads of thick dressings, and covered Robert's upper body with blankets.

Matthew turned his attention to the wound in the right upper thigh. The bandages were removed, and only a few stitches were needed. Thankfully no infection had set in. It appeared that, unless complications occurred, for a few weeks Robert would need the support of a cane, but with time he would walk again normally.

The sheriff had lost much blood, but he was alive, thanks to the healthy strong muscles that had prevented the bullet from penetrating into his internal organs. Doctor Gibbs was not giving any assurances, but at this point, it seemed that there was no damage to the kidney or to any of his vital organs.

"It's small. It doesn't look like the bullet from a Colt, Deputy," Matthew commented when Cody handed the bullet to him. "Whoever shot Sheriff Sanders must have aimed directly at his back and I would guess he aimed purposely toward the kidney. But just before the bullet entered, Robert evidently had started to turn and the killer missed the targeted area. It's a good thing, too. Robert would be dead if the bullet had gone into his kidney."

"I'm riding to the Thorton Ranch," Cody said, his face grave with worry, "as soon as it's light to ask Luis Serrano and Ken to ride out with me. Don't lose that bullet, Doc, whatever you do."

Gina's premonition that trouble was on its way had come all too soon. Robert was unconscious, burning with a raging fever, and he was critical. Cody would be searching for the madman who had shot Robert. She looked at the unconscious sheriff and his apprehensive deputy and dismissed the feeling of foreboding within her.

Maggie cooled Robert's face, neck, and chest with the herbal water. The next few hours would be crucial; infection must be prevented. Robert was a healthy man and in his prime. Now that the bullet was out, his body would hopefully purge the injured area of infection.

Cody sat at his desk and stared out the window of the jail as the sun's first light colored the hills of Sonora. Gina placed a cup with strong hot coffee in front of him.

She was hesitant to ask questions, but she needed an answer. "Cody, do you know who shot Robert?"

"I think so."

He drank the coffee, handed the empty cup to Gina and walked to the rifle cabinet. Gina watched as the deputy removed three Winchesters, several boxes of ammunition, and two extra Colt Army .44 revolvers and holsters. He laid them side by side on the table. Once again, she rejected the growing presentiment.

"I'll be back with Luis, Ken, and the Mayor," Cody said. "William will have to deputize the men riding with me. Robert sure as hell can't do it."

He looked at Gina, feeling a powerful need to hold and comfort her, but instead he reached for his hat and walked out the front door.

Gina walked to the window and watched him mount Sammy and ride away.

47

Robert moaned softly in a deep sleep. Almost eight hours had passed since he was shot. Maggie gently cooled his face, arms, and neck.

Pressing the wound, looking for abnormal swelling and redness, Matthew checked the area that surrounded the incision. It was six-forty five in the morning; he had only left Robert's side during the night a few moments at a time.

"We're going to need more hot water from the hotel, Maggie," Doctor Gibbs said. "It's time to put a poultice on his lower back wound. The area around the incision is inflamed and his body hasn't cooled down enough to my liking. Can you do it?"

"I can and will do it as long as it's needed, Doctor Gibbs."

"Oh, by the way, tidy Miss McLeod, your cleaning the jail was right on time. Hard enough to operate in a jail cell, but it could have been disastrous if we had to operate in a filthy jail cell on a filthy cot. I appreciate your hard work and I know Robert will appreciate it most of all."

Maggie welcomed the kind words from the doctor. "Thank you, Doctor," she replied. "I am happy to be of help."

"Thomas," Maggie tapped his shoulder gently to wake him. "We need more hot water from the Sonora Hotel. Bring all you can carry."

"Sure thing, Maggie," he said, yawning.

The ladies applied the poultice and when Robert was sleeping soundly, it was their turn to rest. They closed their eyes, heads resting on the folds of their arms, and quickly fell asleep.

Doctor Gibbs sat by Robert's cot, dozing. The front door of the jail opened, and John entered the room with two baskets of breakfast food. Myrtle, Millie, and Andrew followed with more baskets.

The chef at the Sonora Hotel's restaurant had recently sent fresh hot coffee, warm bread, and butter to the jailhouse.

Gina reached for a freshly baked warm roll and sat by Millie as she stared at the Winchesters and revolvers on the table.

"Where is Cody, Gina?" Millie asked.

"He left over an hour ago. He went to the Thorton Ranch to get Luis; then he was going to get Ken and the Mayor. He's coming back. Mayor Thorton has to deputize the men riding with Cody."

"I knew he would he need food to take with him, I'm glad I brought it with me. He'll search for the horrible person that shot Robert. I wish I didn't worry so much about my sons."

"I know you worry, Millie, but Cody will find whoever did this to Robert, and he will bring him in for trial. Try not to worry."

"I'll try, Gina. I just hope he comes back safe and sound."

John tapped Matthew gently on the shoulder to wake him and shoved a cup of strong hot coffee under his nose. In an effort to rouse himself, the doctor gulped it down and held the empty cup up. Maggie had read his mind and was on her way to find the coffeepot.

As soon as Maggie was out of hearing range, John broached the immediate problem that faced the town. "What are we going to do without a sheriff or deputy? Cody's tracking a killer and Robert's here, unconscious."

Doctor Gibbs mulled over John's remark and said, "We'll need some kind of visible authority, a good, forceful lawman. Do you have a suggestion? Are you thinking of asking Caleb?"

"I think Caleb would be willing to step in," John said. "But only temporarily. He once told me he was all through being a United States Marshall, but if someone is needed to keep the peace, I think he'd want to help. I'd run the grocery store for him while he stays at the jail. Might be good for him. Sometimes Caleb gets restless; he needs action. Stocking the store with flour, coffee, and sugar doesn't always get his full attention."

Caleb J. Alexander, John's younger brother by ten years, was a retired U.S. Marshall. He had settled in Sonora three years earlier after a long and successful career keeping the peace in the San Joaquin Valley.

This U.S. Marshall towered over most men, and a barrel chest, powerful arms, and especially strong hands added to his formidable presence. He was legendary among culprits for his vicelike grip. No one got ever got away from Caleb J. Alexander.

Another of the Marshall's unique abilities was his piercing stare. Deputies stood in amazement when one of his penetrating glares elicited additional information from a suspect.

In the last two years of his career, Caleb suffered two bullet wounds, several months apart. Afraid the next bullet might claim its victim, his wife, Elsie, along with their two sons, Micah and Mark, persuaded him to retire.

John had suggested that Caleb move to the beautiful hills of Sonora, and become a peaceful citizen in the town. Caleb agreed, but John knew his brother needed to keep busy and suggested he invest in some kind of trade shop.

So, for the last three years, Caleb J. Alexander had provided his customers with their food supplies. He was not known as a retired U.S. Marshall except to a few select and privileged individuals. However, if he agreed to pin a badge back on that massive chest once again, there was a good chance the people of Sonora would look at Caleb in a totally different light.

"That's the best thing to do, John. Caleb's perfect for the job. Does he know that Robert's been shot?"

"No, I don't think he has heard yet about the shooting. I'm going to tell him this morning. He's due in the store early. Myrtle and I need coffee and sugar anyway. I'll tell him what happened and ask him if he'd be willing to take over while Cody's away and Robert's recovering, if he recovers. When Cody comes back with the Mayor, Caleb can give them his answer."

"What do you think, John," Matthew asked, "will he accept the challenge?"

"Yeah. He likes Robert and Cody. He'd want to help out as much as he can and someone has to take over. It might as well be Caleb. Like you said, he's perfect for the job."

Matthew breathed a sigh of relief. Now the deputy could concentrate on finding the man who killed Jose and the man who attempted to kill Sheriff Robert Sanders. The retired U.S. Marshall would concentrate on keeping Sonora peaceful.

48

*L*uis opened the door when he saw the deputy dismount in front of his cottage. "*Amigo*, what has happened? Is something wrong?" Luis demanded.

"Robert was shot late last night." He tried to calm the look of fear on his friend's face. "He's not dead, Luis," Cody said. "The doctor removed the bullet early this morning. He was sleeping when I left the jail. I want you to ride with me to find the man that shot Jose and Robert."

"I will get ready, but first I have to tell Maria and Arnoldo."

Maria and Arnoldo stood in the doorway, listening as Luis and Cody conferred. When Luis approached his wife and brother-in-law, he related to Maria and Arnoldo what Cody had said.

As Arnoldo spoke to Luis in Spanish, he was visibly upset, and was getting more overwrought by the minute. Luis listened quietly to Arnoldo as Maria respectfully interjected her opinion to Luis, and at the same time, tried to calm her brother.

Luis beckoned Cody, "Arnoldo wants to ride with us, Cody," he said with a troubled look. "He wants to help find Jose's killer; he can identify him. My friend, he will not be told he cannot go with us. Arnoldo wants to help. What do I tell him?"

Determined not to paint a pretty picture of what the next few days might hold, the deputy spoke truthfully. "I don't know what to tell him, Luis. I can't tell him how long we'll be gone. We might be in the hills for days. We're tracking a killer. Won't sleep much, we'll have to take turns watching the camp. We eat what little we bring.

"If he comes, I'll expect him to be able to defend himself and fight for all of us if he has too. Can he use a rifle or a revolver? The same man that killed Jose will kill Arnoldo if he gets the chance."

"He can use a pistol and he knows how to use a rifle," Luis answered, "and Arnoldo is a good rider. If we do not take him with us, he says he will follow us, and that would be disastrous. He will not complain or cause us delays, I promise you."

Cody looked at Maria. "Do you want Arnoldo to come with me?" he asked.

In her best English, she answered, "Yes, Cody. Arnoldo will help you."

"Well, the lady wants us to take him with us. He can go along, but he needs a fast horse. Does he have one?"

"Ken will give him a horse," Luis replied, smiling. "Arnoldo will take care of the horse he is given."

"I'll get Ken and the Mayor, Luis. William has to deputize all of you. I'll be back for you and Arnoldo. Bring supplies for at lease five days. The Winchesters and extra Colts are at the sheriff's office."

"We will be ready when you come for us, *Amigo*."

Cody banged on the Thorton's front door. It opened after a few minutes, revealing Mayor Thorton standing in his bare feet wearing his nightshirt.

"What the hell's going on, Deputy? What brings you out here this time of the morning?"

Cody followed the Mayor into the kitchen. He was not fully awake until he indulged himself with hot coffee. Mayor Thorton lit the wood stove, placed the coffeepot on the burner, and sat down at the table. "Now tell me what's going on, Deputy. What's so all-fired important that you rode all the way out here this time of the morning?"

While the coffee heated, Cody related the episode at the North Star Mine, the discovery of William Johns' camp, and the shooting of Sheriff Sanders.

"Is Robert going to live?"

"Hope so. Doc took out the bullet, and the sheriff was asleep when I left the jail. I came for a posse, Mayor. I've asked Luis and I need Ken. Your son's a good tracker."

"He'll ride with you and Luis."

"Get dressed, Mayor. You'll be deputizing Luis, Ken, and Arnoldo."

"Did you say Arnoldo? Why, he can't go with you. He's just a boy, Cody. Are you crazy? He might get killed."

"I know, but he's also an eye witness to the killing and the only one that can identify the killer. I didn't ask him to come; Arnoldo insisted."

Mayor Thorton finished his coffee and stood up from his chair, "I'll see if Ken is awake and then I'll get dressed," he said.

At that moment, Ken entered the kitchen.

"Cody," Ken said, "I heard voices. What's going on? What are you doing here?"

After a brief explanation, Ken's help was requested and promptly given. The deputy asked for an additional favor, "Oh, yeah, Ken, can Arnoldo borrow one of your horses?"

"I have a young Appaloosa that's dying to run," Ken replied. "Hope Arnoldo can control him."

Luis and Arnoldo were ready and waiting when Ken, Mayor Thorton, and Cody approached the cottage. Ken handed Arnoldo the reins to a young Appaloosa, frisky and full of spirit. Luis sat mounted on his horse, while Maria brought food for her husband and brother.

All five men turned their horses and headed toward Sonora at a full gallop. Maria waved and watched them as they disappeared from sight; her lips formed words silently as she prayed for the safety of these brave men.

49

*T*he Sheriff was still unconscious when Cody walked inside the jail.

Matthew told him the latest news. "John's at the grocery store. He thinks Caleb will take over your duties while Robert is laid up and you're tracking the killer. He'll take up his old job as the U.S. Marshall, temporarily."

"Caleb?" Cody said, surprised. "Well, we sure won't have problems when we take over again. Who's going to cross Caleb?"

"Mayor Thorton can swear him into office this morning, if he agrees," said Matthew.

"How is Sheriff Sanders doing, Doc? Will he live?"

"The next twenty-four hours are critical. The bullet missed the spine and kidney, but I had to probe deep into the muscle. It could have been worse. It's a good thing it wasn't a bullet from a Colt, or he'd be dead right now."

Relieved at the doctor's prognosis, Cody confided to Matthew, "Cecil heard two shots fired, one right after the other, but the person that shot Robert must have known a shot from a Colt would wake the town."

"And Robert fooled him," Matthew said. "He had to be turning around when the trigger was pulled. If infection doesn't get him, I'm confident he'll be his old self again."

"Ken will look for tracks and boot prints in the center of the building and by the side of the saloon. I asked Cecil to help him. He was the first person to see the sheriff after he was shot."

Cody scanned the rooms. "Where's Gina and Maggie?"

"Gina's at the hospital getting the office ready for early patients. Maggie, Myrtle, Millie, and Louise left earlier to wash the bloody sheets, bandages, and dressings at Gina's house."

When the front door of the jail opened, those assembled in the room focused their attention to Caleb J. Alexander. Graying at the temples, hair sparse on the top of his head, years of inclement weather, and the last two bullets caused Caleb to look older than his fifty years. A natural furrow between his eyebrows made him look cross and in a bad humor, but his presence filled the room.

Caleb scanned the men sitting at the table and went directly to Mayor Thorton. "I'm ready to be sworn in, Mayor, as the acting U.S. Marshall," he said, wasting no time. "Might as well get the swearing over." He pointed to Luis and Ken and commanded, "You two. Come on up here and be sworn in as deputies."

Mayor Thorton swallowed the food in his mouth and stood in front of Ken and Luis. Arnoldo jumped up and joined the three men.

"What the hell are you doing, boy?" Caleb questioned in his usual boisterous voice. "You can't be a deputy. You're too damn young. How old are you?"

Arnoldo did not move, intimidated by Caleb's words. Any sane person thought twice about crossing Caleb.

The deputy chewed the last of his bread and swallowed it, reluctant to leave his breakfast. He put a hand on Caleb's shoulder and led him to the side of the room.

After Cody's explanation, the Marshall was still not agreeable and announced his opinion for all to hear. "He shouldn't ride with you, Deputy. He's too damn young. But it's your call, and I'll have to stand by your decision. Come on, son, stand in line."

Mayor Thorton handed out deputy badges, but omitted Caleb. Tucked away in a box, was the impressive U.S. Marshall's badge. With pride, Mayor Thorton pinned it onto Caleb's imposing chest.

"Ken," Cody said, "let's look at the area where Robert was shot. There could be horse and boot prints."

Cody left Ken searching diligently and walked over to fetch Cecil from the telegraph office. Cecil could add insight to Ken's investigation.

One-half hour passed, Ken and Cecil approached Cody with their conclusions. "Three horses waited behind that pile of boards," Ken said, pointing to the debris. "One horse had shoes, the other two didn't. I also found two pairs of boot prints by the horses. One pair had a hole in the sole. The other boot prints are by the saloon; they're different."

Ken pointed toward the saloon, and spoke thoughtfully. "Robert had to be looking into the center of the building, because the shots came from behind him. When he fell, his head was toward the saloon. I found two casings from a small pistol by the side of the saloon. It sure wasn't a Colt, Deputy, probably a derringer."

Ken dropped the casings into Cody's hand. The deputy put one into his pocket, the other he carried to the jail. He handed the casing to Matthew with the suggestion, "Don't lose that bullet or this casing, Doc."

$\mathcal{M}$atthew listened to Robert's heartbeats. "Steady and surprising strong," he said, encouragingly. "He'll be awake soon. Did you make any tea for him, Gina?"

"Tea is ready, Doctor."

"Is the office ready for early patients?"

"All ready."

"Good, I'll be there later. I'm waiting for Maggie to return. I want her to stay with Robert while we see to patients. John left a little while ago; he's bringing Maggie back to the jail. The next batch of bloody sheets and dressings will be sent to the Chinese laundry. We need Maggie's help here."

While Cody sketched the entrance and layout of Rattlesnake's camp, Luis and Ken listened. Arnoldo could get the details from Luis.

Deputy Taylor's shrewdness would be tested in this delicate situation and he would require cooperation from all three of his men. The pursuit would be a contest and a contrast of wits. The deputy's keen sense of strategy, his gifts of ingenuity and strength, would be pitted against William Johns, a brilliant, but scheming, deceitful, treacherous, and powerful adversary.

Luis took Arnoldo aside. Cody left Ken at the table and knelt by Robert, speaking softly to see if he was awake.

Ken spotted Gina pouring tea into a cup for Sheriff Sanders. He was subdued, but obviously happy to see her. "Gina, it's good to see you again. How was New York? Did you see all your friends? Did you take care of all your business?"

"Hello, Ken. I had a lovely time in New York, the weather was perfect, and I saw most of my friends, the people who are very dear to me. The visit was really enjoyable. Going through my parent's home for the last time and listening to the will was difficult, but aside from that, I truly did have a pleasant time."

Mayor Thorton called his son. Ken acknowledged his father's summons and concluded his conversation with Gina. "The people of Sonora were afraid you wouldn't want to come back to California. We thought you'd miss your old friends and want to stay in New York."

"I missed Sonora, Ken," Gina said as Ken started to leave. "I could not wait to come back to California."

Gina put the cup of tea onto a small table by the cot, dipped a rag into the pan of warm herbal water, and wiped Robert's face and neck, commenting, "He does feel cooler to me, Doctor."

"I think the fever dropped some after you and Maggie put the poultice on the back wound. He's starting to come out of the chloroform. Try to make him drink that tea, Gina."

One leg bent, his body weight resting on the other leg, Cody leaned close to the sheriff and spoke softly. "Robert, can you hear me? Can you tell me what happened when you were shot?"

Robert opened his eyes, looked directly at the deputy and tried to focus on his face. His mouth formed words, but could make no sound. Cody put his ear close to the sheriff's mouth.

"He's still pretty tired, Deputy," Matthew said, "and he's not fully out of the chloroform. He'll probably be able to talk to you later in the day. You may not get much out of him, but he should be able to speak to you then."

"We're ready to leave now, Doc. I won't be here to talk to him later."

Despair usurped Gina's feelings of foreboding, and tears threatened.

Cody walked to the table and picked up a Winchester. "Ken, Luis," he said, "we're ready to go. Pick out your Winchester and Colt."

Gina wondered what she would do if the deputy did not return alive? How could she live the rest of her life without him?

Luis and Ken walked to the table; each grabbed a Winchester rifle and a holster holding a Colt revolver. Arnoldo watched Luis and Ken, but he did not speak.

The sheriff's belt, holster, and Colt were on Robert's desk. Cody presented the lot to Arnoldo. "It's a loan," he said, "but you do need a Colt."

Arnoldo smiled brightly. All were armed and ready. They walked out the door to their waiting horses. Gina and Matthew followed, her arm linked through his, and stood on the board porch in front of the four mounted men.

Tears filled her eyes, but she did not cry. Somehow, the nurse has to keep her composure until Cody was out of sight.

Gina's uniform was covered with blood from the midnight surgery, her hair was a mass of tangles, and she was tired. A long day awaited her, filled with patients who would need both doctor and nurse's attention. She concealed her inner feelings and smiled confidently to Cody. He was a lawman and would do his job.

Cody looked at Gina and returned her smile. To him, she was beautiful. He touched his hat, pulled on the reins. and turned Sammy around. A quick nudge and all four horses loped north on Washington Street, heading towards the hills of Sonora.

Matthew walked back into the jail. Gina crossed the street and unlocked the door to the hospital. The river of tears she had held back for hours now streamed down her cheeks.

"You cannot help the doctor today looking like this," she said, wiping her eyes while speaking to her image in the mirror. "Wash your face, drink some cold water, tidy your hair, and change this filthy uniform."

But her mind was already somewhere north of Sonora. She stared vacantly at the extra uniform hanging on the hook in the wardrobe. So engrossed in her thoughts, Gina did not hear the bell when the entrance door opened.

Maggie startled her when she walked into the back room announcing, "Millie, Myrtle, Louise, and I washed everything. Matthew says he won't let us wash anything again. But the sheets and bandages are drying on the clothesline. There is a breeze, and I think everything will dry quickly."

The nurse did not acknowledge one word Maggie spoke and resumed her reflections.

Miss McLeod stood directly in front of Gina, placed her hands on Gina's shoulders, and asked bluntly, "What is wrong, girl? Have you been crying? You have been crying. Has the deputy left for the hills?"

Gina answered Maggie indignantly, "Yes, he has. How do you know what I am thinking? What am I? A book for everyone to read?"

Maggie ignored Gina's quip. "Does the doctor want me to stay with Robert or help here at the hospital?"

"He wants you to stay with Robert. I have to change my uniform now; patients will arrive soon. When you talk to the doctor, tell him I am ready."

"You do not have to concern yourself that I will tell the deputy that you are in love with him. I'll never say anything. Although everyone knows it anyway, girl. It's written all over you."

Shutting the front door, Maggie hurried to the sheriff's office, leaving the vexed nurse alone to change her uniform.

The rest of the long day Gina's mind would be on Cody and she really did not care who knew it.

The deputies walked their horses to the opposite side of Johns' campsite where Robert and Cody had scrutinized the miners on the previous day. As before, scrub oak, towering oak trees, buckbrush, manzanita shrubs, and enormous boulders effectively hid William's camp from the casual viewer.

Around the clock surveillance would be easier since this particular terrain was so thick with underbrush. Cody needed rock-hard evidence to use against Rattlesnake. If he, or his deputies, were discovered watching the campsite, not only would the surveillance definitely end, their own lives might also end.

Arnoldo discovered a perfect observation spot. He had gone to the top of the hill overlooking the camp and crawled through a narrow passageway in a huge boulder, which led into an expanse that was large enough for two or three men.

The boulder protruded out and over the camp. On the bottom of the boulder's projection, small portions of the rock had worn away over time. This left open gaps that let in light and air. The deputies peered through the openings on their bellies. From this safe, secure lookout, no one would ever guess that eyes watched from overhead as the miners worked, slept, and ate.

A waterfall cascading into a small stream beneath the boulder muted the sound of the deputies' voices and movements. Away from the entrance of the mine below, the horses were tethered in a large hollow. The deputies were safe for the present time.

While two men slept, two stood guard, and Rattlesnake's camp was observed around the clock for two full days. It was not until the third morning that Cody saw a familiar rider enter the campsite. His attire was the same as previously, a white shirt; black trousers, black vest, clean, and although dusty from the ride, not dirty. A black English bowler hat was perched arrogantly on his head.

Arnoldo peered through the binoculars, and after adjusting them, he was able to identify the rider as the man who shot Jose.

The visitor dismounted and walked toward the miners. Cody and Arnoldo were lying motionless near the boulder's edge. Johns' spoke to the miners, but the deputy could catch only jumbled fragments of the conversation.

Three of the five miners went to various hiding places in the camp, where they collected cloth bags tied with string and took them to Johns. He loosened the strings and emptied gold dust or nuggets into his hand. Cody counted as Rattlesnake checked twenty bags.

Evidently satisfied with the amount of gold dust and nuggets, Johns sat by the wooden shack while five men stood or kneeled and listened to him speak. Again, Cody was not able to hear much of the conversation.

Ken scooted into the boulder hideout and for the next two hours the three deputies watched as Johns spoke to his men. Seldom did the miners move or say anything in return.

Finally, Johns stood up, brushed off his trousers, and walked to his horse. As he grabbed the reins, the sixth miner came out of the entrance of the mine, smiling at the other men who stared back at him with anticipation on their faces. He carried a bundle under his arm wrapped in a ragged cloth.

A sudden look of surprise that appeared on the young man's face told the deputies that Johns had not been expected at the campsite. The miner quickly turned around, but Johns followed and called to him with a loud voice.

Rattlesnake extended his hand; the young miner held the bundle to his chest, slowly inching closer to Johns until he faced him. Rattlesnake waited, and although the young miner was obviously reluctant to part with his bundle, he finally handed it over.

When the cloth was removed, William held up a beautiful oriental gold knife. The handle and sheath were covered with precious jewels, which gleamed brightly in the sun.

Cody wondered what in the world was an artifact worth a king's ransom doing in the mine? Were there other treasures concealed in the privacy of that cave?

Johns wrapped the jeweled knife back in the cloth cover, smiled, and handed it back to the young miner. Relieved that hostility between them had apparently ended, the miner nodded, held the treasure to his chest, turned his back to Rattlesnake, and walked toward the entrance of the cave.

Johns took three steps toward his waiting pony, but he suddenly spun around so quickly that the observers on the rock above, as well as the miners standing around the campsite, did not fully comprehend what was happening.

An explosion sounded. The young miner bent forward, and his knees gave way as he fell to the earth, his face buried in the sand, blood spreading across the back of his dirty shirt. The object under his arm was flung far beyond his dying body.

Johns held the smoking derringer that he had pulled from under the cuff of his right shirtsleeve at his side.

Rattlesnake called out to two men and pointed at the dead body. He picked up the priceless knife from the ground and watched as the dead man was transported to his grave, the deep, dark recesses of the cave.

Holding the ragged cloth bundle, Johns mounted his dapple-gray and rode out of the camp.

52

*L*uis stepped out of the shadows with his Colt drawn as Ken, Arnoldo, and Cody approached the hollow.

"Johns shot one of his men in the back," Cody said, reaching for his saddle. "He left the camp and rode north. Ken and I will follow him."

"What? Why did he kill one of his own men?" Luis asked.

Cody, Ken, and Arnoldo took turns detailing the shooting of the young miner.

Anger mounted in Luis, a person seldom incensed. "This man is dangerous," he asserted. "We have to stop him once and for all. He cannot be allowed to shoot innocent men. What do you want Arnoldo and I to do now, *Amigo*?"

Cody cinched the belt tight around Sammy while Luis and Arnoldo waited for instructions. "I learned that Rattlesnake had been seen in Columbia," he said, "and I'll bet that's where he's headed. Ken can pick up his tracks and we'll ride to Columbia. Keep watching the miners, but have your horses ready, and keep the supplies out of sight. When Ken and I get back, we'll all ride back to Sonora. It's been three days since Robert was shot. If he's awake, I'll see what I can learn about the shooting."

"Do you have a plan, *Amigo*, to capture this Rattlesnake?"

"Yeah. But I need to see where he stays, if he keeps a room in Columbia. I need to ask questions of the right people. We'll sleep in our own beds tonight, and tomorrow we'll leave early in the morning and come back to this hideout."

If Widow Nancy had given Cody the correct information, the

deputy would find William Johns in Columbia. When all the ends were tied, Deputy Taylor would finalize his plan for the capture.

Ken picked up the trail and both men started their ride north toward Columbia.

53

Staying out of sight as much as possible, Cody and Ken rode to Columbia Street and headed south to State Street. After traveling east to the corner of State and Main streets, the deputies left their horses at the livery stable. While they searched for William Johns the horses could feed and rest.

By 1875, the boom was over for Columbia. The population had dwindled from 6,000 in 1860, to approximately 500 men, women, and children. It was a respectable and quiet community. The town boasted a schoolhouse, volunteer fire department, several outstanding hotels, and a post office.

A dry goods store furnished miners tools for digging gold out of rocks and dirt. Rough apparel was also available, for a price. The miners had little choice: gray, red, or blue flannel shirts, heavy-duty trousers, high boots to pull over pant legs, and wide brim hats.

When a bank could brag that it had weighed out fifty-five million dollars in gold over the years, an ounce at a time, it became famous indeed. So boasted the Wells Fargo Bank in Columbia. The bank's scales were so precise that the miners claimed that a written word on paper could get an accurate weight.

Children played tag on the street, men and women strolled into shops, hotels, and the post office. Was this the reason William Johns had chosen Columbia over Sonora? He did stand out in a crowd, but no resident of Columbia would think Rattlesnake to be anything other than a singular individual, an eccentric man who liked eccentric clothes and horses.

Cody and Ken removed their badges and started down the main street, one man on each side. At the south end of Washington Street, stood The Fallon House, a large hotel with an attached theater built shortly after the great Columbia fire of 1857. In the beautiful theater, the miners were allowed to watch the actors or actresses perform even if they were not dressed in fancy clothes. Tethered in front of The Fallon House, Cody and Ken spotted the dapple-gray.

"Rattlesnake doesn't know me Cody," Ken said. "He may know you by sight or reputation; we can't take that chance. I'll walk inside and inquire about the price of rooms. If I can get a look at the guest book, I'll see if his name is written in the register."

"I'll wait over there," Cody agreed, pointing a spot behind a shack, "but if I have to leave and I'm not here when you come out of the hotel, meet me at the livery stable."

The Fallon House was bustling with guests dressed in the latest fashions. Some strolled through the elegant, red velvet drapery to obtain a seat in the hotel's restaurant, and some took the stairs to their rooms on the second floor to rest or freshen up before supper. Other guests sat in the lobby and visited with each other. A performance by Lola Montez was scheduled for that evening and the hotel personnel were making final preparations for her appearance.

Ken stepped to the desk clerk to make his inquiries, but was asked to wait due to another visitor demanding the clerk's attention. He took the opportunity to peruse the register on the counter. No guest named William Johns was listed.

Ken returned to where Cody was standing alongside a large oak tree, and the deputies walked to a spot where any passerby could not overhear their voices.

"I didn't see him," Ken said, "and no one was registered under the name of William Johns. He could be anywhere, on the second floor or in the restaurant. What do you want me to do now?"

"Nothing," Cody said. "We'll ride back to Luis and Arnoldo. Ken, you ever been to the Joss House here in Columbia?"

"Me? No."

"I think that knife came from China. Two Chinese men walked into the hotel, rich Chinese men. I've been in the Joss House. It has gold statues, shields, and knives hanging on the wall. They all have jewels like that knife we saw today. I think I know why rich Chinese men went in the hotel."

"What do you mean?"

"What is a knife like the one we saw doing in the cave? I bet there's more than gold in that mine."

Three hours later, the four deputies were on their way back to Sonora. Clean clothes, hot food, and their own beds awaited them.

Cody believed that to capture this suspect of murder and mayhem, he must get Johns' full attention immediately. There seemed to be only one way to do that, dazzle him with what he loved most in the world, money and a lot of it. That was the trick, but if Cody's plan worked, Johns didn't have a prayer.

There were definitely two sides to William Johns, alias, Rattlesnake. His name and his alias fit his dual personality perfectly. With his newly developed plan, the deputy believed he was leaving no stone unturned.

54

*M*ost of the townspeople had closed up the trade shops for the night when Cody hitched Sammy to the post in front of the jail. The hospital was locked up and dark. From all outward appearances, Matthew and Gina were at home.

A light was burning in the sheriff's office. When Cody entered, the deputy was surprised to see the doctor and nurse checking Robert's wounds. Caleb was at Robert's desk; Maggie was washing the dishes.

Gina smiled as Cody entered. Caleb stood up, and Maggie waved. Matthew left Robert's side; he was anxious to hear how the posse had fared.

"Cody," he asked, "how is the investigation going? What have you found out so far?"

"We know that William Johns is the killer of the Mexican man, Jose. Arnoldo identified him. And, we know there's more to that mine than gold."

Caleb questioned Cody. "What are you talking about, Deputy?"

"A miner carried a knife out of the cave. Gold, valuable, had jewels all over it. It was a Chinese knife, I think."

"What did Johns do when he saw it?" Matthew asked.

"He looked happy, at first," Cody answered, "gave it back to the miner, smiled, started for his horse, then turned around and shot the miner in the back. He wears a derringer under his right shirtsleeve."

While Caleb and Matthew were silently digesting this information, Cody saw that Robert was awake, and walked over to speak with him.

"Deputy, good to see you," Robert said. "Did I hear you say Johns shot one of his men?"

"He did, but I'll go into that later. Sheriff, you able to tell how you were shot?"

"Yeah, I think so. I was doing the rounds, heard a noise, and walked toward the sound. It came from the middle of that burned out building, across the street from the saloon. I went into the ruins to search, but it was too dark to see anything.

"I didn't hear no more sounds. I figured I'd go back after I did the rounds and check again. I started to turn around and felt a bullet go through my leg and then another go into my back.

"I fell down, couldn't move. Then, I heard footsteps running toward me. I think someone stopped to see if I was dead."

The sheriff paused; Maggie spooned broth into his mouth.

"Rest, Robert," Cody said. "We'll talk later."

"No, I want to talk to you now. I can do it," Sheriff Sanders continued speaking slowly to conserve his energy. "Someone stood over me. It may have been a dream, but I thought I heard a man's voice say, 'That has done it; I killed the *bloody* bastard.' Something like that."

"Those are the words an Englishman would use," Maggie said. "The English use the word *bloody* as a curse word, like the American people use damn or hell. Are there many Englishmen living in Sonora?"

"I think I know of one in Columbia," Cody said. "Sheriff, what did you hear after that?"

"They got on their horses and rode away. I figure two, maybe three horses. The voice I heard sounded like Rattlesnake's, so I guess that's why I thought I was dreaming."

Robert's color faded and his head fell back on his pillow. The deputy sat quietly as Matthew listened to his heartbeats.

"Will he walk again, Doc? Is he healing?"

"Yes, he'll walk, with time," Matthew explained. "He's actually doing very well, and he's healing. Fever's down and there is no infection. A few weeks and he'll be back to normal."

Doctor Gibbs put the stethoscope into his medical bag. "We are going to move him to Gina's house tomorrow," he said. "Maggie, Myrtle, and Louise are going to take care of him. Gina will tend to him at night. With all those ladies waiting on him hand and foot, he won't be worth living with anymore."

Robert opened his eyes. "I heard that, Doc."

Deputy Taylor had one more question. "Sheriff, did you look through any wanted posters before you were shot?"

"I left them on the desk, Cody."

As the deputy walked to Robert's desk, Caleb reached for his hat. "Now that you're here, Deputy," he said, 'I'm going home. See you early tomorrow. When are you going back to the campsite?"

"Daylight tomorrow."

Caleb left the sheriff's office, and Cody sat in Robert's desk chair.

Although his head was down, concentrating on the wanted posters, Gina set a plate of food in front of the deputy. He glanced up at her. "Thanks, Gina," he said. "I could use some supper. Is there any water or coffee?"

The nurse was just about to answer Cody's question when there was a commotion in the cell. "You cannot sit up yet, Robbie," Miss McLeod vocalized strongly. "Are you daft, man? Lay back down. Do you hear me? You cannot sit up."

"Put a pillow behind my back, woman. I need to talk to Cody."

Gina gave Cody water and left him to settle the dispute. "Maggie is right, sheriff. You do not want to risk ripping open the stitches, do you?"

"She can stay close to me if I need to lay back down," Robert called out to the deputy, "Cody, come back in here. Tell me what you've found out about Johns."

"Rest a minute, Sheriff," Cody said, winking at the nurse. "Gina says I'm hungry and she's forcing me to eat."

A smile spread across Gina's face. While he ate a late supper, she sat nearby. He handed her his empty plate and glass.

"More?" she asked.

"No, but when this is over, I want you to fix me the Italian eggs you made for me the night we rode Sammy."

She smiled her reply. It was flattering to know Cody remembered that night and the food she had cooked for him.

Cody went into the cell, pulled up a chair, sat down by Robert, and recounted, briefly, the last three days.

Maggie walked into the cell. "You can still talk if you are flat on your back, Robbie," she commanded. "Cody, I think the knife you described came from China. My brother told me about valuable treasures from all over the world that left England for America every month. Small things that could be taken quickly and hid easily."

"And I wouldn't be surprised if some of those treasures are right here in Sonora, Maggie," Deputy Taylor said, then mumbled to himself while thinking of Rattlesnake. "He's clean on the outside, but dirty on the inside."

"I agree, deputy, if you're talking about Johns," Robert noted. "He's dangerous. You and the other deputies need to be careful. Did you find a wanted poster that might fit him?"

"Only the one from Auburn we got a few months back. He's been wanted for over a year. Johns could have drifted south to Columbia after the shooting, if it got a little hot for him up there. That mine of his has appears to have been working close to a year."

"It's a good location," Robert said. "The hills around his camp are heavy with brush, trees, and boulders. We never would have found him if we hadn't been led there. I would have passed right by it."

"Deputy, Robbie needs to rest," Maggie said. "And you need to go home and get some sleep. Robbie, you need to sleep now. You will get too tired if you do not rest."

Robert looked at Maggie and said with a contented smile, "This woman bosses me around day and night, Cody."

Maggie turned to Cody. "You look tired, too, Deputy, go home. Gina and I will see you in a few days. Robbie will be better by then."

As if Maggie remembered, at that moment, whom she was ordering about, she added, "Please take care of yourself when you go back into the hills."

"Robert, swallow this medicine before you lay back down," Gina ordered, holding a bottle of laudanum and a spoon. "Maggie and I will leave soon and I want to make sure you are asleep when we leave, but we'll be back early tomorrow. Cecil is staying with you during the night."

Cody went to the desk, and picked up the wanted poster from Auburn. Gina watched his every move. He turned when he reached the door. "I should be back in a few days," he said. "I'll see you then."

"Please be careful, Cody," she murmured.

Deputy Taylor closed the door to the jail. Maggie grabbed Gina's attention after Sammy's hoof beats had faded away, and just before Gina's tears could gush. "Come on girl, we need to tend to Robbie. He needs our attention before we leave him. The deputy will be fine, you'll see."

"I hope so, Maggie, I truly hope so."

A few short months ago, Gina only remembered aggravation when she thought of Cody Taylor. But today, if he should be killed and she had to live the rest of her life without him, Gina closed her eyes to the wretched pain that would never leave her heart.

55

*K*en and Arnoldo put away the fresh supplies; Luis and Cody entered the boulder hideaway, eager to observe the miners at work. But they saw only one man hunched over by the stream. It was a good time for the deputy to sketch the layout of Johns' campsite.

High around the perimeter of the camp, stately oak trees, redwood, and pine concealed the enclosure. Above the entrance of the mine, a river stream fell over a steep precipice and down the side of a massive boulder, creating a small waterfall. The waterfall became the smaller stream that ran through the middle of the camp and carried the much sought after specks of gold. Here the miner panned; from time to time he looked toward the entrance of the cave.

Caleb would need to know every inch of Johns' camp, the position of every rock, tree, bush, and boulder. Cody's plan to invade this site would take full cooperation from the deputized and trained men who would assist the Marshall in the capture.

A maneuver of this dimension had to be detailed to the smallest degree. After several hours drawing diagrams, documenting the shape and size of the entrance of the cave, complete with sketches of the terrain, there was still only one miner visible.

Leaving Luis in charge, Cody crawled out of the boulder position to stretch and get some food. Arnoldo slept soundly; Ken was on guard duty.

"Pretty quiet, Cody?" Ken asked. "What's going on?"

"Not much. Hope they don't know we're watching."

He grabbed food and water, sat on the ground and rested his back against a rock while he ate. Sheriff Taylor had told Cody, as many other fathers had told their sons, that legend had it that somewhere in the hills of Sonora there was an enormous cavern that contained a subterranean lake so huge it boasted a depth of two hundred and fifty feet.

In addition to the lake, huge chambers with unique mineral deposits hang from the ceilings and walls. These are the gems of the cavern, all the different formations of stalagmites and stalactites that are thousands of years old, flashing vibrant colors, and which have formed unusual shapes that dazzled the mind.

What if William Johns discovered that particular cavern? What if he had accumulated vast amounts of treasures, artifacts, museum specimens, and kept them hidden deep inside? If so, his clandestine operation would never arouse suspicion because little, if anything, was known about this underground wonder.

. . . .

When gold had been discovered in California, it had been purely accidental, but it changed the destiny of a nation, and quite possibly the world at that time.

Up to 1848, Mexicans had settled most of California. But when stories of men finding gold and acquiring vast fortunes spread like wildfire around the world, California swelled. Clipper ships brought the Irish, Italian, German, Dutch, and Chinese by the thousands, all to satisfy the hunger to become rich.

Tales of happy miners stumbling over chunks of gold encouraged teachers, doctors, and lawyers, men of every calling, to board wagon trains and hurry westward.

When the few and favored did strike it rich, their good fortune was evidenced by their raucous shouts of joy and the totals on the assessor's scale. These prosperous men decided to flaunt their wealth. They built the most ornate and lavish homes and decorated them with exquisite and florid museum pieces. But masterworks are not easy to acquire; they are not for the general public to purchase, but are most likely kept in museums and privately owned castles, or displayed in stately homes.

However, covetous individuals intent on acquiring their heart's desire, are willing to let unscrupulous men purloin masterworks from homes, castles, or museums, knowing that deceit and violence would be the only way to part a treasure from its owner. Thus, a vicious cycle was created. Precious, expensive, and priceless masterworks are pilfered from museums and private residences, often at the cost of the lives of the innocent and unsuspecting, and sold to the highest bidder.

. . . .

"Ken, have you ever heard of a cavern that has lakes two hundred and fifty feet deep, with chambers hundreds of feet high?" asked Cody.

"Yeah, Dad has described such a cavern many times. It's supposed to be somewhere in these hills, but he said no one knows the exact location. Why? Do you think this might be that cavern instead of just a mine?"

"Could be," Cody said. "I'm going back to the rock."

"Arnoldo's sleeping," Ken said. "When he wakes up I want to get a closer look at that cave."

If this was truly the famous cavern, the extent of Johns' valuable holdings exceeded imagination. What untold wealth had been brought from other countries to this site? And, how many people had parted with the treasures that might fill the cavern unwillingly, victims of murder and theft?

"Anything happen while I was gone, Luis?" Cody asked.

"No, that miner is still in the same spot."

Ken entered the lookout. "Arnoldo is awake and hungry," he said, "I left him on guard. Anything happen yet?"

Ken slid down on his belly, and all three men focused their attention on the opening of the cave when a wagon pulled by four mules rolled out. One man rode shotgun and one man with a rifle sat behind a man that held the reins. The weight of the wagon carved deep ruts in the dirt and was loaded with different sized crates tied up with rope.

Cody signaled for Luis and Ken to retreat. All three men left the rock and walked down the hill to their horses. This wagon had to be followed.

Safely in the hollow, they strapped the saddles on their horses. "Luis, you and Ken will follow the wagon," Cody said. "Arnoldo and I will go to see Caleb. I want the Mayor and Marshall to hear from Arnoldo that Johns is the man that killed Jose. We'll take all the supplies; we won't be coming back, at least not as lookouts."

Within fifteen minutes, Cody and Arnoldo were headed toward Sonora. Ken and Luis waited for the heavily loaded wagon to gain ground before they followed.

The deputy would present his plan for the capture of William Johns to Mayor Thorton and the U.S. Marshall. It was a risky and dangerous plan, but with the right people playing the right parts, this scheme might just work. The stratagem was almost completed, with only a loose end or two to tie up, but when that was done, William Johns would be in for a surprise.

56

*A*t a safe distance, Luis and Ken followed the northbound wagon until it stopped by a stream south of Columbia.

Trees by the stream gave the men shade while they rested and ate.

One hour after the miners arrived, Ken and Luis saw a fancy horse-drawn carriage approach, followed by a larger wagon. Alongside the carriage, on a dapple-gray horse, was a man wearing black trousers, a vest, and an English bowler hat.

He greeted the miners as he walked toward the wagon. The three men pried the lids off the crates. From the carriage, two men alighted, each holding a large satchel.

Johns removed one article at a time from the crates and allowed the men from the carriage to hold, caress, examine, and decide what their hearts desired. Obviously affluent, these men were dressed in top hat and tails, and could purchase anything that struck their fancy. William Johns prided himself as the only man in Columbia or Sonora able to supply what the heart fancied.

Elaborate hand-painted English or Italian vases, small statues, exquisite paintings, chairs, tables, ornate cases studded with jewels, all worth a fortune in gold, were held up and admired. Even from a considerable distance, quality showed in the workmanship of all the different and beautiful objects.

In the fancy carriage, the affluent men held and admired their smaller purchases on the way back to Columbia, accompanied by the larger wagon, which was filled with the bulkier purchases of luxury and opulence. The miners turned their wagon around and headed for the camp. William Johns smiled shamelessly as he rode alongside the carriage.

Luis and Ken had watched the proceeding in amazement and each man wondered to himself: Where did this man obtain such remarkable articles to sell? How many treasures were yet to be discovered in that cave? How were all of these fabulous art objects being transported to the cavern in the hills near Sonora apparently completely undetected?

57

"Deputy, I didn't expect to see you for a couple more days," Caleb said, surprised when Cody walked into the jail accompanied by Arnoldo. "What's happened at the campsite? Where are Ken and Luis?"

Anytime the U.S. Marshall asked a question or questions, he expected an answer without delay.

Deputy Taylor was quick to respond. "Ken and Luis should be on their way back to town. Marshall, Arnoldo wants to tell you about a killing that he witnessed at the North Star Mine. Do you have time to listen?"

Early in Caleb's career, he had spent two years in the south of Texas and northern Mexico. Although not fluent, Caleb spoke and understood the Spanish language.

When he was sent to the San Joaquin Valley, populated heavily by people of Mexican decent, his capability with Spanish was a great aid to him.

The questions he asked, either in English or Spanish were promptly answered, but Caleb knew that Arnoldo was young and shy, and hesitant to speak to him. He addressed Arnoldo first in English, "Sit down, son, and tell me what you have to say."

Minutes passed as Caleb, Cody, and the mayor waited for Arnoldo to start speaking. Caleb's impatient stare finally made the young man draw a deep breath and begin his story.

As Arnoldo narrated his experience, he slowly gained confidence. Caleb listened carefully as Arnoldo detailed the cold-blooded killing of Jose. "Three men drew their pistols when Jose walked toward his tent, afraid he was going to get his weapon. But the one that shot Jose was

William Johns. He used a Colt revolver which he drew from a holster strapped to his hip, not with the derringer under his shirtsleeve. I saw him again at the campsite. I will never forget his face."

Caleb sat back in his chair, questioned Arnoldo about some of the details of his account, turned to the mayor and Cody, and repeated Arnoldo's complete story in English.

"Arnoldo, go get something to eat at the cantina," Cody said as he handed Arnoldo money. "I'll tell Luis where to find you when he gets here."

"Well, Deputy," Caleb said after Arnoldo had closed the front door, "what do you have to tell me?"

Cody recounted the last few days of surveying the campsite, and then asked if either Caleb or Mayor Thorton knew the location of a large cavern in this area of California. Neither man knew the exact location of the cavern, only the stories.

"Correct me if I'm wrong," Cody said, "but, I think Rattlesnake can store stolen merchandize in that cave and no one would know. His camp is protected on all sides. If Robert and I hadn't been led to the entrance, we'd never have known where Johns was mining."

Deputy Taylor showed his sketches and diagrams of Rattlesnake's camp to Mayor Thorton and Caleb. He went to the map on the wall and pointed to the location of the cave.

"I can't believe it, Deputy," Mayor Thorton said. "I never would have believed that a working mine was in that area."

"Must have rode by that spot a hundred times," Caleb said. "Didn't know it was there either."

"It's time to tell you both something that's highly confidential," Mayor Thorton said, sitting down at the table. "Not even my wife knows. Only my four boys know what I'm going to divulge.

"My son, Edward, moved to San Francisco last summer. He was transferred there to investigate, secretly, the loss of many masterworks, highly prized and expensive treasures. The items had been stolen from wealthy residences, museums, castles, or archeological diggings throughout the world. These items are crated in their country of origin, carried to a central port, and presumably taken by ship to England and America.

"These artworks are not only valuable, they are national treasures. Reported stolen to Edward, are paintings by masters, along with statues, tapestries, urns, small chairs and tables, and jewelry cases overlaid with gold, also old, and exquisite jewelry. Later, anyone who can pay the prices that unscrupulous men demand can own the treasures; no questions are ever asked."

"What has he found out so far?" Caleb asked the mayor.

"Not much I'm afraid. Representatives of the British Parliament have traveled to America to plead with Edward to help find the extremely rare, expensive national treasures and return them to the proper authorities. They authorized him to use whatever means are necessary to uncover this secret international conspiracy and close it down permanently.

"Deputy, you may have found what Edward has been trying to uncover for these last few months. It may be the final link that connects all the other links. Have you finished surveying the campsite?"

"For now," Cody said, "there are four eyewitnesses that saw the operations of the mine. Three of us saw William Johns shoot the miner and ride off with the ceremonial knife."

"Then you will not need Ken," Mayor Thorton said, "at least not for a few days. I want to send him to San Francisco with a letter telling Edward what you have uncovered, everything we can prove up to this point."

It was time for Cody to advise the Marshall and Mayor Thorton of his plan to capture Johns. Also, Cody will inform them who the actors will be in this charade and game of wits. The deputy reserved only the information where the final capture of William Johns would take place.

Cody had selected two women to act out their parts for the capture and gave his attentive listeners a brief description. "A rich Scottish widow, Maggie McLeod, has come to the gold country to purchase expensive treasures. The bait to lure Johns will be a piece of jewelry worth thousands of dollars that she gave to a close friend who lives in Sonora."

"You're going to use Maggie McLeod? Seems risky, Deputy. Who's the friend?" Caleb inquired.

"Widow Nancy," Cody answered, grinning.

Mayor Thorton and Caleb stood speechless as the deputy continued. "Mayor, in your letter to Edward, ask him to loan us jewelry, a necklace, earrings, or a bracelet, I don't care what it is, but I need Nancy to wear something that is museum-quality jewelry, something you can see a mile away. Once he finds out Maggie purchased it to give to Nancy, he'll know she's got a lot of money."

"I can write him, and ask him to pick out an elaborate piece," Mayor Thorton said. "I understand San Francisco has places that display priceless, beautiful old jewelry. There must be something he can get on loan, temporarily at least."

More was required from Mayor Thorton's son. "Tell Edward we need money and a lot of it," Cody said. "We need to prove to Johns that Maggie is serious about what she buys."

"I'll ask, Deputy," Mayor Thorton replied, "but if I know Edward, he'll want to bring the jewelry and money himself."

"Better yet," Cody said, "and tell him to bring men he trusts with him. Now, Marshall, you need to plan how you're going to break into the camp and search that cave."

For the next two hours, Caleb, Mayor Thorton, and Cody were enjoined in a lively discussion. Refinement to the plan were put forward by each man, but it was Cody's grand design that was agreed upon.

A surprise raid on the camp would allow the Marshall to arrest the miners and seize any illicit goods stored inside the cave. The brilliant strategy that was mapped out by Caleb would involve fifteen qualified men. At the same time, at another location, Johns would negotiate his wares with a woman and her accomplice.

"Is Robert at Gina's house?" Cody asked.

"Took him this morning, early," Mayor Thorton said.

"I'll go to Gina's tonight and tell Robert my plan to trap Johns."

"And, I'll tell you something, Deputy," the mayor said, "Robert sure didn't chafe when Maggie fussed around him here at the jail."

"No, he sure didn't. When she wasn't standing over him," Caleb added, "he'd look all over the jail for her."

The front door opened, and Ken and Luis walked in and sat at the table. The objects in the crates on the wagon were described and the man who sold the items was identified.

"Ken, we have all agreed to tell Edward what's happening here in Sonora and Columbia and ask him for his help," said Mayor Thorton. "You will carry a letter to Edward in San Francisco as soon as I write it."

Leaving Caleb, Luis, Ken, and the deputy in consultation at the sheriff's office, Mayor Thorton mounted his horse and rode home. He had an important letter to formulate.

It was late in the afternoon when the deputy headed home eager to see his mother and brother. They had been neglected during the past few days because of duty.

Someone who was constantly in his thoughts lately had also been neglected. But he will make it up to her later.

58

*W*hile her son ate warm apple pie, Millie told him the latest gossip about the townspeople without omitting the smallest detail.

Refusing a second piece of pie, Cody asked his mother about his absent brother. "Where is Andrew? Is he with Billy?"

"Oh, I forgot to tell you. Billy and Andrew left a little while ago. They went to Gina's house to help John with something, I can't remember what now. Robert will be convalescing at Gina's, in the same room where you stayed after you were shot.

"Myrtle, Louise, and Maggie decided to cook supper so the sheriff would have company and feel indulged. As if he needs to be indulged. Maggie is constantly at his beck and call. Gina has invited Andrew, Billy, Matthew, and me. I'm taking apple pies for dessert.

"The sheriff is really doing quite well," Millie added, as she filled Cody's coffee cup. "He does get very tired still, but he is eating well and he can even walk a few steps. With help, of course."

Millie set the pot back on the stove. "When Matthew and Gina are finished at the hospital," she said, "they will pick me up. Are you riding out to the hills again, Cody?"

"No, Mom. I need to talk to Robert. I'll be at Gina's house tonight. Thanks for the pie. I'm going to clean up now."

"Cody, before you go, Son, I am so glad you are safe at home. Everyone will be surprised to see you at supper tonight."

He grinned at his mother, kissed her cheek, and went to change clothes. The bed looked so inviting that before he cleaned up for the evening, he decided to close his eyes.

He flopped on top of his grandmother's quilt, kicked off his boots, and rested his feet on the wrought iron footboard. As his body melted into the softness of the mattress, he heard a wagon approach the house. He put his hat over his face, listened to the voices in the kitchen, closed his eyes, and stared into the velvety blackness.

Two hours later Cody awoke abruptly, glanced around and realized he was home in his own bed. The evening shadows had descended. He needed to talk to Robert; it was too late now to clean up.

When he removed his boot from the stirrup and tethered Sammy in the grassy area by the front gate, he heard laughter and masculine voices coming from the backyard. Delicious aromas drifted out of the open kitchen windows. The evening was still warm although the end of summer was near. He looked forward to spending time with his family and his friends.

The screen door was unlocked; Cody let himself into the entry hall. He saw Robert propped up in bed in the guestroom behind the stairs.

"No! You will not sit up any longer, Robbie," Maggie scolded. "You have been up too long now."

She removed two pillows and helped the sheriff lay down. Cody lingered in the doorway as Maggie attended to Robert.

"Deputy," Maggie said, as she looked up, "you are finally back. Gina has been impossible to live with the last few days. She worries about you constantly. Do not, under any circumstances, tell her what I just said. Sit down and talk to the sheriff. I have to help in the kitchen with supper. I'll tell Gina you're here."

Cody sat on the chair next to the bed. "Before you go, Maggie," he said, "there's something I want to ask you and I want the sheriff to hear what I have to say. Come back in and shut the door."

"This sounds serious, Cody. Is there something wrong?" Robert asked.

"I'm getting a plan together, Sheriff, to trap and arrest Johns, but I need to use a woman as a ploy. I want to use Maggie."

"No, Deputy, you can't use Maggie," Robert said. "I won't stand for it. Whatever it is, it's too dangerous."

"What do I have to do, Cody?" Maggie asked.

"Act out the part of a rich widow who wants to buy something from the gold country for her home in Scotland," Cody said, grinning.

"Absolutely not," said Robert, "I don't want Maggie placed in a dangerous predicament. Why don't you use Gina? She could be a rich

Italian widow here to buy something for her house in Italy."

"I don't want to use Gina in this plan, Sheriff. If Johns says something Gina doesn't like, she'll start talking in Italian and throw something at him. The capture would be over. I need Maggie."

"Robbie," Maggie interrupted, "remember I was raised in Scotland. You have not seen dangerous until you have lived there. I want to help the deputy. I know how a rich widow acts when she sees something she wants to buy. Remember, I worked for rich women."

"I'll give you the details of my plan later, Maggie, after I've made the arrangements," Cody said. "You can't say anything to anybody, not even Gina."

"Good enough, Deputy." Maggie said.

Cody added for emphasis, "Remember, not a word to anybody. You're the type that commands and demands what she wants; I need that."

"Cody, I don't like it," said the sheriff. "I don't want her in any danger. You can't watch her every minute. What if she gets hurt?"

"Robbie," Maggie breathed, "what a nice thing to say. Does this mean you are worried about me?"

"I said I don't want you to get hurt. And, yes, I am worried about you. If you get hurt who'll boss me around?"

When Maggie left the room, Cody gave Robert a briefing of the last two days and explained what he had learned from Mayor Thorton about Edward heading an investigation into stolen art.

"Ken's taking a letter from the mayor to Edward in San Francisco. If the information we have is the link Edward needs," Cody added, "then I start my plan. In a week, Ken will have Edward's answer, so we will have to wait a few days."

"Do you think Rattlesnake will realize Maggie isn't a rich widow?"

"She can pull it off. Maggie has a way about her. She knows how to give orders and how to demand her own way. You must know that, Sheriff."

"You're right. But I don't want her in any danger, Deputy."

"Sheriff," Cody promised, "she'll never be out of my sight. Luis and Arnoldo will be armed and watching. If I know Edward, he'll send trained men. She'll be safe, I give you my word."

"Edward should come to Sonora himself if he wants to assist in the capture," Robert said.

"I think he will. He's got orders to break up this smuggling ring. Mayor Thorton is asking Edward to wire us a lot of money. We want to be able to prove that Maggie's serious, willing to spend her money.

"Wealthy people live right here in Sonora, Sheriff, and they want to spend their money. Rattlesnake's a greedy man. He wants money and power. Edward knows the type of man he's looking for and that man could well be Johns."

"What can I do?"

"Convince Maggie she's wealthy, have her act the part. I have to go to Nancy's house tomorrow. She'll be used in my plan. Nancy has fancy clothes that Maggie needs to borrow."

"You better watch Widow Nancy, Cody," Robert warned, "she can make a man do something he shouldn't do. You know what I mean."

"That's exactly what I need, Sheriff," Cody answered. "She's the one that has to convince Johns that her friend is rich. So rich that her pleasure in life is traveling all over the world looking for expensive things to buy.

"I'll be back to see you before I leave. By the way, Sheriff, Maggie seems to be paying a lot of attention to you. I hear she waits on you hand and foot."

"Never you mind, Deputy. Maggie's helping me get well and that's all."

Cody left Robert and walked into the kitchen. Food was shifted from pans to serving dishes and transferred to the dinning room table. Surprised and pleased to see the deputy grace their presence, all the ladies flocked around him. Everyone was delighted that he was staying for supper, especially Gina.

59

The evening was almost a celebration. Chicken, perfectly battered and fried, fresh carrots, blanched and buttered, eggplant fried the Italian way, in bread crumbs and olive oil, homemade rolls, along with homemade Italian wine, made the men, including Robert, amble lazily into the parlor. There they lounged in the large comfortable chairs until the ladies finished with the dishes.

When it was time for dessert, Millie and Gina dutifully cut up apple pies. "Gina, the dinner turned out wonderfully," Millie said, coming out of the pantry holding a large tray in her hands. "Everybody was talking at the same time. It was like we hadn't seen each other for weeks."

"I hope Cody can relax now that Robert is feeling better. I was so worried about him when he rode off to the hills the morning after the sheriff was shot. He is so serious about his work."

"As was his father. If my husband did not come home in the evening for supper when I expected him," Millie related, "I walked the floor. The night he was killed was the saddest, most frightening night of my life. Now, I worry about my son."

Their conversation was interrupted by the deputy himself walking into the kitchen. Cody positioned his well-built body between Millie and Gina, putting his arms around their shoulders. "What are my two favorite women doing in the kitchen?" he asked.

Millie kissed her son on his cheek and quipped; "Cutting you men some pie, not that you deserve it, and saying how happy we are that the deputy of Sonora is with us tonight."

She handed Gina a plate with a large piece of apple pie for Cody, and lifted the heavy tray to serve the other guests.

Gina questioned Cody as she put the plate and a fork on the table in front of him, "How was the surveillance of the camp? Were you in any danger?"

This evening the deputy was mellow, contented, and felt free to relate to Gina the information that was not confidential. "Arnoldo found this boulder with a space inside it big enough for two or three men. We looked out over the camp through gaps in the bottom."

As he continued with his tale of the past few days, Gina listened quietly. When Cody spoke of the miner who was killed, she became totally absorbed in his unusual and exciting narrative. She loved to watch him while he spoke, and her attentiveness kept the deputy speaking.

Maggie burst through the kitchen door, interrupting Cody. "Here you are, Deputy, thank goodness. I have been looking for you," Maggie announced as she pulled the fork from Cody's hand just when he was about to stab the last of the pie on his plate. "Robert wants to talk to you before I settle him into bed for the night, and he's waiting for you." She grabbed his dish and set it on the sink. "Gina, you should find Matthew so he can check Robert's back wound."

Cody said with a snicker in his voice, "Maggie, I wasn't finished with my pie. Can't he get himself settled in bed for the night?"

Maggie flashed him a warning look. "You are finished with your pie, and remember it was only three days ago that the sheriff was shot in the back and thigh," she retorted. "Have you conveniently forgotten how quickly infection sets in?"

Always the nurse, Gina tried to soothe Maggie's irritation at Cody. "It's time the doctor and I looked at the back and thigh area. I'll go find him."

Maggie held the kitchen door open to let Cody pass by. "Shall we go?" she asked, haughtily.

"That's exactly the way I want you to talk when you meet William Johns, the man you're going to help capture. Just be your usual irritating self."

"That's what I do best, Deputy."

Matthew replaced his stethoscope. "He's healing well, Maggie," he said, "no need to worry, there's no infection. What do you think, Gina? Will he live?"

"Yes, I think he will, doctor," replied Gina, grinning broadly.

After making sure Robert had water and the bell in case the nurse was needed during the night, Maggie prepared to leave the room.

Robert grabbed Maggie's hand before she walked out and asked, "Can you stay for a minute?"

"I thought you wanted to speak to the deputy alone."

"What I have to say concerns you, Maggie," Robert said. "Shut the door, Deputy."

Maggie sat on the end of the bed. Cody sat in a chair by the sheriff.

"Cody, you wanted Maggie to use one of Nancy's fancy dresses. I don't want her to borrow a dress from Nancy. I want to buy the dress and I don't care how much it will cost."

"Robbie! I will never let you do that. There is no need. I can buy my own dress. I have money," countered Maggie.

"You have been helping me constantly since I was shot; you wait on me all the time. I want to do something for you."

"It was necessary to pitch in," Maggie said. "Matthew and Gina were busy with patients at the hospital. I wanted to help."

"Then, Maggie," Robert pointed out, "I want to help you. If you can find something at one of those fancy shops in town, I'll give you the money for it, as long as the deputy approves."

Other than her immediate family and Gina, no one had ever been this charitable to her. "Thank you, Robbie," she said, sincerely, "I will never forget such a noble gesture. I am truly at a loss for words."

Deputy Taylor was always ready to put a bee in Maggie's bonnet. "I didn't think that could ever happen to you, Maggie."

"Now you watch your tongue, Deputy. Robbie, I will come back after he leaves the room."

Margaret closed the door to the bedroom as Cody grinned mischievously. "She's quite a woman," he said. "Wouldn't you say so, Sheriff?"

"Yes. She is quite a woman, Deputy. Quite a woman."

"Get some rest. After I talk to Nancy, I'll let you know if she wants to help."

"You just remember who you are dealing with when you see Widow Nancy. She can take a man by storm and he won't even know he's drowning. I don't want you to risk the affection Gina feels for you."

"Don't worry, everything's under control." Cody touched his hat, grinned, stepped out of the room, and closed the door. Maggie was waiting for him.

"Let me know when you want me to look for a dress. I do not want Robbie to spend his money on a dress that I am going to wear."

"You deserve it. You're helping him get well, and now he wants to do something for you. If you can leave the sheriff for an hour or two, I want you to ride with me to Nancy Johnson's house. She'll be the one to arrange a meeting with you and Johns. I want you two to meet and talk."

"Widow Nancy? I've heard of her. Myrtle and Louise told me all about her wild ways. I can leave Robbie, but not for too long. Myrtle and Louise will sit with him. When were you thinking of talking to Nancy?"

"Tomorrow morning," Cody said. "Can I pick you up in the afternoon?"

"I can be ready. The ladies told me Nancy is a handful. You need me to protect you."

"Thanks, but I can handle Nancy. See you tomorrow."

Cody located Gina at her front gate waving to Matthew and Millie as they pulled away from the house. He leaned against the front porch post and watched her.

Before Andrew and Billy rode off together on one horse, she gave them orders. "You boys be careful on the way home; it's dark on the road. Andrew, hold onto Billy, *Hai capito? Capisci?"*

To give warm hugs to women friends and to embrace children and boys like Andrew and Billy, was part of Miss Tufano's inherited Italian characteristics. More reserved to men, she kissed their cheek.

At supper, Cody saw her beautiful smile as she spooned out food to the ones sitting at the table, listened to her laughter, and observed her use of gestures to emphasize certain words. Gina was unaware the deputy was drinking in all of her quirks and mannerisms as she went about her duties as hostess throughout the evening.

Missing everyone already, Gina walked slowly toward the front porch to say good-bye to Cody. In the past, whenever the deputy was at Gina's house, it was his custom to walk out the gate, mount Sammy, touch his hat to Gina, grin, and ride off.

But what he had in mind for Gina this evening before his departure was nowhere nearing customary. He met Gina on the walkway, between the gate and the porch.

"It was such a wonderful evening, Cody," she said. "I was surprised, but pleased you were able to be with us. I did not think you would be out of the hills for days. We all missed you...."

The next words she was about to say stuck in her throat. Cody stood directly in front of her, and his intense blue eyes penetrated deep into

Gina. His right arm reached around her waist, and his left hand enclosed the back of her head. She was pulled forward, pressed firmly against him, locked in his arms. His left hand brought her head forward, close to his face, and restricted it from twisting away. The force of his embrace caused her unwittingly to catch her breath. At that instant, Cody's lips found hers and Gina was kissed fervently.

Surrendering to his strong arms and embrace, Gina once again was awakened to the pleasure of Cody holding her close to his body.

Her Mama's words echoed in her brain, "When a man holds you like he owns you, then, *la figlia*, you will know that man loves you only."

Cody released her, but held her hands. Gina opened her eyes and tried to focus on his face.

"Thanks for the supper, Gina," he said. "I've missed you."

"You are so welcome," she could barely answer, swooning from breathlessness.

He walked to Sammy, mounted, sat for a minute looking at her, touched his hat, and nudged Sammy onward.

Maggie threw the screen door wide open, anchoring it with her body and glared at Gina, "Where have you been? Are you coming in sometime tonight?" she demanded harshly. "We still have a lot to do in that kitchen and I need your help. Hurry up, girl."

Gina smiled, and with a dreamy-eyed expression on her face, she climbed the porch stairs slowly as Maggie looked on. "Maggie, I have just kissed the man who loves me. Cody loves me."

$\mathcal{M}$ayor Thorton waited until the stagecoach turned off Washington Street and disappeared from view. If the connections on the trains from Stockton to Sacramento, and Sacramento to San Francisco were on time, Ken could be sitting in Edward's office as soon as the following day.

"Ken is on his way to San Francisco," Mayor Thorton said, as he joined Caleb and Cody at the table in the jail. "It took me damn near two hours to write that letter to Edward. I still can't believe there's a smuggling ring and it's right under our noses."

"If Edward doesn't show up in Sonora carrying a satchel of money and a piece of jewelry for Nancy to use as bait on Johns," Cody said, "I'll be surprised."

Caleb shoved a piece of paper to Cody; he read it, sat back in his chair, and handed it to the mayor.

William read the paper and looked at Caleb. "Got the plan to invade the camp all worked out?" he said. "I like it."

"The deputy drew up the plan, I added a tactic or two," Caleb answered. "Cody knows the surrounding hills. Now all I have to do is round up good men who can be trusted. If Edward brings men with him, I'll use them, too."

At a time chosen by the deputy and Caleb, after meeting with Edward or the representatives he would send to Sonora, the U.S. Marshall would direct a band of fifteen men to surround the camp.

The first band of four men would advance east into the hills around the campsite and would go to their predetermined hiding places. The other band of four men would spread out west around the camp and remain unseen and wait. Two days later, when the camp and mine were to be seized, seven more men, including the U.S. Marshall, would hide close to the entrance of the camp and wait for Caleb to give the final instructions and signal to ride in and encircle the camp.

If only one or two men were visible inside the camp, Caleb's men would move in and arrest these miners. The other deputies, including some of Edward's men, would stand as lookout or guards and remain on the surrounding hills.

Caleb, Micah and Mark, and two of Edward's men, would enter the mine, search out, and arrest the remaining miners inside the cave.

With lookouts on guard at the entrance of the enclosure, and all the miners shackled, men experienced in exploring a large cavern would begin their search for the illicit goods.

"Deputy, while I secure the mine," Caleb said, "you'll be in Columbia at the hotel with Nancy and Maggie."

Cody acknowledged Caleb with a nod in the affirmative.

Caleb continued, "Mayor, you need to deputize my sons. Cody, who are you going to use to assist in your arrest of Johns?"

"Luis and Arnoldo and a few of Edward's men. Rattlesnake killed Arnoldo's cousin, Jose. I want Arnoldo to put the shackles on Johns."

"How many miners are in the camp now?" Caleb asked

"Robert and I saw six men and Johns. But he killed one miner. That leaves five miners unless other members of Johns' gang have arrived."

While Caleb was quietly jotting down the final notes for his plan, Mayor Thorton questioned Cody, "Have you talked to Nancy Johnson about helping you?"

"Not yet, I'm going to talk to her today," Cody said. "If she agrees to help, Maggie and Nancy will get acquainted this afternoon.

"Dealing with Maggie won't be easy for Rattlesnake. He likes to give orders, doesn't like to take orders. Johns will have to yield to Maggie, own up to her demands."

Mayor Thorton chuckled, "He's a killer and she's a buyer," he said, "and if Margaret McLeod can dupe Rattlesnake, it'll be a fitting end to his career."

"And he won't even be able to shoot her," Caleb added.

61

*N*ancy opened the front door, exposing a lounging robe of blue satin material that clung tightly to all of her lovely curves. Her long, wavy brown hair cascaded down her shoulders and back. Her brown eyes gleamed with pleasure when she saw the deputy standing on her porch. Without question, Nancy was a beautiful, desirable woman.

"I saw you ride up, Deputy," she murmured. "I was wondering when you were going to turn up again. You haven't been by at this time of the day for a long time."

Cody walked into the entry hall and left the front door open. "Well," she asked, seductively, "what can I do for you?"

"I want you to do me a favor."

"Now, Deputy," she said, reaching up to pull off his vest, "you have only to ask. You know I always want to make you happy."

Cody pulled her arms down to her sides and held them there. "I need you to help me capture a man, a killer."

Nancy stepped back and tried to wrench free from Cody's grip as she questioned him. "You want me to do what?"

The deputy held her firmly by the arms. "You will need to distract a man in your usual way," he said, "by making him notice you. He's got to want to strike up a conversation with you."

"What killer am I suppose to distract? And, what if I don't want to help?"

"His name is William Johns, alias Rattlesnake. You're the only one that I know of who can make him notice you just by walking into a room. I need you to help me, Nancy."

"You are talking about that man I met at the Chinese laundry, aren't you? He's a killer? You're crazy, Deputy. He's no more a killer than I am."

She glared, while Cody explained, "We've discovered a smuggling ring in Columbia and Sonora, and we think Rattlesnake may be the leader. We know expensive and rare art works are being stolen from other parts of the world, then smuggled here to the gold country, and sold for a lot of money.

"He'll want to start a conversation with you because of the jewelry you'll be wearing the first time he sees you. He'll ask you about it and when he does, you tell him your friend, a widow woman from Scotland bought it for you. I guarantee, he'll want to meet her."

Nancy wrenched herself free from his grip, piqued at him. She hoped he had stopped by to resume their former romance, but instead he wanted her to do an official favor for him.

"It sounds dangerous, and I don't want any part of it."

"Since when were you afraid to meet a man, Nancy. I can't ask anyone else; you're the only one that can turn a man's head and make him talk to you. With or without expensive jewelry."

This uninhibited lady had a willing heart, sometimes too willing. Whenever the deputy had asked her to do him a favor in times past, official or otherwise, she had never refused.

"Johns noticed you at the Chinese laundry in Columbia," Cody continued, "and you didn't know he was watching. He went out of his way to help you. This man kills people Nancy; he needs to be stopped. But he's smart. Before I can arrest him, we've got to catch him selling his stolen goods."

Nancy took two steps away from Cody, folded her arms across her breasts, and stood with her back to him. Soft, blue satin material flowed around the contour of her firm, young body. He was pleased to stand back and admire the view she presented.

Nancy turned abruptly to face the deputy, asking, "You're sure I'm going to wear expensive jewelry?"

"I'm sure."

"And I'll be protected. You'll be there watching me, won't you?"

"I'll never take my eyes off you."

"When do I meet my friend, the rich widow?"

"This afternoon."

Her irritation dissipated, and she smiled at him, flashing her usual charm. "You do have a way about you, Cody Taylor," she cooed. "It's those blue eyes. I never could resist a man with blue eyes. Especially not you."

"Thanks for the help, Nancy; you're a special lady. I'll see you later." Cody grinned, touched the brim of his hat, and left Nancy standing at her open front door looking almost irresistible in her clinging blue satin robe.

62

*C*ody called for Maggie later that afternoon. He complimented her as they rode to Nancy's house. "You've been a big help to the Doc and Gina, Maggie. They've been able to work at the hospital and see patients while you have watched over Robert. He looks better."

"I like the sheriff, he reminds me of my father," Maggie said. "There are a few men who deserves good care and Robbie is one of them."

As they rode to Nancy's house, Cody told her what she was going to be up against when she finally faced William Johns.

"You will be protected at all times, Maggie. We won't let you or Nancy out of our sight. There'll be government men, trained men, watching you every minute, and not only because you'll be carrying lot of money and Nancy will be wearing expensive jewelry."

"Oh, I am not afraid in the least," Maggie said. "The women in my family did brave things, secret things during the feuds in Scotland. We are not a fainthearted lot."

"No, you aren't what I'd call timid."

"Did Nancy agree to help, then?"

"Yeah, I told her I'd give her the details when I came back with you."

"What will Nancy do to make William Johns notice her?"

"He'll notice right away, because of what she'll be wearing," Cody said, "and anyway, she can turn any man's head just by the way she looks at him, walks, and dresses. She's already met Johns once at the Chinese laundry in Columbia."

Cody continued to lay out the plan to Maggie. "I've asked Edward Thorton to loan us a valuable piece of jewelry, something expensive and rare. When Rattlesnake sees what it is, I'm sure he'll want to talk.

"You, Maggie, you've got to make him believe you are a wealthy woman. Try to remember the beautiful objects owned and displayed by rich people, especially the ones you used to work for. Ask for those types of things. Maybe he can't supply them, but he'll know that you have expensive tastes. When he describes something that you think is right, and he provides it and you pay him, he'll be the seller of stolen goods, and we'll be able to arrest him."

Maggie was pensive as she looked at the deputy. "I do not have to invent the type of things I want, Cody," she said. "The McLeod's own a castle in Scotland. After I arrived in New York several years ago, my brother wrote me that the new residents in the castle had reported a robbery. Old, irreplaceable and beautiful items worth a fortune were stolen from our castle."

"The McLeod's have a castle in Scotland?"

"Yes," Maggie responded. "It's the McLeod Castle. The McLeod clans have been the only residents since the eleventh century. I lived most of my life in that castle.

"But, unfortunately, a heated argument between my father and his cousin left my father dead. Mother, my brother, and I were forced to leave McLeod castle and find permanent lodging elsewhere. I brought my mother to America because she was devastated when father was killed. Terence still lives in Scotland. Yes, Deputy, I know fine, old, handmade works of art."

"Maggie, I'm sorry," Cody said.

"Oh, it was a long time ago. But I can recall vividly the type of art and furniture and decorations that royalty own. I know every piece of furniture and every painting that has ever been in that castle."

Maggie sat quietly, lost in memories, and stared in front of her. Cody complimented himself silently to have chosen Maggie to play the role of the rich widow. She was going to be perfect in the part. She had the personality for it. After all, she had been a rich woman herself once.

"We can talk in here," Nancy said, as she led them into the parlor.

Upon entering the room, a massive sideboard struck Maggie. It was beautifully carved and took up one long wall. Mahogany tables with ornate curved legs were located in front of each window. Two settees and four matching chairs, all done in exquisite needlepoint upholstery, were positioned in the center of the room. Placed on the tables and sideboard were beautiful hand-painted oil lamps, vases, and figurines. Heavy damask drapery layered the tall windows that completed the parlor.

Although it was an old house, the placement of the furniture and the richness of the accessories gave the room an elegant, formal look.

Maggie sat on the settee by Cody. Nancy sat on an overstuffed chair facing them.

"Can I get either of you some refreshment?" Nancy asked. "Cake? Tea? Anything?"

"No, thank you, Nancy," Cody answered, and he proceeded to introduced Maggie.

He started the conversation by describing every detail of what their roles in the apprehension of Johns would be, without disclosing any confidential information. The ladies listened and asked intelligent questions. After they accepted their roles and showed astuteness, Cody immediately appreciated one truly outstanding quality in both of these women: The willingness to help even when danger threatened.

"Maggie's ancestry," Cody continued, "the McLeod clan, has a castle that goes back hundreds of years. Maggie can name and describe all the master-works that were stolen from that castle, so in conversation Johns will realize that she is familiar with first-rate merchandise."

Taking over the conversation from Cody, Maggie described furniture, paintings, exquisite frames, and priceless accessories that had been a part of the family's heirlooms.

Nancy listened, fascinated. "It must have been a splendid castle, Maggie," she said. "I would love to see it some day."

"I hope to show the castle to you, Nancy. Even if I cannot show you the castle, my brother lives in Scotland still, and he would love to tell you all about McLeod castle."

A chemistry had developed between Nancy and Maggie; each seemed to know what the other was thinking. They were perfect for their parts and would compliment one another in the role each played.

Cody and Maggie were preparing to leave when Maggie decided to ask Nancy a final question. "I need to wear a dress and a large hat for this occasion, Nancy, that will call attention to me when I meet with William Johns. I have not been in Sonora long. Do you know where I can find a dress a rich widow might wear? The deputy wants me to wear something imposing and grand."

"I met my late husband while I was in San Francisco," Nancy recalled, "working in the theater. I have several costumes in my wardrobe and trunk that were made for me when I acted the parts of wealthy women on the stage. You look about my size; why don't we look there first?"

Nancy stood up and started for the stairs. Maggie conveyed a thought to Cody before she followed Nancy. "We should not spend money to buy a new dress if it is not necessary. Is that not true?"

$\mathcal{M}$ayor Thorton greeted Edward and Ken as they stepped down from the stagecoach. Ten men, trained in secret governmental intrigues, were also merging into the Columbia and Sonora areas.

Traveling on stagecoaches, buggies, trains, or horseback, Edward's men arrived with little notice. Their instructions were to watch for anyone dealing in expensive goods.

Caleb opened the front door to the jail as Edward, Ken, and Mayor Thorton entered. Cody ushered two black men, Clint and Roland, who were wearing city clothes, through the back door of the jail.

Legend had it that Clint was about forty-five years old, although other than a few gray hairs at the temples he did not look any more than thirty. He was six feet tall, with an expanse of shoulders that seemed to go on forever, and enormous, powerful hands. His eyes were iron-black, sharp and biting. While in his early teens, he had been coerced into boarding a sailing ship and forced into hard labor. Living amid such wretchedness, with meager food rations and daily beatings, Clint had to become tough as nails and quick as a cat. Criminals had no chance to flee when Clint was around, he could outrun any man, and when he caught the culprit there was no chance of escape.

The second man, Roland, was also middle age, but taller, leaner, and pure muscle. Like Clint, Roland had taken his share of cruel, savage atrocities from his youth onward, but Roland had learned discipline and patience through all the mistreatment. He could endure prolonged physical or mental strain without noticeable fatigue.

The one singular characteristic of any criminal is that they tend to boast about their despicable deeds. Roland would disappear into the shadows watching and listening until the ruffian bragged about his diabolical, underhanded accomplishments, and, in the end, it was the culprit that put the noose around his own neck.

Edward recognized in Clint and Roland their potential to be valuable agents, and he had hired them to be part of his team when he was transferred to San Francisco. Even though most people distrusted and degraded the Black race in 1875, Edward had promoted both of these men to positions of trust and authority.

When all the men had gotten acquainted and had taken their seats, Edward placed the satchel on the table and opened it. Imprest to him for the apprehension of William Johns was $50,000.00, in one thousand dollar bundles. A necklace and an exquisite hair comb had also been commissioned.

The necklace, of considerable size and weight, had twisted gold links that formed a chain. Each link was set with precious gems, pearls, rubies, emeralds, and sapphires, four different gems per link. All twenty links were secured by a beautiful gem-embellished clasp.

The rectangular-shaped hair comb made of tortoise shell had a gold-hammered decoration on the front. The decoration was set with ten opals circling the perimeter. In the center of the opals, were two peacocks, one of gold, with exquisitely carved feathers, and the other of elaborately carved lapis lazuli.

Both pieces were works of art, unique and priceless. When Nancy wore the necklace and comb at the initial meeting with William Johns, she would be noticed by anyone who possessed knowledge of one-of-a-kind, precious items.

"The United States government is aware that certain artifacts have been smuggled into the port of San Francisco," Edward began, "and then they have been moved to other states in the East. Our efforts to locate the people responsible have been unsuccessful.

"Our men have positioned themselves in the cargo holds at the shipping docks, and they have examined numerous crates. They found nothing out of the ordinary nor illegal.

"A wealthy Englishman was nabbed in Chinatown recently by our agents buying an oriental statue," Edward related. "Obviously rare, it was solid gold and in impeccable condition. In exchange for identifying the persons who sold him the item, he will not be prosecuted. His true name is Wallace Alastair Richardson. Have any of you heard of him?"

Caleb, Ken, Cody, and Mayor Thorton nodded negatively.

"The names he gave us were Daniel and Simon, with no last names. But these men had told Richardson that they were from the gold country. Three weeks later, two men left his house and walked toward Chinatown. Our men followed, but lost them.

"One month ago, we sent two of our agents to Chinatown, but they never returned, and we presume they are dead. We are at a loss, gentlemen," Edward continued, "as to how these goods are being transported without detection into the gold country."

Caleb ventured an opinion. "Have you tried the trains? Have you looked into the crates that go as freight and can be left at different railroad sidings where the owners may claim their goods?"

"Yes," Edward answered. "We have checked the freight at the San Francisco depot and the Sacramento depot. Nothing. And yet, gentlemen, Mr. Richardson says he purchased a valuable statue from men who came from the gold country, and specifically, from Columbia. Where did they get it? It had to come into California somehow."

Frustrated, Edward looked to the men for answers. "Our efforts to obtain information always leads to a dead end. Merchandise is reaching the gold country from somewhere; we just do not know how it is being transported."

Cody introduced another avenue of thought. "There are stops the trains make south of Sacramento, at Galt, Stockton, and Lathrop. In fact, there is a spur train to Milton from Stockton. Have you checked the freight at any of those locations?"

"No, Deputy, we have not checked any out-of-the-way stops," Edward replied. "That would be too obvious. If crates were left at a station where there is no activity, people would get suspicious."

"If I were sneaking something valuable into California," Cody put to Edward, "I wouldn't send it to a big city like San Francisco or Sacramento. I'd send it where nobody expects it to go."

"The deputy has something there, Edward," Caleb interrupted. "You need to check the freight at the depot in Stockton or Lathrop and at that spur train that stops in Milton. Galt's too far away from Sonora."

Caleb thought for a moment and then said, "If there was a crate left at one of those out of the way stops, eventually someone would have to claim it. If a crate was left in Lathrop or Milton, there isn't a house or a building around for miles. It could stay there a month."

Edward sat staring at Caleb, sensing a flaw in his thinking. Big cities might not be the drop-off point for stolen art; it might be just the opposite.

Edward stood up and motioned to Clint and Roland to follow him to the back door. He issued quiet instructions, and both men left by the back entrance.

"I'm sending Clint and Roland with two other men to check the depots at Stockton, Milton and Lathrop. If there was any freight dropped off at any of those towns, one will report back to me, and the other will stand guard. We now have to wait gentlemen, for my men to return with answers. Excellent suggestion though, Deputy."

"Since we have to wait until we hear from your men, Edward," his father said, "I suggest we head for the Sonora Hotel and have lunch. Madame Pamela Dumont is expecting us and has reserved a quiet table. After lunch we can resume our discussion."

Mayor Thorton stood by as Cody locked the satchel of money and jewelry into the safe. All five men reached for their hats and walked out of the sheriff's office.

64

At the Stockton depot, Roland and his assistant found nothing was tagged for the gold country. Lathrop depot was a one-day ride on horseback to and from Sonora, but they found no crates that lay in waiting. They rode back to Sonora.

Clint and his assistant investigated the spur train to the Milton depot and found two crates corded and tied with heavy rope. Clint's assistant rode back to Sonora.

Edward left immediately for Milton accompanied by Ken and Cody.

"Has anyone claimed the crates?" Edward asked Clint.

"Not yet," Clint said, stepping out of hiding. "They're still there."

Edward was allowed to opened the crates after he displayed his credentials to the attendant.

Pushing aside the packing material, the agents lifted out a doll-size candleholder hand-painted in an exotic oriental dress made out of Chinese porcelain. Other precious works of art packed in the crates included three vases covered with beautiful, delicate flowers. At the bottom of one crate was a pair of musical, Italian porcelain figurines of a man and a woman, which was equipped with a key. When the key was turned, a lovely melody was heard. There were three marble statues made to sit upon a tabletop, all were different in design. The last items to be removed from the crates were five paintings in ornate, gold frames, their sizes ranging from small to medium.

Cody uncovered a jewelry case made of wood, overlaid with gold and studded on all sides with jewels, magnificent piece. In fact, all of the objects were masterworks.

"Ken, you and Clint stay here, and see if anybody comes to claim the freight. If and when it is claimed," Edward advised, "follow them. I want to know where those crates are delivered. Ken, you're familiar with the location of Rattlesnake's mine; don't ride away until the wagon rolls inside, if that's where the crates are intended for delivery. Report back to me as soon as you find anything out."

Cody and Edward rode back to Sonora, now confident about how some of the merchandize was reaching the gold country, but they were still plagued with questions: Who was the mastermind behind this smuggling ring? How did he direct the shipment of the merchandize? Where did he get the goods he shipped to this country?

After almost twelve hours of waiting, Ken and Clint spied a wagon approaching the Milton depot. Four mules pulled the wagon. As the wagon drew near, Ken recognized the drivers as men from Rattlesnake's mine. After the miners had claimed the freight, Ken and Clint followed the wagon on the long road until it disappeared into Johns' mining camp.

They rode back into Sonora, bringing their information to the eager ears of Edward, Caleb, and Cody. Now the final strings were tied and the stratagem could begin.

Posing as visitors in Columbia, three of Edward's men reserved rooms at the Fallon House; two other agents booked rooms at the Columbia Boarding House. In Jamestown and Sonora, five other agents were dispersed in various hotels. Whenever William Johns left the Fallon House, and wherever he went throughout his day, he would be watched by at least two government men around the clock.

Fortunately, Johns was a man of habit. He invariably consumed a full breakfast at eight o'clock, tea and cakes were taken at eleven, and lunch was served promptly at two in the afternoon. Supper was always placed before him at seven in the evening.

On more than one occasion, during the surveillance, Edward's men watched as formally dressed men carrying satchels, often accompanied by extravagantly dressed ladies, approached Johns' table. They spoke quietly, and eventually all went upstairs, presumably to his room.

Armed with this information, Nancy fine-tuned her plan to saunter into the Fallon House, captivate William Johns, and set up an appointment for Maggie. At the same time in the hills of Sonora, the first eight of fifteen men would hide themselves in the surrounding brush and trees above the Rattlesnake's mine.

Cody's strategy needed precision timing to make sure all involved in the smuggling ring were accounted for, either at the Fallon House in Columbia or in the hills of Sonora. On the day when William Johns meets with Margaret McLeod, after Nancy had successfully negotiated the appointment at the Fallon House, the U.S. Marshall will arrest the miners at Rattlesnake's camp in the hills of Sonora, one by one.

The time now had come for Nancy to invade the restaurant wearing her showy accessories. William Johns, in his usual apparel, minus the hat, was taking tea. Cody watched the scene unfold from the shadows, with Edward at his side. Clint and Roland had taken up positions at the back entrance of the hotel; their assistants were watching the front entrance. Johns was so astonished by both Nancy's hair comb and necklace, and her seductive appearance, that when she was escorted to a table close to his he ignored his cakes and watched her every movement.

Entering the restaurant unescorted, presented no problem for Nancy Johnson. She said demurely to the hotelkeeper, "I am visiting your lovely town, but I am so tired. May I take a seat in your restaurant and have some tea? I really feel the need to rest."

The attendants were only too happy to escort Mrs. Johnson to a table.

Johns was dazzled. In order to grab his attention immediately, Nancy had chosen her raiment carefully. She had finally settled on the lovely blue velvet dress with the tight, low-cut bodice that displayed most of her ample, perfectly shaped breasts. Johns stared shamelessly.

And when tea and cakes arrived at Nancy's table and she reached for the teapot, her napkin accidentally fell onto the floor.

Johns burst out of his chair. "Please! Do let me assist," he said, picking up the napkin and placing it on her table.

"Why, thank you," Nancy cooed.

"I see you are alone, Madam. I would be honored if you would join me at my table for tea."

"How kind of you. Thank you again. I do hate to eat alone, don't you?" Nancy purred.

"My name is William Johns," he said. "I hope I am not being too bold, but may I have the pleasure of knowing your name?"

"I am Mrs. Nancy Johnson," she breathed.

"What brings you into Columbia today? Are you a frequent visitor to our town?"

"My sister-in-law lives here and I try to visit her regularly. She is older and doesn't have much company. I think it is sad for people to be lonely, so I try to visit as often as possible."

"Pray tell me, Mrs. Johnson," Johns began, going directly for the kill, "wherever did you get that lovely necklace and beautiful hair comb? France would be my guess. I am fascinated by the workmanship and outstanding quality of both items."

This was Nancy's queue and she was off and running, "What would you like to see first?"

"The comb," Johns answered.

Nancy inclined her pretty head and smiled. William removed the comb and fondled it gently, turning it over and over in his hands.

She replaced the hair comb and leaned forward, giving William the opportunity to reach for the necklace that nestled on her breasts. "I'll leave it on my neck," Nancy said, "the clasp is difficult to open. Please, take your time; examine it to your heart's content. You have such nice hands."

While he examined every jewel on each link, Rattlesnake looked up now and again into Nancy's big brown eyes. "Where did you say these two pieces were purchased, Mrs. Johnson?"

"Oh! Didn't I say? These were gifts. I have this friend, you see, Mrs. Margaret McLeod. She lives in a castle in Scotland, but she is visiting California, and she stopped in Sonora for a visit. She gave me this necklace and hair comb as a gift. She is quite well-to-do."

After several pots of tea and more than one serving of cake, Nancy had won Rattlesnake over, hook, line, and sinker. Johns had ascertained that Mrs. McLeod was a lady of influence and great wealth. Nancy also alluded to Margaret's interest in buying unique one-of-a-kind items to decorate her castle.

As Nancy bid farewell and stood up to leave, Johns took her hand, held it, then bent and kissed her fingers. "I look forward to seeing you again," he said. "The day after tomorrow would be nice. You and I should take tea together, hopefully along with Mrs. McLeod. I have some beautiful items that I would like to present for her approval. How should I recognize her?"

"She has very red hair, natural red hair, and she will be dressed in the finest, most expensive fashions. She always wears a large hat with feathers. You cannot miss her. I look forward to our next meeting, Mr. Johns."

As Nancy took her leave, Johns absorbed her sway around the tables, and then he drew in a deep breath as she turned back to smile before she picked up her skirts to saunter out the front door.

Led to the site by Ken, Caleb had his first group of men at the camp at the very same time that Nancy was dazzling Johns. If all went as planned, when William Johns was arrested and Edward was tying up ends at the Fallon House, the U.S. Marshall would secure Rattlesnake's camp at exactly the same time on the same day.

*W*hile Edward had been driving Nancy to Columbia for her meeting with William Johns, Cody had called upon Maggie.

The attire Maggie had borrowed from Nancy's wardrobe was flamboyant, but appropriate for this occasion, and she looked absolutely elegant. It was a green velvet dress that accentuated her skin and hair. A tight bodice with a low neckline exposed a generous part of her creamy white breasts. The long, abundant skirt flowed to her feet revealing matching shoes. Maggie had piled her hair on top of her head and had covered it with a luxurious green velvet hat with bold, vibrant-colored flowers, complete with ostrich feathers. A parasol out of the same material was also provided.

"I will just step in and say good-bye to Robbie," Maggie announced to Cody. "He is so worried about me. I do not think he approves of me helping you, deputy."

Maggie's appearance shocked Sheriff Sanders; he did not speak, he only stared. Was this the same lady who was usually at his bedside, assisting in his healing process?

"I promise to not take any chances," Maggie said. "I will be careful, Robbie. Do not worry about me. You rest now, and I will see you when this job is done."

Cody supplied detailed information about the imminent capture of Johns to Miss McLeod as they neared Columbia. Clint and his assistant, along with Roland and his assistant, lingered unobtrusively as Cody pulled the horse to a halt near the Columbia Boarding House.

Luis and Arnoldo, dressed in their finest clothes, tied their horses to the hitching post in front of the Fallon House, while Edward helped

Nancy out of the Mayor's buggy. Edward carried the satchel and spoke to Maggie as they walked into the Fallon House.

At precisely eleven o'clock in the morning, the time scheduled for the apprehension of Johns at the Fallon House and for the assault on the mine, the action got underway. If cooperation and perfect timing were not hindered in any unforeseen way, a certain person would be incarcerated for both murder and for receiving money for stolen artifacts.

Maggie sipped her tea, pinched off small amounts of cake, and listened as Mr. Johns gave her choices as to the array of items he thought she would be eager to purchase. Unconcerned with what Rattlesnake thought of her, she acted rude and demeaning as she bargained for the items.

Her voice rose when her discontent grew. "No, I do not want to spend that much money on a common chair. How dare you insult me. The chair I want is exquisite, a carved harp for the back of the chair, and all the wooden parts should be covered in gold. The seat that I envision is magnificently done in needlepoint, silk needlepoint. If you can present a chair of that description to me, I will gladly pay your price."

Nancy sat placidly, seemingly unconcerned as Maggie haggled, in no way concerned when Mr. Johns' gaze toward Maggie turned unpleasant. Nancy looked at him in her most seductive way and flashed her beautiful smile until it appeared that his mind had been diverted, and his temper had cooled.

For nearly two hours the discussion proceeded as Maggie demanded, Nancy allured, and William Johns condescended. Finally, Maggie stopped interrupting his every word and sat silent; she realized he was near the end of his patience.

Johns took a deep breath, looked at her, and said in his kindest voice, "I have three items that you must approve before you agree to their purchase, Mrs. McLeod. The first, a chair for your desk with silk tapestry as you requested, wood parts covered in gold. The second item, I think you will be surprised and happy with when you see the jewelry case. Exquisite. A magnificent piece! And the last item, the statue of a robust man carrying a large cluster of grapes."

"The statue must be carved from marble. Italian marble. Nothing less will do," stipulated Maggie.

"Yes, Mrs. McLeod. I'm sure it is quarried from the finest Italian marble."

"It had better be, Mr. Johns."

"Now, Mrs. McLeod, I trust you are happy with your choices?"

Maggie turned her head toward Johns, gloved hands resting on the handle of her upturned parasol. "How on earth am I to know if I will happy or not? Have I seen the pieces? Do I not have to approve them before I make the purchase?" Maggie said, arrogantly.

Johns' voice betrayed his anger. "I have the items upstairs, adjacent to my room, what I call my viewing room. Please, my dears Mrs. McLeod and Mrs. Johnson, will you follow me? The viewing room is large, and you will sit comfortably in chairs and be in a private place. There you can hold and examine your purchases."

Johns rose from his chair to assist Maggie.

"I do not go into the room of a man, Mr. Johns," Maggie said, rooted firmly in her chair, and loudly enough for all in the room to hear. "That sort of thing is not done in Scotland."

"But, Mrs. McLeod, there is only one other gentleman in the room, my valet, and you will be accompanied by Mrs. Johnson. I promise no harm will come to you."

"It is not harm that I question," Maggie retorted. "It is my virtue. If you cannot abide by my wishes, I shall take my leave."

Maggie glanced at Nancy, and the ladies collected their personal belongings. From their places, Cody was taut and Edward poised. If Maggie left, Johns was sure to lose a lot of money. But the aggravation he had suffered up to this moment might cause him to let Maggie depart and take her money with her.

Seething, Johns now sat back in his chair, and covered his feelings with words of honey. "May I bring the items you are eager to purchase to this very table?" he asked. "Would not that be to your liking, Mrs. McLeod?"

"In this hotel, primitive though it may be," Maggie said insolently, "there must be a place somewhere that one could sit unobserved and carry out business. Is there not a room with tables and chairs where we can sit without intrusion?"

There was, in fact, such a room just off the main lobby at the opposite of the stairs. It was a private area, made accessible to the officials of Columbia for monthly meetings. The space could accommodate comfortably up to ten people around an oval mahogany table. A large closet for coats and hats was located in the corner behind a door.

When Nancy left the Fallon House, after the initial meeting with William Johns, Edward and his assistant, Clint had approached the proprietor of the hotel, Mr. Joseph T. Downey, for a quiet, little conversation.

Edward displayed his credentials and introduced Clint. "We will be conducting an investigation, Mr. Downey," Edward stated, "along with a possible criminal apprehension that could take place here at the Fallon House. Your full cooperation will be expected, along with the cooperation of the most trusted members of your staff. The man in question is a guest of your establishment, a man named William Johns. We have reason to believe he is a very dangerous individual."

"You will have my full cooperation, Mr. Thorton," Joseph T. Downey said, "I did not approved of the way Mr. Johns has been conducting business in our hotel. This is an old and respected establishment, and I feared something was amiss. The cleaning staff was not allowed into his room, and he had his valet do everything. He is a most private person. It has been very unnerving not to know what was really going on in his upstairs room. Please tell me your wishes, and we will do everything we can to assist you in the apprehension of this most unsavory character."

Edward requested the use of the private room off of the lobby and opposite to the stairs for the apprehension procedure, far away from the eyes and ears of guests. Mr. Downey assured Edward the conference room would remain unlocked.

Edward told Clint and Roland to wait in the closet provided for coats and hats. Maggie would draw money from the satchel and place it on the table. As Johns counted his profit, he would become the seller of stolen art treasures.

Edward had given Maggie final instructions while they walked into the Fallon House. He had specified that she was to choose that particular room for the apprehension. Maggie was also instructed to treat Edward as her servant, and the keeper of the satchel.

"I saw a room opposite the stairs when I entered the hotel today," she said, firmly. "That is where I will tell Edward to bring my satchel." As she prepared to leave the restaurant, Maggie gathered her parasol and purse.

Johns strained to be patient. "Mrs. McLeod," he said, "I would much rather we view the articles for your approval from my viewing room."

Maggie narrowed her eyes and spaced her words. "Mr. Johns, bring one item only to the room opposite the stairs. Bring the Russian jewelry case. That should be easy for you to carry alone. If I am happy, I will pay you for that item. Then, and only then, will I accompany you to your private viewing room. Do you have the mental capacity to comprehend my instructions?"

"I will talk to Mr. Downey," replied Johns, with obvious indignation. "Hopefully, he will allow us the use of the meeting room. Please excuse me, ladies."

Mr. Downey turned up the gaslights immediately. Mr. Johns waited as the ladies drifted inside the room. They sat at the table, their backs to the wall opposite the door.

"Please excuse me another moment," Johns said.

He returned minutes later with a covered box and set it on the table in front of a less than pleased Maggie, but he kept it close to himself. When the lid of the box was removed, Maggie and Nancy gasped as Johns lifted the object from its receptacle.

The jeweled case was approximately eight inches tall, twelve inches long, and six inches deep, and contained three, velvet lined, separate drawers. A beautifully enchanting melody sounded when the cover was raised. Maggie marveled. She pulled it from him and set it in front of herself, caressing the top and sides with her gloved hands.

Made of ebony wood, the legs, lid, and edges of the case were inlaid with hammered gold. Studded on all sides and the top were alexandrites, beautiful Russian gems that glistened as if on fire, which seemed to dart and dance within the stone, along with perfect diamonds and emeralds.

The lock was in the shape of a flower, and the petals were of pure gold. Johns held the key to the lock in his hand, a key of pure gold, and passed it under the noses of Maggie and Nancy. Johns was right, the workmanship was in a class by itself. It truly was a magnificent piece.

Edward gave Johns time to fetch the jewel case from his viewing room and carry it downstairs to the meeting room for Maggie's approval, before he approached the door to the meeting room, satchel in hand, and tapped softly. Johns left Maggie admiring and caressing the jewel case at the table, and opened the door allowing Edward to enter.

"I want this jewelry case," Maggie announced, her voice rising. "Whatever the amount, I want it. Edward, come forward, hand me my satchel. Mr. Johns, how much did I agree to pay?"

The price had not been negotiated, but Johns announced the amount; "The case will cost $10,000.00, Mrs. McLeod."

Edward walked around the table and placed the satchel in front of Maggie, and waited until she opened it. Edward bowed slightly, then left Maggie's side, and stood in front of the door that had been left slightly ajar.

Rattlesnake leaned forward, his hands flat against the surface of the table, and watched Maggie remove bundle after bundle of money from the satchel.

Edward pulled out his Colt Single-action Army, .45 caliber revolver. Silently, Clint and Roland immerged from the cloakroom as their assistants appeared without a sound through the door to the meeting room, and waited behind Edward. With Colt revolvers held steady, guarding the door and the culprit, Edward stepped forward and stood directly behind Johns.

Five bundles lay side by side on the table. Johns reached for the closest bundle. As his fingers curled around the first packet, he felt the pressure of cold hard steel on the back of his head just above his right ear. Silence rocked the room, following the simultaneous cocking of five Colt hammers.

Rattlesnake was thunderstruck. He stared, gaping, unable to retaliate, and then he twisted with fury, his eyes turned hard and evil, and his body shook violently. The ladies looked up and screamed when they saw Johns' in a spasm, and Edward's men in the room, revolvers held steady. It was a perfect performance.

Edward's authoritative voice reverberated in Rattlesnake's ear. "William Johns, put your hands flat on the surface of the table."

Roland grabbed Johns' left arm, and Clint seized his right arm and removed the derringer from Johns' sleeve. Johns' was quickly frisked for other weapons, none were found. Clint was just forcing Johns' arms behind him when the deputy walked into the room, followed by Luis and Arnoldo.

Cody presented the handcuffs to Arnoldo, and as he snapped them in place around Johns' wrists, Clint swung Johns around to see the young Mexican man who had shackled him. Outwitted at his own game, he became livid with rage and disbelief. He vocalized his detest for Arnoldo and Luis, then thrashed with all his strength to reach for them. His face reddened and his veins distended in his temples as he blurted out abusive remarks and expletives to Clint and Roland, the two Black men that constrained him.

Edward gave the final instructions. "William Johns, you will be escorted to the Columbia jail. Men, secure him in one cell and put his valet in the other."

Clint and Roland dragged Johns from the meeting room and out the front door of the Fallon House, while their assistants were arresting Rattlesnake's valet.

Cody approached the ladies, who were looking quite shattered. "Mrs. McLeod," Deputy Taylor said, "you have been apprehended in the process of buying stolen art treasures." Luis and Arnoldo walked around the table, and stood behind Maggie and Nancy.

"Mrs. McLeod, Mrs. Johnson," Cody said, officially, "will you please stand up and follow me. You both have serious questions to answer."

Maggie reached for the money, attempting to replace it in the satchel. The deputy grabbed her hand and held firmly. "Leave the money and the satchel, Mrs. McLeod," he warned. "That will be evidence against you, Mrs. Johnson, and Mr. Johns."

Subdued and humiliated, Maggie and Nancy reached for their parasols and purses. Cody led the ladies, heads lowered, from the room. Luis and Arnoldo walked in back of Maggie and Nancy.

A buggy waited for them behind the Columbia Boarding House.

Cody helped Maggie and Nancy into the Mayor's buggy, and complemented them for the outstanding way in which they acted out their parts.

"We couldn't have trapped Johns without the help of either of you, Maggie and Nancy. The town of Sonora and Columbia is obliged, and Edward's department will be indebted to both of you. Thanks for all your help."

Maggie and Nancy agreed to help in the capture of William Johns, without concern for the danger they would both face. The praise from Cody and Luis, and a smile from Arnoldo, was appreciated and fitting, it brought smiles of relief for a job well done.

67

*W*hen Edward opened the door to Johns' viewing room, he discovered a variable museum of paintings in frames carved from mahogany wood, done by masters, and hung in different places on the wall. Vases, urns, and statues filled the room, along with beautifully made chairs and small tables.

Each item had to be tagged. Some of the items were from distant parts of the world. Edward carried with him a list of valuables that had been stolen from China, England, Scotland, and Italy. A few on the list were here in Johns' room.

Clint held and admired a small English vase and handed Edward a crumpled paper that was used as buffer against breakage. "Look, Edward," Clint said, "this paper gives the address of a warehouse. It says, 'DELIVER TO: 428 Grant Street, San Francisco, California.' That's the same area where we lost those two men when they left Richardson's house, and the same area we sent the two agents who never returned."

Edward looked over the paper. "Go to the telegraph office," Edward commanded, "and wire this address to the department. Have them send someone to investigate that building immediately. Better have them send more than one man. I'll bet that's where they're hiding the merchandise when it comes off the ship. Until it's sent to Milton on the train."

Edward was desperate to learn who the mastermind was in this scheme. Who was stealing masterworks from all over the world and sending them to California? What devious, greedy individuals were the brains behind this whole enterprise? If his department got inside the building at 428 Grant Street in San Francisco's Chinatown, what would they find? If it were a place that still held stolen art treasures, and there were crates still unopened, maybe, just maybe, he would find a name or address that would lead him to the genius behind this conspiracy.

Until that time, he was grateful for the help he had received from the deputy of Sonora. There was no way William Johns would be able lie his way out of selling Russian jewelry boxes, English vases, or Chinese porcelain. Rattlesnake had been caught red-handed.

Edward resumed his work tagging the items he knew was on the list of stolen merchandise. Crate by crate, this vast amount of treasure was going back to the countries of origin, and, hopefully, to the proper owners.

Caleb had Rattlesnake's five miners in custody, the old man who had threatened Robert and the three men who had been with him, now known to be his sons. Members of Johns' gang of thieves, they were assigned to stockpile treasures and they used their dig as a front. Instead of spending the rest of their years living in grandeur and self-indulgence, nine miserable men waited to be incarcerated in the Sonora jail.

While Edward and Caleb's men were guarding the miners, Ken, Micah, and Mark, and two men with extensive knowledge of caverns, explored the cave looking for hidden treasures. The cavern was enormous, with deep, dark openings that tunneled into various parts of the mountain. Torches illuminated the darkest areas, where they found larger articles.

There were paintings visible, two swords with jewels on the handle and sheath, large vases, tables, chairs, statues, and ceremonial weapons of every kind. A staggering amount of work was in store for the men who would identify, crate, and transport the wares to San Francisco.

Cody's hunch had been correct; this mine was a cavern millions of years old. It contained stalagmites, stalactites, and lakes of untold depths.

Caleb was successful in getting one of the miners to talk. Eager to tell all he knew, Caleb took him aside with Ken, Micah and Mark, and one of Edward's men, "We couldn't do nothing," the miner related, "unless Rattlesnake told us to do it. We had to stay right here; we couldn't leave the camp, he would've killed us. He told us when to ride to Milton and pick up the crates. He killed my brother, shot him in the back just because he didn't ask before he took something out of the cave. My brother just wanted to show us what he had found, that's all."

The miner's anger at Johns also spurred his confession about the attempted murder of Robert. "Rattlesnake made my brother and me go into town with him and make noise in the burned out building so he could shoot the sheriff. He's a coward! Shoots everyone in the back. What do you want to know? I'll tell you everything."

From another miner it was learned how the larger objects were transported. "Those statues and tables there came to America in large crates by ship. Before it docked at the shipyard in Frisco to offload its legit cargo, it put down its anchor south of Frisco. Barges sailed out to meet the ship, and our goods was lowered to the waiting boat. The barges would go up to Stockton by the river. Then we'd take some of the goods to Frisco by wagon, and some crates we'd bring back here. We never saw who picked the boxes up in Frisco; we left them in Chinatown."

The lawmen also learned that some crates held treasures packed in burlap sacks with coffee beans. This was done in order to confuse any authorities that searched the ship for the stolen merchandise.

Shrewdly and cleverly planned, no one suspected valuable art works inside a load of coffee beans. To demonstrate, the miner reached inside the coffee beans and pulled out a vase, a small candleholder, and a wooden case with inlaid work, small things hidden without detection.

Over a period of time, Mr. Johns had amassed numerous art objects from England, China, Russia, and Italy. He was a brilliant innovator and used only underhanded methods to acquire stolen goods from all over the world.

A total of fifteen men had raided the North Star Mine the day Jose was shot. Eleven men were being held for trial, including Rattlesnake and his valet. That left four men not yet in custody. Who were they? Caleb was determined to find them.

The deputy thought the miners might attempt an escape en route to Sonora. "If we shackle them in pairs, Marshall," Cody suggested, "they won't run far even if they get away."

"I agree. I'll have the wagons start sending the prisoners to Sonora tomorrow."

Caleb turned and walked toward the men who were in safekeeping. "Shackle those men in pairs," he said to the men guarding the miners. "I don't want any of them getting away before they reach Sonora. We won't be moving the prisoners until tomorrow. They better make themselves comfortable for the night, it's going to be a long one."

*O*n board three separate wagons, nine shackled miners left Rattlesnake's campsite to await their trial and certain conviction.

With the help from the miner who volunteered information as to how the merchandise reached the gold country, evidence mounted and all of it pointed directly to William Johns.

Edward had eyewitness testimony from three men.

Arnoldo, identified William Johns as the one who killed Jose in cold blood, and with malice. Cody, Arnoldo, and Ken testified that William Johns' shot one of his miners in the back at the cave. Also, the bullet removed from Robert's body matched the bullet and casing found near the saloon, and was a positive match for the bullets in Johns' derringer.

Edward Thorton had the most incriminating evidence of all; he had witnessed William Johns receive money for stolen goods.

Whether Johns would remain in jail for the rest of his life or suffer death by hanging, Rattlesnake would never sell stolen goods again.

*E*dward placed Caleb, Micah, and Mark in charge of vacating the first campsite run by the old man with the long white beard and his three sons. Caleb and his sons would also tag and ready for transport, William Johns' campsite and the cavern, of all the valuables hidden away.

Since Caleb was assigned to the cavern, Cody resumed his duties as deputy of Sonora, in addition to acting as advisor to Caleb.

The sheriff requested one thing from Miss Margaret McLeod when he was ready to return to full-time duty. "Maggie, I want you to bring me lunch every day and stick around for an hour or two. Can you do that for me?"

"I can and will do it as long as you want," Maggie affirmed, "but I have a request for you."

"What's your request? Ask me."

"I want to clean the jail while I am there. If you think I will bring food to a place as dirty as it was before we cleaned it, you do not know Maggie McLeod."

During the last few weeks, this Scottish lady with the beautiful red hair had become an essential part of the sheriff's daily routine.

After all the terrible occurrences in this town, starting with Harris and Clark, and culminating in the secret maneuvers of William Johns, the residents of Sonora needed time to relax and return to normalcy. No one would deny that the summer of 1875 had been out of the ordinary. People would speak about the unusual occurrences during that summer in Sonora for years to come.

Mrs. Thorton was pleased to have two of her sons, Edward and Ken, temporarily back into the family home. "Before Ken leaves for Coulterville," she said, as the family sat at the supper table one evening,

"I want to have guests come for a special dinner and dance. This will be Ken's final season learning the breeding of horses. He'll soon be the director of his own ranch.

"David is expected in Sonora to compile information on the smuggling that was carried on during the past few months, and since he will be the prosecutor in charge for the case against William Johns, I think he would enjoy such an evening. I don't have to ask you, Edward. I know you want to invite everyone who helped in the capture."

"Because of the special work that Ken has performed for Edward," Mayor Thorton said, "I suggest something a bit more glamorous. Why don't we reserve the room on the top floor of the Sonora Hotel, my dear, and have everyone, including their families, who helped capture Johns and who assisted Edward come to a pitch-in-supper and dance? That will be something for Ken to remember when he leaves for Coulterville."

Mayor Thorton put down his fork and walked to the calendar hanging on the wall. "I think the event should be held at the next full moon," he advised, "which will be in two weeks time, and coincidentally will fall on a Saturday evening. Would that give you enough time, my dear, to complete all the arrangements?"

Mrs. Thorton was ecstatic. "It will give me plenty of time, William," she said, "and in addition, it will mark the end to a most disagreeable summer. So much has happened in just five months. Thank you, dear, for an outstanding suggestion. I am going to start compiling my list immediately.

"I will need help. Let me see, I can ask Juanita, Wesley's wife, Millie, Myrtle, Louise, Maggie, and Elsie, Caleb's wife. If Gina can get time off from the doctor's office, I'll ask her to help."

Mayor Thorton watched his wife mumbling to herself as she left the table. "Look at your mother," he said to Edward and Ken, "she bounced out of the room and she didn't finish her supper. I will never understand how women can get so inspired about planning an event, especially if dancing is involved."

"Pop, you wouldn't have suggested it if you didn't want her to plan it," Edward reminded Mayor Thorton. "You will be looking forward to the dance and food yourself. Everyone who is invited will have a good time and you know it."

"You're right, son. With the evening activities in the hands of your capable mother and her helpers, we can all look forward to this special occasion."

71

*I*n an earnest attempt to make this dance a gala affair, something to remember during the long winter months ahead, Mrs. Thorton and her helpers started their pleasant task the very next day.

Elsie, Millie, Myrtle, and Louise would bake bread and rolls. Mrs. Thorton and several women renowned for their creativity as cooks, were to bring various dishes that would include meats, along with an assortment of vegetables.

Millie was elected to convince Chef Pamela Dumont at the Sonora Hotel to make the dessert. Mrs. Taylor's technique was flawless. "But your apple pies will be the highlight of the evening. Pamela, you know how much Robert loves your food," she mentioned, "especially your apple pies. For that matter, Robert loves all your desserts. Can you imagine how pleased he would be if you were the one to end this wonderful and delicious supper with your dessert?"

"How many guests will you be expecting, ma'am," Pamela asked, blushing, "because a large cake with a custard filling could be the main dessert, and I can bake some additional apple pies. What do you think?"

One other important matter had to be addressed: What would the ladies of Sonora wear to such a formal occasion? The dry good shops were busy altering the fancy dresses and accessories that were in stock. Material was purchased by the bolts for women adept in sewing.

Nancy insisted Maggie and Millie search through her numerous trunks and select the apparel of their choice to wear at the dance.

Gina had decided against wearing the emerald green taffeta she had brought from New York City. However, she removed the long flowing garment and shoes from her wardrobe and put them on her bed, recalling the night she first slipped the dress over her body. She loved the color and feel of the material, if only Gertrude had not chosen this particular style.

Maggie entered her room. "Good," she said, "I hoped you would wear that gown. It is so beautiful."

"No, Maggie, I do not want to wear this dress," Gina said. "It shows the top of my breasts. I wish Gertrude had not been so set on this style."

"You should have told her you did not like the cut of the dress, not that it would have mattered to her one way or the other. Gina, you look absolutely beautiful in the gown; please wear it to the dance.

"I remember when you danced that night. The men all looked at you, especially when you danced with Mr. Nathan. He was such a wonderful dancer."

"I'll be too embarrassed to wear it now," Gina said, frowning. "I think I shall wear the gray wool; it's my favorite anyway. I picked that style."

As usual, Maggie voiced her opinion. "You will faint dead away from the heat in that thing. No, you will wear this green taffeta. You mind me now, girl."

Gina laid the wrap beside the gown.

"No, Gina, not the cape," Maggie wailed. "Please tell me you are not going to take that thing to the dance."

"Maggie, the evenings are beginning to get cool. I will wear the green taffeta if you stop going on so about the cover that goes with it. *Capisce?*"

"I understand. Now, come, see what Nancy is lending me for the evening."

An elegant black velvet gown was draped over Maggie's bed. The neckline was low, but modest, and trimmed with white French lace. The fitted bodice would accentuate the waist, and the sleeves, which ended at the elbow, were trimmed with lace identical to the neckline. The skirt was gathered with yards of material that fell softly to the floor.

"It is lovely, Maggie," Gina said. "You will look absolutely stunning in it. It was kind of Nancy to lend it to you."

"She forgot it was in her trunk. She told me to keep it, but what would I do with a dress like this hanging in my wardrobe. Now, promise me you are going to wear the green taffeta."

"I promise," Gina answered reluctantly.

"Then we are ready. I'll let the dresses hang for a day or two and then I will press them." As an afterthought Maggie added, "Do you realize, Miss Tufano, this will be my first elegant dance since I arrived to this country? I will not be working as a servant, mind you, I will be a guest. Can you imagine that?"

$\mathcal{D}$avid Thorton arrived in Sonora two days before the red-letter day. Mrs. Thorton was beside herself with worry thinking her son would not attend the dance. But with David's arrival, final preparations commenced.

The auditorium had been cleaned and decorated. Elegant costumes chosen by the guests were pressed and ready. There were last minute annoyances, but nothing that these women were not able to correct.

Because strong drink was being served at the dance, the sheriff and deputy were on duty. Robert was not able to dance, due to his recent injury, and Cody did not dance, so they were to be in charge if any person became inebriated and needed to sit away from the main group.

Gina's escort to the dance was Andrew. Maggie would accompany Billy. The boys were to be taught the waltz by their partners. So ten days before the formal gathering, Andrew and Billy were at Gina's home every evening struggling to learn the steps. One problem had presented itself, however; neither Gina nor Maggie played the piano. One must have music to dance, so Myrtle was chosen. She loved to play Aunt Mary's piano anyway, and the boys had sworn her to silence.

It was difficult for Billy to twirl Maggie, keep in step with the music, and remember which foot to use first. But Andrew, with his arm around Gina's waist, waltzed her around the floor like he had been dancing most of his young life. Unlike his brother, Andrew loved to dance, and he adapted the correct posture in his own style. As Maggie watched him, she mentioned to Gina that Andrew danced much like James Nathan.

"Who was James Nathan, Gina?" Andrew asked.

"Oh, someone I use to know before I came to California."

"You danced with him?"

"Yes, Andrew, I did. The family I stayed with in New York had music one evening before I left, and I danced with James. Maggie was also at the dance."

"Did you dance with James Nathan too, Maggie?" Billy inquired.

"No. I was serving tiny, tiny tea sandwiches and keeping an eye on Gina. She was very popular that evening."

Billy and Andrew gained confidence with each session. The night before the dance, the ladies knew the boys were ready. All in attendance would see their skill in leading a partner in a waltz.

While Gina towel dried her hair, she remembered her grandmother's tortoise shell comb. It was formed in the shape of a bird, with two diamonds sparkling as the eyes, and a mouth accentuated by a brilliant ruby. It complemented the ebony color of Gina hair.

Before Gina's graduation at Bellevue Hospital in New York City, where she trained to become a nurse, Tina showed Gina the comb and asked her to wear it when she received her certificate. Gina did as Tina asked. The comb was from Florence, Italy, and had only been worn for grand occasions.

Now, as Gina rolled her hair into a coil and fastened it with this special tortoise shell comb, she felt that her evening attire would be perfect.

The auditorium was spacious. French doors opened wide onto both the front and the back of the building, allowing fresh breezes to circulate throughout the room. A veranda extended out and over Washington Street. All in all, it was a very romantic setting. Couples could snuggle up to one another under the stars and full moon.

When the guests arrived in their best formal attire, Millie directed that the food be laid out on three large separate tables.

Gina placed a steaming fragrant stew in a Dutch oven on the table designated for main dishes. As she centered it, she felt a man's hand on her bare shoulder. She turned her head and followed the hand to the face. "Ken, it's you," she exclaimed. "I was frightened for a moment. I did not hear you approach."

"You look ravishing in that dress, Gina," he said, surveying her from the hair comb to her feet. "You take my breath away." He cast a momentary look around the room. "Who brought you to the dance? Are you with anyone special?"

Gina got that uneasy feeling. "Maggie and I came with John," she answered. "Our escorts for the evening will be Billy and Andrew."

She moved away from Ken to another table. Her wrap was lying by her purse on a chair across the room. Gina wished it were around her shoulders. Ken followed her around the table; he was not his usual self tonight. Gina wondered if he had something to drink before he left home; there was a definite shine to his eyes.

Maggie came toward Gina with two serving dishes. "Take one of these plates and follow me," she commanded.

She handed Gina a dish and walked to the table used for the vegetables. Gina followed with a frown on her face, seeing Ken lingering by the dessert table.

"Gina," Maggie asked in a whisper, "what is wrong?"

"Ken seems different tonight. He keeps looking at me. It makes me a little uncomfortable."

"I will speak to John and Matthew. If he comes too close, they will rescue you."

"I would have felt better if I had on my gray wool dress."

Maggie set her platter on the table and turned to face Gina, nose to nose. "Listen to me, girl," Maggie cautioned, "no matter what you wear, people are going to stand and stare, at least the men will. It is the natural thing for them to do. Will you relax, enjoy the dress, and your evening, please?"

Gina smiled at Maggie. "You told me the same thing several weeks ago, remember?"

The ladies giggled and walked back to speak to Millie.

Gina realized, however, that Ken was standing at the back of the room and tracing her every step. His noticeable advances worried her. She made a promise to herself to stay far away from him during the evening.

73

*A*n impressively attired and groomed Andrew and Billy entered the room. They had dressed with care and attention to the smallest detail.

Feminine lighthearted laughter, along with the gentlemen's deep tones, echoed around the room.

When the music started and couples filed out on the floor, Andrew and Billy walked toward Gina and Maggie. The boys bowed, took the ladies by the hand, and led them to the dance floor. The evening festivities had commenced.

Although he was dressed informally in a black coat, black trousers, and a white shirt, the young single women blushed as they turned their gaze to the ruggedly handsome deputy when he entered the room. Tonight his sandy-colored hair was trimmed, and his usual two-day stubble had been shaved away. He walked easily through the crowd, listening to conversations and laughter.

Cody saw six young men in a group on the side of the dance floor. Billy was the tallest of the group. Andrew was near Billy, both of them talking to a young woman partially hidden from the deputy's line of vision. Cody did not recognize her and walked away.

Millie spotted her son and came toward him, asking, "Cody, can I get you a plate of food? Mrs. Martin and Louise made your favorite, beef stew. Just the way you like it."

"Not yet, Mom; I'll wait awhile."

"Let me know when you're hungry, dear."

"Millie, can you come here please?" Mrs. Alexander called. "We all want the recipe for this wonderful chicken pie. Your crust is absolutely outstanding. It is so flaky."

"It really is so easy," Millie cooed, leaving Cody's side. "I don't even need to write down the measurements. I know the recipe by heart."

If food was required, Sonora's choice was Cody's mother. Millie always put her heart into anything she did, but especially when food was of the primary importance.

Pretty widow Nancy spotted the deputy standing in the back of the room. Her bright, soft yellow dress flowed gracefully around her irresistible feminine figure as she walked toward him.

"Hi, deputy," she whispered, linking her arm through his. "I'm glad to see you've finally arrived. I've been waiting for you. Will you save me a dance tonight?"

"Nancy, you know I don't dance," he replied.

"You don't have to dance," she breathed, "just hold me. Close."

"I won't be dancing tonight, Nancy. I'm on duty."

"Well, if you change your mind, Deputy, you'll know where to find me. I'll never be far away from you."

Cody grinned, inclined his head slightly in Nancy's direction, and touched his hat. As she drifted around the room, all the guests she passed smiled and greeted her. Since her part in the capture of Rattlesnake, the people of Sonora realized Nancy was more than just a woman with a pretty face and figure.

Deputy Taylor made his way over to Robert who was seated at the back of the hall, close to the French windows.

Edward raised his right arm; the musicians stopped the music and the dancers stood in a circle watching Edward. He motioned for all who were to receive honor to come and stand at his side.

"Thank you, ladies and gentlemen," he said to all the guests, "for accepting our invitation and coming to this dinner and dance.

"As you know, tonight we give special merit to the men and women who helped in the capture of William Johns and who finally put the elusive Rattlesnake behind bars.

"First, merit and appreciation to Arnoldo Guzman and Luis Serrano, for their bravery in alerting Sheriff Robert Sanders and Deputy Cody Taylor of the brutality of William Johns. Unknown to Luis and Arnoldo, a lot more than killing was going on under Rattlesnake's direction. With their help, we were able to uncover and put an end to his secret conspiracy and to prevent the further deaths of innocent people who stood in his way.

"Next, special merit to Sheriff Robert Sanders and Deputy Cody Taylor, the men who found the location where stolen national treasures and museum artifacts were being held for sale. Johns piled up astronomical amounts of money for the items that he sold.

"Not to be forgotten is Caleb J. Alexander, who stepped in as U.S. Marshall for Sheriff Sanders after Robert was shot. He kept Sonora peaceful, and this enabled Cody and his deputies free to smoke out Rattlesnake. Ken, Cody, and Caleb were tireless workers, instrumental in securing the final captures.

"Not many of you are aware," Edward said to the guests, "that the mine worked by William Johns, alias, Rattlesnake, was under close observation by four men. Ken Thorton, Cody Taylor, Luis Serrano, and Arnoldo Guzman. These men watched, undercover, night and day for three days until they obtained the evidence to use against Rattlesnake. If William Johns had discovered that these men were watching his camp, death would have surely been the lot for each of them.

"Cody deserves special merit for his brilliant plan to invade Rattlesnake's camp in the hills and make the capture of William Johns in Columbia on the same day, at virtually the same time. Another of his brilliant ideas was to use two women, Nancy Johnson and Margaret McLeod to trap William Johns.

"Nancy used her lovely feminine appeal to distract Johns and get his attention. She did this by wearing a necklace and hair comb worth thousands of dollars. She lured and duped Rattlesnake into believing he would make a lot of money if he sold Maggie McLeod, Nancy's friend and a rich widow from Scotland, something of exceptional quality to adorn her castle in Scotland. And, because of the bravery and astuteness of these two women, Maggie and Nancy were the ones who finally put this shrewd devious man behind bars."

Edward beckoned Nancy and Maggie to move closer. "Ladies and Gentlemen," he said, and turned to look at Nancy, "this woman was facing untold danger when she approached the hotel where William Johns was known to sell his merchandise. After Mr. Johns became enthralled by her appearance, he initiated a conversation. Mrs. Johnson suggested he meet Mrs. McLeod, a rich widow looking to acquire priceless works of art for her castle. I will add at this point, William Johns was completely won over by Nancy's charm, beauty, and grace."

Edward turned toward Maggie. "Like Nancy, Margaret McLeod did not flinch at the danger she knew she would encounter in this charade. On the day she met William Johns, what she said to him and how she made him meet her demands, was exactly right. He was completely fooled by her arrogant, overbearing demeanor, and caught off guard by her irritating, aggressive behavior. He worried so much about pleasing this superior lady that he forgot to be careful. I might add, he never pleased her, no matter what he said, but he kept trying.

"William Johns did not have a chance to speak. Maggie put him in his place by interrupting him constantly. Actually, every time he opened his mouth. And, to be perfectly honest with you, ladies and gentlemen, I was amazed at Mr. Johns' control. She annoyed him so much that I was surprised when he didn't shoot her. I think he was tempted, on more than one occasion."

The audience roared with laughter, but the lighthearted bickering was not over. Maggie was not one to let this observation of her character pass her by.

"Mr. Thorton," Maggie commenced, haughtily, "I did not see you squeezing into an elaborate gown and donning a hat and sitting in a restaurant eating cake and drinking tea until I thought I was going to bust. I did not hear you instruct me on how to ask for my purchases. Neither you, nor any of your men told me what I was supposed to say to this blackhearted demon. Maybe if you had enlightened me, I would not have been so exasperating to Mr. Johns, or I might add, to you."

Maggie closed her mouth and glared at Edward with her hands on her hips. Again, boisterous laughter filled the room. Finally, Edward and the audience regained control. Oozing with kindness, Edward thanked Maggie and Nancy again, as well as the brave men who had helped his department obtain the capture.

The speeches over, a round of applause was heard, and the music began.

Cody watched Robert, his arm around Maggie's waist, as she accepted thanks and praise with humor. Edward offered Nancy his arm, she accepted graciously, and together they walked toward the front of the hall. They stepped out on the veranda, arm in arm, for a private conversation.

As the music started, and couples filed out on the dance floor, the deputy fixed his attention on the boys standing with Andrew and Billy. As the group parted, his brother led a young lady onto the dance floor.

She had dark hair piled high on her head, long curls hung down her lovely swan like neck, and a magnificent comb crowned the top of her hair. She wore the most beautiful green dress, a perfect fit for her exquisite figure, curving around the fullness of her upper body, and accentuating the tiny waist and naked shoulders. Matching green satin shoes peeked out from beneath the long skirt as she floated to the center of the dance floor on Andrew's arm.

The couple faced each other, Andrew put his right arm around her waist, and she raised her left arm to his right shoulder. Andrew took her right hand in his left and guided his partner over the dance floor in perfect step to the music.

Cody riveted his gaze to the couple dancing together. This young woman was Gina. Jealously and envy seeped into every fiber of his body. Men looked at her dancing with his brother; each step was pure elegance. Cody beat down the urge to walk out onto the dance floor and drag Gina away from the prying eyes, when he felt someone's gaze boring right through him.

"Well, Deputy," Robert said, as he put his hand on Cody's shoulder, "our nurse looks different tonight. Doesn't she?"

Cody ignored him.

Andrew escorted Gina to the side of the dance floor. She sat down behind Matthew and removed one of her shoes to rub her toes, while Andrew went to the dessert table with Billy. Gina heard a scuffling sound behind her. She turned to see Ken pull up a chair.

Gina put on her shoe and sat upright. Ken's arm extended around her back, his hand caressed her shoulder. He leaned close, and Gina knew for a fact Ken was inebriated. Gina stood up, but Ken grabbed her by the hand and pulled her down on the chair.

When the music started again, Ken ushered Gina to the dance floor without her approval. Embarrassment turned her cheeks crimson. Ken's right arm kept her body so close to his that her movements were limited.

After what seemed like hours, the music stopped. Gina left Ken and walked away, seeking refuge again behind Matthew and John. But Ken followed her. He grabbed Gina's arm, pulled her in front of him, and held her close to his body.

Robert watched Ken. His advances toward Gina needed to be controlled. Sheriff Sanders thought it was time for Ken to get some fresh air.

Cody thought the same thing and took a step forward, but Robert held him back. "Cody," he advised, "I'll handle this."

The deputy looked at Robert with a glare of defiance, and raged inwardly. Another man held his Gina. This was intolerable.

The music started once again. Gina pushed Ken's arms away and took a step toward Ted and Sue Martin. But Ken dragged her back toward the dance floor.

The sheriff started toward Ken, but this time Cody held him back. Robert saw a mischievous grin light up the deputy's face as he winked at Sheriff Sanders, and walked out onto the dance floor. It was the time to let all in attendance know Gina belonged to Cody.

Ken's right arm circled Gina's waist, and he pulled her close. But as Ken reached for Gina's right hand, Cody seized his left wrist in a vicelike grip and maneuvered Gina away with his left hand. With Gina at his side, he released Ken's wrist and announced, "This is my dance."

Ken disappeared down the stairs when the music started. Cody took Gina's right hand with his left, and with his right arm, he enclosed her waist. Then to the amazement of all who were watching with rapt attention, Cody whirled Gina in perfect step to the music, while he looked deep into her lovely, luminous eyes.

How was this possible that the deputy was waltzing with poise and style? The audience stood in wonder, gaping.

Gina floated in Cody's arms; together they danced alone, no other couples on the floor. Then, after what seemed like only seconds, the music stopped and the dance ended.

Cody kept his arm around her waist and walked her toward Andrew who was standing by Millie and Matthew. Cody's mother beamed at her son.

"I don't dance, Gina," Cody whispered in Gina's ear. "Don't expect me to ever dance again."

For the rest of the evening, the deputy stayed at Gina's side. He was attentive and gracious to all that approached, but only Andrew or Billy was allowed to be her dance partners.

The music continued well into the night before Mayor Thorton announced, "This is the last dance, ladies and gentlemen. Get your favorite gal or guy, and we'll end the Gala Event of 1875."

A unanimous groan was heard from all the guests. Musicians started in playing "The Blue Danube"; the dance floor was full, including Andrew and Gina, Billy and Maggie.

Food was lifted from the tables and wrapped for transport. The ladies who organized the event were reluctant to leave; with such a gala affair no one wanted to bid adieu. When the last guests walked down the stairs to their waiting buggies, the sheriff and deputy were free to complete their rounds.

Cody held Gina by the upper arms and kissed her cheek. "I want you to come to my house tomorrow," he said. "John will bring you and Maggie."

"May we cook something to bring with us?" Gina questioned.

"You can ask Mom. I'll see you tomorrow." As Cody walked down the stairs, behind the sheriff, he called out, "Don't forget, Gina, my house tomorrow."

"I will not forget," she answered. "I promise."

Gina watched as Robert and Cody disappeared into the town below. Forget? Not this nurse. Not a chance.

74

Cody was not at home when Gina and Maggie arrived for Sunday dinner. Edward and Caleb had summoned him to the cavern. Old relics, including suits of armor, weapons, silver helmets, and shields had been found in a remote section of the cave.

When Deputy Taylor walked through the back door into the kitchen, Millie's guests were just about to sit at the table. He beckoned John, Matthew, and Robert to his side. The men acknowledged Cody's conversation with nods and broad smiles.

Guests and family members around Millie's table surprised her by consuming the mountain of fried chicken, warm rolls, mashed potatoes, and vegetables she had prepared. The gentlemen were in a most agreeable mood. It perplexed the ladies.

Matthew stood up from his chair. "I suggest that we leave this table," he announced firmly, "and all of us can sit in the comfortable chairs in the living room. We will help you ladies with dishes later, after we rest a bit. Won't we, gentlemen? I don't know about any of you, but I'm too full to wash the dishes, I want to rest, and I'm looking forward to having several pieces of Millie's famous custard pie."

"Are you mad? There is nothing you can say, Doctor," Maggie responded, tersely. "We are doing the dishes now." She stood up and began to clear the table. "Dirty dishes cannot be left for any length of time. The food will dry on the plate and have to be scrubbed off. What can you be thinking?"

"Put down that dish, Maggie," Robert said, "and follow me to the parlor. I want to talk to you. Is that clear, woman?"

Robert spoke directly to her in a tone of voice she had never heard him use before, and he watched her reaction with a determined look.

"Oh, all right, Robbie," she said, quietly, "if you want me to fol-low you."

"I do."

Matthew helped Millie out of her chair; John led Myrtle and Louise into the living room. Maggie followed Robert to the parlor meekly.

Andrew and Billy ran to set up the game table in the living room.

Gina was about to follow the boys, but Cody stopped her. He took her by the hand. "You and I are going outside in the yard," he said, pull-ing her to the back door, "I want you to sit with me on the swing."

"I was put on that swing by you once before. Remember? I struggled to stop that swing while someone I know stood by and watched me. If I remember correctly, I think you were told in two languages and still re-fused to help."

Cody grinned, and led her out to the yard.

Gina sat on the swing and held onto the ropes. She gazed out at the yard, stable, and up into the large oak tree. It was autumn, October 1875. Her memory slipped back to April when she first arrived in Sonora, and she recalled all the events that had occurred since the moment she stepped off the stagecoach.

While lost in thought, she was transported back in time to when she had met the Taylor family five years before. She pushed the swing for-ward and backward, reliving little Andrew's efforts in trying to sit on her lap while she sat on the swing. She recalled, too, the first time she saw Cody. So much sorrow, tragedy, but also happiness, had come and gone since the last time she occupied this seat.

Cody waited patiently while she reflected on the past. Seeing her expression change, he spoke. "Gina."

"Yes, Cody?" she answered, looking up at him.

"You looked beautiful in that green dress last night, more than beau-tiful. When we danced around the room, I could see every man staring at you. For the first time in my life, I was jealous; I didn't want anyone else looking at you."

"It was a mistake to wear that gown last night, Cody; it's too, too…" Gina fumbled for the right word to use. Finally her Italian language an-swered, "*A basso*," then in English, "low."

He smirked and kept speaking. "You were sitting on that swing the first time I saw you. It was five years ago. But you left Sonora and went back to New York. I thought about you after you left. I remembered your eyes when you looked at me that day. I didn't think I'd ever see you again. But when you came back to Sonora, I couldn't stop thinking about you. Especially after the night that we rode Sammy together and I held you close to me and kissed you."

Gina's lowered her gaze from Cody's face and blushed at his frankness.

"I couldn't stand it when Ken held you close last night. From now on, I'm the only one that will ever hold you that way."

Cody pulled Gina from the swing. "Gina," he said, his intense blue eyes focused on her face, "I love you. I want you to be my wife."

"Oh, Cody," Gina said, smiling happily, "I want to be your wife with all my heart. I love you so much."

Cody held Gina in his arms and kissed her tenderly, but with longing. On their wedding night, Cody would cool the blazings of love that had kindled inside him five years ago on this very swing, the day he first set eyes on Gina.

"We'll be married soon, before anything else terrible happens," Cody said as he held his beloved in his arms. "I'll wait two weeks. No more."

After Cody and Gina's wedding, two more marriages would be performed in Sonora, but the deputy and nurse would be the first to say their vows.

Matthew was alert to the pair when they walked into the room, hand in hand. He rose from his chair, followed by Robert and John, to congratulate the happy prospective bridegroom. High spirits and tears flowed when Gina told the ladies of her upcoming wedding.

75

Gina Angela Tufano was to wed Cody Benjamin Taylor, a man she dearly loved. She looked forward to her wedding day with happiness, but it also was a time of sadness. Not one member of her family would be in attendance to share her joy.

She had chosen to marry a man who was willing to risk his own life to save her virtue and her life, and someone who loved her very much. Cody was a brave, kind, noble man.

The deputy and nurse would repeat their vows in twelve days. Her future husband, not one for anything fancy or elaborate, preferred a small, quiet wedding. As the arrangements fell into place and the days slipped by, Gina awoke one morning to realize it was her wedding day.

In a dress of pure white, borrowed from her mother's trunk, Gina carried a handkerchief for the gush of happy tears she would shed, and one rose. Her grandmother's hair comb held the white lace veil in place as she walked down the aisle arm in arm with Matthew. She was a gorgeous bride and her happiness was radiated to all of the guests in attendance.

Myrtle cried as she played the "Wedding March" on the piano. Millie and Maggie stood waiting for Gina, Luis and Robert stood alongside Cody, as Andrew and Billy ushered last minute guests to their seats.

The deputy looked so handsome in his new black suit, but he was focused on his beautiful bride coming toward him. Matthew released his arm and gave Gina's hand to the deputy. Cody wrapped her arm through his and held her hand tightly. They faced Minister Parsons for a brief discourse.

The bride and groom turned toward each other, and held hands to repeat the vows.

Minister Parsons' voice filled the room, "Do you, GINA ANGELA TUFANO, take CODY BENJAMIN TAYLOR to be your lawful wedded husband? To love, honor and obey him, through sickness and in health, until death do you part?"

Gina looked at her soon-to-be-husband, a man she loved very much. Her answer was loud and clear, "I DO."

"Do you, CODY BENJAMIN TAYLOR, take GINA ANGELA TUFANO to be your lawful wedded wife? To love and honor her, through sickness and in health, until death do you part?"

Cody raised her fingers to his lips and kissed them tenderly. His heart overflowed with love for this beautiful maiden and he wanted all to hear his reply. "I DO," he said firmly.

"I now pronounce you MAN and WIFE. What God has yoked together, let no man put apart. Cody, you may kiss your bride."

The deputy lifted her veil. He held Gina's tear-streaked face with both of his hands, placed his lips on Gina's lips, and kissed his wife.

About the Author

 *T*era Lee Mattera was born in Fresno, California. After she graduated from Fresno High School, she continued her education by attending Fresno City College. She started her career as a stenographer for the Bank of America in 1962. In December of 1962, she married husband, Ralph Lainez, in San Francisco. Their union produced two beautiful daughters and, finally, one granddaughter. For a number of years Tera Lee has been a Fire and Casualty Insurance Agent.

She has continued her secretarial career to the present time, but Tera does enjoy writing novels, especially those with a western theme. A sequel is planned for *The LAWMAN and the LADY*, and she is currently working on a murder mystery set in San Francisco in the 1950 era.

The author is currently a member of "Win Win" writers group in Fresno, and the V.I.P. (Valley Independent Publishers) group.